Fatal Cajun Festival

Also available by Ellen Byron

CAJUN COUNTRY MYSTERIES

Mardi Gras Murder

A Cajun Christmas Killing

Body on the Bayou

Plantation Shudders

Fatal Cajun Festival

A CAJUN COUNTRY MYSTERY

Ellen Byron

CROOKED LANE

NEW YORK

Copyright © 2019 by Ellen Byron

All rights reserved.

Published in the United States by Crooked Lane Books, an imprint of The Quick Brown Fox & Company LLC.

Crooked Lane Books and its logo are trademarks of The Quick Brown Fox & Company LLC.

Library of Congress Catalog-in-Publication data available upon request.

ISBN (hardcover): 978-1-64385-129-7
ISBN (ePub): 978-1-64385-130-3

Cover illustration by Stephen Gardner
Book design by Jennifer Canzone

Printed in the United States.

www.crookedlanebooks.com

Crooked Lane Books
34 West 27th St., 10th Floor
New York, NY 10001

First Edition: September 2019

10 9 8 7 6 5 4 3 2 1

Dedicated to Elizabeth DiVirgilio Seideman, a wonderful mother and nonna who has no idea how much she inspired the humor and warmth of Grand-mère.

"We do not need to know everything in this world. There are times to treat mystery like wildness and leave it alone."

—Oliver A. Houck, *Down on the Batture*

The People of Fatal Cajun Festival

The family
Magnolia Marie—"Maggie"—Crozat, our heroine
Tug Crozat—her father
Ninette Crozat—her mother
Grand-mère—her grandmother on her dad's side

Law enforcement and adjacent
Bo Durand—detective and Maggie's fiancé
Rufus Durand—Pelican PD police chief
Cal Vichet—officer
Artie Belloise—officer
Jace Jerierre—assistant district attorney
Oliver Gaudet—a judge

Friends and frenemies
Gaynell Bourgeois—friend and coworker
Ione Savreau—friend and coworker
Lia Tienne Bruner—Maggie's cousin
Kyle Bruner—Lia's husband
Vanessa Fleer—frenemy turned friend . . . adjacent

Quentin MacIlhoney—defense attorney, Vanessa's
    fiancé
Xander Durand—Bo's seven-year-old son
Whitney Evans—Bo's ex-wife
Lee Bertrand—Grand-mère's boyfriend
Chret Bertrand—Gaynell's boyfriend
Kaity Bertrand—another teen
Clinton Poche—a local high school student
Brianna Poche—Clinton's younger sister
Zenephra—shop owner in a nearby town
Esme—a young friend of Xander's

The singer and her entourage
Tammy Barker—country star, local girl made good
Pony Pickner—Tammy's manager
Sara Salinas—Tammy's assistant
Bokie Phlen—the band's drummer
East MacLeod—guitarist
Uffen Irgstaad—bassist
The Sound—keyboardist
Toulouse Delaroux Caresmeatrand—accordionist,
    modified washboard (frottoir)
Valeria Aguilar—backup singer
Gigi Barker—Tammy's cousin
Narcisse Barker—Gigi's husband

Chapter 1

"So, we agree we're not getting married in the summer," Maggie said.

"Not unless you want me to walk down the aisle in shorts and flip-flops."

Bo grinned and squeezed his fiancée's hand. The couple had just finished a tour of their future home, an apartment above the plantation's 1920s garage, which was being remodeled as a spa facility. Despite an engagement already two months old, Bo and Maggie had yet to set a wedding date. This delay was due to a brainstorm on the part of Charlotte Crozat, Maggie's beloved grand-mère. "Pelican should do a musical festival that runs Sunday through Thursday," Gran had announced at a meeting of the tiny town's equally tiny tourism board. "Those are the slow days in our business. We can advertise our festival as a way for New Orleans Jazz and Heritage Festival attendees to get a dose of music and local flavor on their way to New Orleans."

The board members, who usually saw meetings as a

chance to imbibe and gossip, were stunned by Gran's brilliant idea. They put down their Sazeracs and got to work. But pulling off such a major undertaking in such a short time required herculean efforts on the part of pretty much everyone in town, so Maggie and Bo put their wedding plans on the back burner and pitched in. Maggie took charge of graphics for the *Cajun Country Live!* Music and Culture Fest while her detective beau coordinated security, which would be provided by on- and off-duty members of the Pelican Police Department. The only matrimonial detail confirmed by the couple was Maggie's bridal attire. She'd be married in the 150-year-old gown worn by her mother, Ninette Doucet Crozat, and generations of Doucet women before her. Due to its age, the dress would remain in storage until as close to the wedding date as possible. Whenever that date might be.

"We could do a Halloween wedding or a Christmas wedding," Maggie said as she and Bo strolled past the plantation's garçonnière and carriage house, both renovated to serve as guest lodgings.

"Or a wedding where the only holiday we're celebrating is our actual wedding."

"Or that. So many choices. But none involving flip-flops, please, oh please."

They reached the back door of the Crozat manor house. With its thirty-two square columns and galleries encircling the home on both the ground and second floors, Maggie's family home was a gracious example of Greek Revival architecture and a landmark on Louisiana's Great River

Road. Overwhelmed by the cost of maintaining a majestic but centuries-old compound, many locals turned their plantations over to the state or a nonprofit historical foundation. Some historic homes became derelict, the victims of a family's internecine fighting over their shared inheritance. Others were sold to and eventually razed by one of the oil or chemical corporations lining the lower Mississippi River. But the Crozats opted to hold on to their ancestral land and run it as a bed-and-breakfast. Like many small businesses, Crozat Plantation B and B rode a roller coaster of ups and downs. However, unlike many small businesses, most of the recent downs at Crozat involved murders.

Bo held open the door for his bride-to-be. "*Merci*," she said with a flirtatious smile, which he returned. He then followed her inside and into the kitchen. Maggie's father, Tug, was there, unpacking groceries, while her mother, Ninette, brow furrowed, examined a computer printout. The headliner for *Cajun Country Live!* was Tammy Barker, a native daughter of Pelican who'd won *Sing It*, a hugely successful TV talent show. Her manager had booked the whole B and B for the length of the festival, so the Crozats were prepping for a crowd. A tray of pecan pralines sat on top of the kitchen's old stove. Maggie took two and handed one to Bo. "Everything okay, Mom? You don't look happy."

Ninette continued to study the paper in her hand. "Our guests sent a list of food demands for at least three of them. One is a pescatarian—"

Tug stopped unpacking. "Pesca what now?"

"Pescatarian," Maggie said. "It means someone who doesn't eat meat or poultry. Only fish."

Ninette waved the paper in the air. "But Tammy is allergic to seafood, so she can't eat it at all. She's a vegetarian. And her manager is following something called the Paleo Diet."

"Paleo what now?" Tug looked befuddled.

"Okay, I'm not even sure what that is." Maggie pulled her cell phone out of her jeans back pocket and did a quick search. "Hmmm . . . might be better to list what you *can't* eat on this diet. Dairy, potatoes, grains, legumes, refined sugar, refined vegetable oil—"

Ninette groaned. "Stop right there. Tug, honey, we're going back to the store." This elicited a groan from her husband. "Thank goodness I made enough pralines to get us through tomorrow." Crozat B and B was sponsoring a booth at *Cajun Country Live!* that they'd titled Pelican Pralines, which would sell Ninette's homemade treats as well as Maggie's paintings and a souvenir line she'd created featuring her illustrations of local plantations.

Maggie opened the refrigerator door and peered inside. "Pralines, pralines, and more pralines. Is there a pecan left in the state?"

"Probably not, thanks to your mama," Tug said.

Maggie's father grabbed his car keys off the kitchen's large trestle table, and then he and Ninette left for another round of shopping. Bo helped himself to a second candy. "I think I'm gonna go on the praline diet and only eat your mama's fine sweets. Get my protein from those pecans." He finished the praline in two bites. "So, are y'all excited about having a famous guest? Whitney's a big fan of Tammy's," he said, referencing his ex-wife. "Did you know her at all when she lived here?"

"No. I've never met Tammy. She was a kid when I left for New York. I knew of her family but didn't know them personally. As soon as she won that TV contest, pretty much all the Barkers took off to Los Angeles with her. Brothers, sisters, parents, stepparents, grandparents, even a few ex-grandparents. I hear she's got some cousins left in Pelican, but that's about it." A shadow crossed Maggie's face. "Gaynell went to high school with her. But she isn't at all excited about her coming back. She actually seems unhappy about it but won't say why."

"Maybe Gaynell's jealous. They're both singers."

Maggie shook her head. She'd met Gaynell through her job as a tour guide at Doucet, a plantation once owned by Ninette's family. Although a dozen years younger than thirty-two-year-old Maggie, Gaynell quickly became one of her closest friends. The multitalented musician was as kind and bighearted as they came and possessed an intelligence that belied her angelic blonde looks. "I think it's more serious than that. She gets this look like something bad happened, but she doesn't want to go there. I'm a little concerned."

"You know what concerns me?"

"What?"

"That we're alone for a change and not doing anything about it."

With that, Bo pulled Maggie in for a kiss.

* * *

The next day was Maggie's last before taking a week off from her new position as Doucet's art collection specialist. Late April brought the lush, damp warmth of a south Louisiana spring, and she drove across the Mississippi River with the top down on the 1964 Falcon convertible she'd inherited from Papa Doucet, her late grandfather. A few bars of a Trombone Shorty song alerted her to an incoming call, and she pressed a button on the Bluetooth device straddling her ear. She was greeted by her grand-mère's tinkly voice. "Hello, chère."

"Hi, Gran. How'd the meeting go?" Her grandmother, a pillar of the *Cajun Country Live!* festival committee, had been called to an early-morning confab to finalize details for the event, which would start the next day.

"Oh, the usual last-minute panic. But I've got some great gossip. Rufus Durand and Quentin MacIlhoney both dropped out of the mayor's race." Pelican's current mayor had abruptly announced he was moving to New York to pursue his dream of being an actor. Besides mutterings about whether or not Broadway was crying out for a rotund sixty-five-year-old with a thick Cajun accent, his departure generated a race to replace him.

"Both of them? Why?"

"Neither realized it was an unpaid position."

Maggie burst out laughing. "Seriously?"

"Oh, yes." Gran giggled.

"Wow. That was some poor research on their parts." Maggie heard Gran giggle again. "Gran, are you drunk?"

"No." There was a pause. "All right, maybe a little. We had a bit of champagne to celebrate the festival's approach. Anyway, since no one's running against her, Eula Banks is our new mayor. And that's your Pelican scuttlebutt update for the day. Hold on, young man, where are you going with that bottle? Bye, chère." Gran ended the call and her granddaughter shook her head, amused.

Maggie pulled into the driveway leading to Doucet, a large, stately home on the west side of the Mississippi. She parked in the small employees' lot and strolled to her office in a newer building designed as a mini version of the Doucet manor house. The room, bathed with natural light from a bank of windows, served as a studio where Maggie could restore damaged artwork, as well as a transitional space for pieces being rotated in or out of the plantation's collection. She spent the morning cataloging a portfolio of sketches she'd found squirreled away in the manor house's cavernous attic. The drawings, in exceptional shape, depicted rarely seen images of post–Civil War plantation life. Maggie's boss and close friend, Ione Savreau, was thrilled with the discovery and planned to display them in a special exhibit.

Maggie broke for lunch at noon, joining Ione and Gaynell at a bench under the plantation's most majestic magnolia tree. Her friends still wore the antebellum costumes Maggie had happily shed for her new job. A group of part-time new hires, teens from the local community college, approached them.

"Hi, Maggie." The greeting came from the group's leader, a thin, frizzy-haired redhead.

The girl made a move to sit on the bench next to Maggie, and the three other teens followed suit, but Ione held up her hand. "Nuh-uh, girls. We're talking business. You can take it over there." She pointed to a picnic bench in the distance.

The redhead stood up, disgruntled, then recovered with a smile. "Okay. We'll see y'all later." The teens then took off.

"And by *y'all*, she meant you."

Ione said this to Maggie, who responded with an eye roll. "Ever since word got out that Tammy Barker is staying with us, I've become the most popular gal in town. At least with teens and tweens. If I'd been this cool when I was a teenager, I might never have bolted for New York. It took Tammy to put me on the social map in Pelican."

"Did you hear we have a new mayor?"

This out-of-left-field comment came from Gaynell. Maggie and Ione swiveled toward their friend. "Gaynell, chère," Ione said, her tone soothing, "every time this Tammy's name comes up, there's a sadness to you. I think you'll feel better if you tell us what's going on."

Gaynell stared at the uneaten sandwich in the container on her lap. "It's silly. I mean, it was just high school stuff. Tammy was a junior when I was a freshman. She dated my older brother Arnaud a little. We were both into music. I've never been that competitive, but she kinda was, and . . ."

Maggie cut to it. "Did she bully you?"

Gaynell sighed and nodded. "She was one of the cool kids, so she could get people to not sit with me or believe rumors she started. During a school talent show, when it was my turn, she got up and walked out. A ton of kids followed her. She got called out on it by the principal, but that never makes things better. Only worse."

Maggie gritted her teeth to suppress her emotions. Few things made her angrier than bullying. Bo's seven-year-old son, Xander, who was on the autism spectrum, had suffered such relentless teasing at his old school in northern Louisiana that it motivated the family's move to Pelican. "We officially hate Tammy," she declared. "Right, Ione?"

"Oh, yeah," Ione said with a vigorous nod.

Gaynell smiled. "Y'all are too much. But really, it's okay. It's silly that it still bothers me. It's been a long time since high school. Like, two years."

"Ouch," Ione said. "Thinking on how young you are reminds me how old I am."

Maggie sighed and nodded. "Me too."

"I'm sure Tammy's changed," Gaynell said, sounding like she was trying to convince herself this might be true. "I mean, she's a big star now and I'm a nobody. There's nothing to compete for."

"Whoa." Maggie took her friend by the shoulders. "You are *not* a nobody. You are an awesomely talented musician who just needs someone to see that and do something about it."

"Well . . ." Gaynell took a deep breath. "I haven't told

anyone this yet, but I filled out a Jazz Fest application for Gaynell and the Gator Girls. Someone's coming to hear our set, and if they like it, they'll give us a slot next year."

Maggie and Ione whooped, drawing attention from the teen cabal at the picnic table. "Did Tammy show up at Crozat?" the redhead called to them hopefully.

"No," Maggie called back. "We've got something way cooler to be excited about." She hugged Gaynell, and then her cell phone buzzed. Maggie checked and saw a text message. "It's from my mom. Tammy did show up. Along with a bunch of buses and trucks." She held up the cell phone so her friends could read Ninette's message:

GET HOME NOW!

Chapter 2

Maggie arrived home to find Crozat packed with trucks, buses, and lookie-loo cars. She drove to the back of the plantation, parked by the shotgun cottage she shared with her grandmother, and hurried to join her parents at the front of the house.

"Where are we going to put all of those?" she asked, scanning the phalanx of vehicles.

"The trucks are heading over to the festival grounds at the airfield," Tug said. "We don't have to worry about them."

"Just the busloads of guests," Ninette said. "I never did get a final head count from Tammy's people. I hope I don't run out of food."

Gran sauntered up to the others, holding a champagne flute. Maggie gestured to Gran's glass. "Still celebrating?"

"It's Louisiana, chère. When do we *not* celebrate?" Gran checked out the growing crowd of onlookers. A group of young girls huddled together, pointing to the buses with excitement and whispering to each other. "What's the proper word to describe that group of young women? A gaggle of girls?"

The door of the first bus opened, generating squeals and jumping up and down from the cluster of teens. "A giggle," Maggie said. "I think you'd call it a giggle of girls."

Gran raised her glass to toast Maggie. "Nicely done. I like it."

A young woman who wasn't Tammy Barker stepped out of the bus. She was in her midtwenties, with olive skin and black hair cut in a severe but fashionable hairstyle. She wore a man's white dress shirt, artfully ripped jeans, and open-toed ankle booties. She was followed by a man in his fifties, bald, lean, and exuding authority. Yet there was something odd about his body. After a moment, Maggie's artist's eye homed in on what it was: his torso was unusually long while his legs were short. *He'd be hard to shop for*, she thought.

There was a pause that Maggie could swear had been choreographed. The waiting fans held their collective breath. And finally, *Sing It* star Tammy Barker appeared in the bus doorway. Pelican's most famous daughter was waif-like slim, with a thick thatch of chestnut-brown hair that hung long and shiny to the middle of her back. She was taller than she appeared in photographs, a few inches above Maggie's five-foot-four-inch height. Then Maggie saw that the singer was wearing the kind of giant platform shoes actors had worn in Ancient Greece. Without them, Tammy Barker might not have cleared five feet.

Tammy came down the bus stairs, and Maggie couldn't

help being impressed by how gracefully she moved in the giant shoes. Her fans would have swarmed the singing star had her handlers not formed a human barricade. "Make a line," the bald man barked, and they did so.

The man stepped away, and Ninette gave her husband a nudge. "Go talk to him; he looks important."

"Right," Tug said, nonplussed. He walked toward the man and held out his hand. "Hey there. Tug Crozat. Welcome to our home."

The man took his hand and shook it. "Pony Pickner. I'm Tammy's manager." He pointed to the woman in the open-toed booties managing the crowd. "And that's Sara Salinas, her assistant."

The introductions were interrupted by a loud screech of "Tammy, baby cousin!" A doughy woman a few years older than Tammy barreled toward the singer, followed by a man about the same age with dark, lazy good looks. Sara looked ready to tackle the charging woman, but Tammy threw her hands in the air and screeched, "Gigi! Narcisse!" The three engaged in a round of hugs. Tammy's fans pressed forward. Gigi motioned for them to step back. "Go on now, shoo."

Sara's eye's narrowed. "That's my job. I'm her assistant."

Gigi threw back her shoulders. "I'm her cousin. *And* president of her fan club."

Pony stepped between the women and pushed them away from Tammy. "I'm her manager and I outrank both of you." If he noticed the dirty looks coming from Gigi and Sara, they didn't appear to bother him. "Our star needs to rest now," Pony said. He waved off the buses and trucks, and the convoy lumbered down the driveway toward the River Road.

"Where's everyone going?" Ninette asked, confused.

"To Belle Vista," Sara said. "Pony, me, and Tammy are the only ones staying here." She didn't look too happy about the arrangement.

"But . . . there are only three of you. And you booked the whole place." Ninette was even more confused.

"S.O.P." Pony said.

"S-O what now?" Ninette said.

"Standard operating procedure," Tug whispered to his wife. He looked a touch self-satisfied that he knew this.

"It prevents fans from booking rooms in the same hotel and causing problems," Sara explained.

"Yeah, they can get *poco loco*." Gigi twirled her fingers in the universal sign for crazy. "Believe me, as her fan club president, I would know."

Sara glared at her.

Tammy approached the Crozats. Her fans, sensing they were being dismissed, melted away. "Hi, I'm Tammy," she said with a warm smile. "I grew up in a trailer along Back Road 41. Until I got the platinum ticket to go to Hollywood for *Sing It*, I spent my whole life going by your place and wondering what it was like inside. I dreamed of staying here one day. And now I get to. Thanks for making my dream come true."

There was a moment of silence as the Crozats took this in. Then Gran held up her champagne glass in a toast. "Nicely done."

"*Mother*," Tug admonished her.

"Well, it was."

Ninette regained her wits. "We're honored that you've chosen to stay with us, Tammy, and will do whatever we can to make your stay everything you dreamed of. Tug will get your bags, and our daughter Maggie and I will show you to your rooms. We thought we'd put you in the Rose Room. It's our very best room and it's inside the manor house."

"That sounds so nice, but would you mind if I stayed in the garçonnière? It always looked so cute to me, like a dollhouse. And that way I won't drive y'all out of your home with my vocal exercises."

"The garçonnière it is," Ninette said, her tone polite.

Tammy clapped her hands, delighted. "Thank you so much. I forgot how nice civilians can be." She turned to her manager. "Pony, I asked Narcisse here to be my bodyguard while I'm in Pelican. My regular guy is guarding some Oscar winner on a press tour and can't meet us until New Orleans." She directed the last comment at show-biz neophytes Maggie, Ninette, and Gran with a sigh that said, *the trials and tribulations of being famous.*

"Whoa," Pony said. His lips formed a grim line. "He hasn't been vetted."

"He's family. That's all the vetting I need."

Narcisse flashed a smug smile at Pony. "Can't argue with that, can ya?"

Tammy's manager gave him a cold stare. "Can and will. I wouldn't get too attached to the job."

"Why don't we settle y'all in?" Ninette said, eager to break the tension. She motioned to Maggie and Gran, and the three headed toward the garçonnière. Sara extricated Tammy from a few autograph-seeking stragglers, and they followed the Crozat women, Gigi and Narcisse on their tail. Pony stayed behind, holding a phone to his ear while directing Tug on how to separate the massive amounts of luggage extricated from the bowels of the bus. The manager radiated a dismissive attitude, which Maggie found annoying.

Gran tapped her granddaughter on the shoulder. "What do you think of our illustrious guest?" she whispered.

"She's okay, I guess. A little taken with herself."

"You sound skeptical."

Maggie didn't respond, reluctant to share that she was predisposed to dislike Tammy. The group reached the garçonnière. In centuries past, it had housed boys once they became teens, separating their raging hormones from the plantation's susceptible young ladies. The Crozats had turned it into a lovely, if small, lodging, with a living room downstairs and bedroom upstairs.

Tammy gasped. She clapped her hands to her mouth, then dropped them. "It's as beautiful as I dreamed it would be," she said in a quiet voice. "I can't believe I finally get to stay here."

She impulsively hugged Ninette, and Maggie was forced to consider the possibility that fame had changed Tammy in a good way.

* * *

The superstar and her entourage declined dinner and holed up in their rooms, much to Ninette's relief. Maggie joined her mother in the manor house kitchen and helped prep for their guests' myriad of breakfast food demands. She chopped vegetables, cut up fruit, and thumbed through the family's cookbook to find at least one recipe that would make everyone happy. After a half hour, she admitted defeat and gave up the search. Maggie placed the food she'd prepared for the morning in the refrigerator, then took off her apron and hung it on a hook by the back door. Ninette checked out her daughter's outfit of black boots, black miniskirt, and tight white T-shirt. "You look rather rock 'n' roll. Trying to impress our music industry guests?"

"To be honest, I was out of clean clothes. But I guess I don't mind coming across as something more than a backcountry bumpkin."

"Good luck with that Pony fellow. He wrote us off the minute he saw us."

"I noticed." Maggie checked the time on her phone. "Oooh, gotta go. We're all meeting up at Junie's. Gaynell and the Gator Girls are running through the set they're doing at the festival."

She took off for Junie's Oyster Bar and Dance Hall, Pelican's favorite hangout. Maggie parked in the picturesque village center, where banners welcoming visitors to *Cajun Country Live!* hung from the decorative iron balconies of the centuries-old buildings that ringed the town square. Bayou Beurre, its banks green and lush with spring flora, lay beyond it.

Maggie stepped inside Junie's, a hangout brimming with charming if faded elegance. An ornate bar, carved by craftsmen in the late 1870s, ran the length of one wall, topped with a gilded mirror. Above it rested a mounted alligator who had once been the constant companion of the original owner, Junie. Her son JJ had inherited the bar along with his mother's closetful of colorful caftans. The place, which always smelled like a combination of booze, Cajun food, and mildew, was humming with activity. Locals mixed with tourists who'd arrived early for the festival.

JJ, clad in a caftan patterned with alligators playing saxophones, blew Maggie a kiss, which she returned. She glanced around the crowded room and saw Bo, who waved her over to a large table he and their friends had staked out. The group included Rufus Durand, who was Bo's cousin and town police chief. Next to him sat his girlfriend, dance studio owner Sandy Sechrest. Across from them was Vanessa Fleer, Rufus's former fiancée, and sixty-something defense attorney Quentin MacIlhoney, Vanessa's current fiancé. Relationships in Pelican were nothing if not complicated.

"Maggie, you made it." This came from Gaynell, who was on stage tuning her guitar. She jumped down from the stage and gave her friend a hug. "It's gonna be a fun night. We're doing a bunch of traditional Cajun—"

Gaynell stopped midsentence. Maggie followed her gaze to the front of the restaurant. Tammy Barker had just entered. The singer was flanked by Sara, Gigi, Narcisse, and several hipsters Maggie assumed were musicians based on their multiple tattoos, piercings, and man buns, a look she despised. She gripped Gaynell's hand. "It's okay. You're okay."

Gaynell took a deep, shuddering breath. "I know." She hopped back on stage and grabbed the mic. "Hey, y'all, settle down now." The crowd quieted. "Welcome to Junie's. As a lot of you know, we're Gaynell and the Gator Girls. Tonight we're doing the set we'll be playing at the festival, which'll also be our audition for Jazz Fest."

"Woo-hoo, go Gaynell and the Gator Girls!" Maggie's shout-out earned whoops from her own table and beyond.

Gaynell smiled. "Thank you. But first, there's someone special here. Someone who's super talented and has done our little town proud. Tammy, come on up."

Tammy hesitated. A wave of recognition swept through the crowd. Murmurs of "Is that Tammy Barker?" turned into "OMG, that's Tammy Barker!" followed by applause, then cheers. Narcisse, Tammy's newly minted security guard, waved his arms around in an unnecessary display of power. Gaynell reached out to Tammy, who took her hand, deftly negotiated the stage stairs, and came to the mic.

"How does she walk in those shoes?" Sandy, the dancer, wondered.

"I don't know, but I want me a pair," Vanessa responded, her eyes on Tammy's spiky gold heels.

Tammy addressed the diners. "Hey there, Pelican. It's good to be home." The crowd roared their approval of this sentiment. "I just wanna say . . . sometimes you have to leave a place to know how much it means to you. You look back and realize you didn't appreciate how wonderful it was. And how good and kind the people were. I'm sorry about that."

Tammy aimed the last two lines at Gaynell, who smiled and gave a slight nod. Gaynell spoke into the mic. "Who wants to hear the winner of *Sing It* do some singing?"

The loud affirmative response made the restaurant walls vibrate. It morphed into a chant of "Sing it, sing it, sing it . . ." Tammy and Gaynell huddled for a moment, and then Tammy said, "All right, y'all asked for it. I'm going with a classic." Gaynell strapped on her guitar, nodded to her band, then strummed the familiar chords of Hank Williams's "Jambalaya."

"Goodbye, Joe, me gotta go, me oh my oh . . ."

Maggie knew nothing about music, but she couldn't deny Tammy's voice was spectacular—powerful and crystal clear. The country star threw in a couple of note runs more appropriate to some pop diva's top-forty rendition of the tune, but she finished the song to a standing ovation. Tammy motioned for the crowd to sit down. "Thank you. But I'm just a singer. Y'all wanna hear a real musician?" She hugged Gaynell and handed her the mic. "Give it up for Gaynell Bourgeois!"

The crowd did as instructed. Tammy left the stage and settled at a table whose occupants had been evicted by Narcisse. Gaynell launched into a rousing rendition of the classic Cajun tune "Allons à Lafayette." She followed this with a song of her own composition that brought people out of their seats and onto Junie's dance floor, where they laughed and twirled as they two-stepped. Gaynell sang in a voice that was unique yet as powerful as Tammy's pipes, and deftly segued between guitar, fiddle, and the single-row diatonic accordion many Cajun musicians preferred to the multiple-row piano accordions found in zydeco bands. The Gator Girls finished the song with a flourish. The response was deafening, louder than for Tammy. But the *Sing It* winner was the first to jump to her feet, cheering. Bo leaned over to Maggie. "Whatever happened in the past, she seems to be over it now."

Maggie frowned. She'd spent the entire number surreptitiously watching the country singer, and the ugly expressions she'd witnessed confirmed what she'd feared.

Tammy Barker, contest winner and superstar, was still jealous of Gaynell.

Chapter 3

"Why would Tammy be jealous of Gaynell?" Bo asked when Maggie shared her suspicions with him.

It was a good question, one that gave Maggie a fitful night's sleep as she searched for the answer. True, Gaynell was younger, but only by a couple of years. Could that make such a big difference, even in age-averse Hollywood? Was it a competition based on musical ability? Gaynell played a range of instruments and Maggie didn't know what Tammy's gifts were beyond singing. Still, it was hard to imagine the platinum-selling country diva resenting Gaynell's skill with a frottoir, the washboard featured in Cajun and zydeco bands. Was it over some high school heartthrob? Given that Tammy probably had her pick of Hollywood hunks, that seemed the most unlikely possibility. Maybe it was simply a case of something Maggie once read in a magazine article: no matter how old you get, you never really leave high school.

In the morning, Maggie padded into the living room of the shotgun cottage to find Grand-mère, dressed in beige slacks and a white silk top, surrounded by an assortment of boxes. "Morning. What's all this?"

Gran held up a photo album with a faded cover. "The festival committee insists on doing a poster honoring my contributions to the community, so I'm digging up some pictures for them. While I was at it, I decided to do a death cleaning."

Maggie gaped at her grandmother. "A death what now?"

"*Döstädning.* It's the Swedish tradition of paring down your belongings when you're in the home stretch of your lifetime so that they aren't a burden to the loved ones you leave behind."

Maggie made a face. "Oooh-kay. But can we please call it something else?"

Gran shook her head. "No, we cannot. I admire the Swedes' honesty. Death cleaning they call it, and death cleaning it shall be." Gran held up an odd-looking metal apparatus. "Should we keep this?"

"What is it?"

"An egg beater." Gran turned the eggbeater's handle. "And your response makes the answer a no."

Maggie left her grandmother to her disturbing sorting and retreated to the bathroom for a shower. She then fed Gopher, the family's adopted basset hound, and Jolie, their Chihuahua mix. Maggie had rescued Jolie from the home of a murderer. She'd also saved Jolie's cat bestie, Brooke, as well as both animals' puppies and kittens, from near starvation when she discovered them in the woods behind Crozat plantation. Maggie found wonderful homes for the pups and kitties, while Jolie and Brooke had become much-loved additions to the Crozat family.

"Oh, no you don't," she warned Gopher. The basset, whose stomach was a bottomless pit, was eyeing the almost-full bowl of picky eater Jolie. "No double helpings for you, mister. You're dancing real close to the edge of diet kibble as it is." Gopher gave an annoyed bark but backed away from the bowl.

Maggie put on jeans and a *Cajun Country Live!* T-shirt featuring the logo she'd designed of an accordion and fiddle inside a triangle whose three sides spelled out the name of the festival. Then she headed over to the manor house kitchen. The room smelled like butter, baked bread, and for some odd reason, broiled steak. The trestle table was covered with plates, while multiple pots simmered on the stove. It was only seven thirty in the morning, but Ninette already looked exhausted. Maggie took in the scene. "This is for three guests?"

Ninette nodded. "Regular bread and gluten-free bread. Shrimp and grits on the stove for the pesca-whatever. Egg-free breakfast casserole with veggie sausage for our star guest. Steak and many eggs for Mr. Paleo, her manager." Ninette pulled open the oven's broiler, removed a sizzling hunk of steak, and plated it. "It was easier cooking for that kosher family who stayed with us. That only required two sets of dishes."

Pony Pickner suddenly appeared in the doorway, startling Maggie and her mother. "I've got a form I need you to sign."

"And good morning to you," Maggie said, her tone sarcastic. "What kind of form?"

"Just your basic NDA."

"ND what now?" Maggie and her mother said simultaneously.

"Nondisclosure agreement." He didn't have to add, *How can you not know this?* The thought was implied by his tone.

"What are we nondisclosing?" Maggie asked.

"You'll know when I sue you for whatever it is you're disclosing." Pony handed them each a piece of paper. "I'll need your husband and the older lady who lives here—"

"I assume the older lady you're referring to is my mother-in-law, Charlotte Crozat, who came up with the idea for this whole festival in the first place," Ninette said, her tone laced with a tartness unusual for her.

"If that's her, I need her to sign an NDA, and your husband, too. You can have your lawyer check it out, but it's pretty much boilerplate for the industry."

"No need for a lawyer." Ninette rummaged through a junk drawer, retrieving a pen from the tangled mess of doodads. "When it comes to our guests, we pride ourselves on discretion."

"That's fine for civilians, but we're talking A-list here. Whole different ball game."

"Not loving constantly being called *civilians*," Maggie murmured under her breath.

Ninette signed the form, then handed the pen to Maggie, who took a beat and then signed her own form. They handed both back to Pony. He pocketed them and pulled out his cell phone as it pinged an incoming text. He read the text and fist-pumped the air. "*Yes.*"

"Good news?" Ninette asked, trying to be polite.

"My lawyer just shot down a couple of nuisance lawsuits."

"A little unwelcome disclosing?" This came from Maggie, with an edge.

"Harassment stuff. Total BS. It's the music business. Everything is consensual."

"The women involved might not agree," Maggie felt compelled to point out.

"Trust me, they did. Just groupies trying to make a fast buck. Yeah, managers have groupies. Even roadies do. Can't think of anyone in the business who doesn't. Breakfast ready yet? I need protein before my run."

Ninette picked up a spray bottle filled with oil and gave a plate of eggs and meat a few shots from it. The tempting meal glistened. "Here you go."

Pony sniffed the plate. "There's no refined oil in here, right, only healthy oil? None of that crap you get at the grocery store."

Ninette gave the manager a sunny smile. "Don't you worry about the oil one bit. Just enjoy your breakfast."

Pony took the plate and exited without a goodbye. Maggie eyed her mother. "You used refined oil, didn't you?"

Ninette flashed a devilish grin. "Chère, that oil's so refined it could be a debutante."

"To quote Gran, nicely done."

"Just don't 'disclose' it, my sweet civilian."

Maggie laughed. "I can't. I signed a form." Her cell phone announced an incoming text. "It's Gaynell. I'm HERE. You FREE A SEC?"

Ninette waved her off. "Go. I'm fine. One breakfast down, two more to go."

Maggie left her mother and headed out the front door to the manor home's wide veranda. Gaynell stood outside her pickup truck holding a guitar. "I'm sorry it's so early, but I wrote a new song this morning. It just come to me like that, and I'm real excited. I think it's the one that could put me over the top with the Jazz Fest folk." She stopped to breathe.

"That's wonderful. I can't wait to hear it."

Maggie sat on a rocking chair as Gaynell leaped up the front steps two at a time. "It's kind of about letting go of stuff that haunts you and holds you back. I'm telling myself to move on with my life. I call it 'Forget the Past'—'Oublie le Passe.'"

Gaynell strummed an intricate introduction, then began to sing.

She danced away the evening as the glowing gold sun set
Dancing like a wild child, hoping to forget
That yesterday she ran away from a life that stilled the
*   soul*
She dances like a wild child, hoping that will make her
*   whole*
Forget the past, just clear your mind,

Forget the past, let me be kind.
Elle a dansé le soir alors que le soleil brille
Danser comme un enfant sauvage, en espérant oublier
Qu'hier, elle s'est enfuie d'une vie qui a calmé l'âme
Elle danse comme un enfant sauvage, espérant que cela
    la rendra entière
Oublie le passé, efface ton esprit,
Oublie le passé, laisse-moi être gentil.

Gaynell held the last note and then released it. Maggie burst into applause. She thought the sound was echoing, then realized someone else was clapping. She turned around to see Tammy Barker standing behind her. The singer's thick head of hair was pulled into a tight, high ponytail. Maggie's artist's eyes picked up a scar on one side of Tammy's head. Then she realized she was looking at a seam, not a scar. The TV star's impressive mane was the product of hair extensions; manufactured, like the illusion of her height.

"OMG, Gaynell, that was gorgeous," Tammy gushed. "You sing, you write, you play a ton of instruments. What don't you do?"

"Uh . . . be as successful as you?"

"Ha. Well, that's about to change." Tammy took the cell she held in her hand and tapped out a message. "I just told Pony he *has* to meet with you. He's always on the hunt for new talent."

Gaynell's eyes widened. "Now it's my turn to OMG. Thank you so much!"

Tammy gave an embarrassed shrug. "'*Oublie le passé,*

laisse-moi être gentil.' 'Forget the past . . . let me be kind.'"
There was a pause as Gaynell—and Maggie—took this in;
Gaynell with hope, Maggie with skepticism. "Anyhoo, I'm
giving my band a kinda greatest-hits tour of Pelican. You
know, places I hung out when I lived here. I rented a minivan.
If y'all are free, I'd love to have you come after breakfast."

"That'd be so much fun," Gaynell said. "Thank you."

Both women looked to Maggie for her response. "Sure.
It does sound fun."

"Awesome. The van'll be here in about forty-five minutes. Meet you back here." Tammy's cell had been beeping
text alerts throughout their entire conversation, and she
checked it. She dismissed them one by one. "No. No. No.
Nope. Oh, you wish. Ah, Pony got back to me. He'll meet
with you after lunch."

Gaynell gasped with delight. "Oh my. That calls for a
special thank you." Gaynell strummed a vibrant chord and
sang out the words. Tammy joined in, harmonizing on the
you, and the two high-fived each other. Maggie forced herself to applaud—and wished she could shake off the nag-
ging feeling of foreboding that always preceded disaster.

Chapter 4

As promised, a minivan pulled into the driveway forty-five minutes later. Tammy had rented three cars for the band to share while in Pelican. "Purple, like for Mardi Gras," she told everyone, bragging about how she managed to track down the rare car color and how much she laid out for it. But she insisted her entourage travel together for the journey down her memory lane, hence the minivan.

Maggie boarded behind the singing star and Gaynell. She checked out those already loaded in and couldn't imagine a less likely group traipsing around picturesque Pelican and its rural environs. Tammy's band members slouched in their seats, most barely awake. Only one, a chubby-cheeked, ginger-haired young man who looked a good ten years younger than the others, seemed happy about the excursion.

"Hey y'all, wake up," Tammy ordered. "I want you to meet my old friend Gaynell and my new friend Maggie." Monosyllabic greetings were uttered, except from the titian-haired musician, who said "Nice to meet y'all" with a distinctly local accent. Tammy pointed to a different musician as she introduced each one. "That's East MacLeod, Bokie Phlen, Uffen Irgstaad, The Sound." Tammy finished by pointing to the redheaded young musician. "And Toulouse Delaroux Caresmeatrand."

"Finally, someone with a normal name," Maggie said under her breath to Gaynell, who nodded.

An attractive woman with light-brown skin and a mass of dark curly hair waved her hand from the back. "Uh, hello." She looked annoyed. "Remember me? The one who hits the high notes you can't?"

"Sorry. That's my backup singer, Valeria Aguilar. Ignore the attitude. It's what'll get her fired by the time we hit Nashville." Tammy clapped her hands together. "So, we all ready to pass a Pelican good time?"

"Y'all know it," Toulouse said. Maggie had to smile at his genuine enthusiasm.

Toulouse turned to Gaynell. "You were awesome last night. *Awesome.*"

"Thank you," Gaynell said, a little embarrassed. "I appreciate that."

"*Laissez les bon temps rouler,*" Toulouse said. He held up his hand. "Up top. From one Cajun musician t'other."

Gaynell gave him a quick hand slap, then retreated to an open space a safe distance from the ebullient Toulouse. Maggie settled into her seat and refused the nine AM beer offered with a flirty smile by her seatmate, Uffen.

*   *   *

After an hour of drifting past locations that meant something to Tammy and no one else, Maggie dozed off. She started awake when the van meandered onto a bumpy road and then lurched to a stop. "We're ending the tour at my most favorite place of all," Tammy announced to her drowsy semi-prisoners. "Everybody off the bus."

There was muted grumbling as the group disembarked. They were parked on top of the river levee. Valeria held up her cell phone and turned in a circle. "No signal," she grumbled. "We're in the middle of flipping nowhere."

Maggie looked below and knew exactly where they were. "It's the Harmonie Plantation batture," she said, pronouncing the word so it rhymed with *catcher*. This drew blank looks from the visitors. "That's the fertile land between the river and the levee."

The batture was thick with a variety of overgrown brush. Branches of black willow, bald cypress, and sugarberry trees elbowed each other. Buttonbush and swamp privet bushes grew underneath the trees as vines crept up their trunks. The rotted wood remnants of a dock extended into the river. A battered pirogue, the flat-bottom canoe generally found on bayous, lay on the shore. A rope swing still clung to the branches of a Chinese tallow tree denuded of leaves. Maggie pointed to the stone foundation of what had once been a large house. "People lived here from the mid–eighteen hundreds through the Depression, when floods took almost everything away. The ruins appear when the river's low."

"We played here a lot as kids," Tammy said. "Gaynell,

remember that time in high school a bunch of us came here at night with beer we stole from my daddy's garage fridge?"

Gaynell nodded but didn't say anything. Maggie noticed her friend looked tense.

"Come on, everyone." Tammy started down the levee bank's slippery slope. *Even her sneakers have platforms*, Maggie thought as she watched.

"This was not in my contract," Valeria groused.

Toulouse offered an arm. "Here, I'll help."

The others reluctantly followed their meal ticket's lead. Gaynell, however, hung back. "What's wrong?" Maggie asked her friend.

Gaynell looked down at the ground. "That time in high school she brought up. I thought Tammy had accepted me into the group. I thought I was finally friends with the 'cool' musician kids. We were all goofing around. The old house was still there, and they dared me to go inside. I was scared, but I did it. When I came out, everyone was gone. They left me there alone. It was so dark. I found my way out of there and made my way home."

"You live miles from here."

"I know. But my family couldn't afford cell phones, so I couldn't call anyone. I got in big trouble, but I didn't want to tell my folks what happened because my dad was like to punch someone. Instead they grounded me, which was okay. Gave me an excuse to go straight home after school and stay away from people and not be made fun of." Gaynell raised her head. "You go. You don't have to wait here with me."

Maggie leaned against the bus. "No way. In fact, maybe if we're lucky, that diva will fall off her giant shoes and break something."

"Maggie, that's not fair. I really do think she's changed. I'm sure she doesn't even remember what happened back then. I'm sorry I brought it up. I need to do like I say in my song—forget the past."

Maggie harrumphed. Instinct told her that Tammy remembered exactly what happened and had engaged in a little stealth bullying to throw Gaynell, her perceived competition, off balance. She was about to share this with Gaynell when the others trooped back up the levee. Valeria was trying to detach some leaves stuck to her thatch of hair. "That was fun," she said. "As in not fun at all."

Tammy ignored her. "Okay, tour's over. We need to get back. I want to rest before the festival opens tonight. And someone has a real important meeting."

She winked at Gaynell, put an arm around her, and gave her a squeeze. Gaynell flashed Maggie an *I told you so* look, then boarded the bus.

* * *

While Gaynell met with Pony Pickner about possible representation, Maggie bagged pralines for the Crozats' festival booth. She filled two boxes, but there were still enough pralines to fill a third. She left the manor house for the shotgun cottage to see if her grandmother had a spare box.

"Take what you need," Gran said, motioning to the boxes both full and empty that surrounded her. She held up a pressed gardenia. Her pale-blue eyes were misty. "This is the first flower your grandfather ever gave me. It's from a corsage I wore to a Mardi Gras ball on one of our earliest dates." Gran sighed. "It's hard to part with anything that reminds me of him."

"Then don't, Gran. The Swedes may be spartan, but I'm sure they wouldn't begrudge you some sentimental mementos."

Maggie took an empty box and departed. She was loading her car with sweets when she saw Gaynell leave the carriage house where Tammy's manager was staying. Gaynell strode to her car, a furious look on her face. Maggie ran to her friend. "Are you okay? What's wrong? The meeting didn't go well?"

Gaynell gave a choked, mirthless laugh. "You could say that. Mr. Pickner told me . . . ugh, I can't say the dirty word . . . he told me I'm not eff-able."

"*What?*"

"Yup. He said that to make it in the music business, you need to give off a sexy vibe. His words, not mine. He said I don't, but if I wanted to work on it, he'd be happy to help me out." Gaynell shared the last nasty tidbit with disgust.

"*He said that?* Does he know what century this is? What *year?*"

"I brought that up. And he said, 'The music business has its own set of rules. I'm just telling you the truth. You should thank me.' He was massaging my shoulder as he said this."

Maggie's entire body pulsed with anger. "That sonuva—"

She started for the carriage house, but Gaynell pulled her back. "No. I'm just gonna forget this ever happened and focus on my new song. I was going to rehearse with the Gator Girls, but Tammy invited them over to jam with her band before tonight's show, so I'm just gonna go home and practice on my own."

"She didn't invite you?"

"Said I didn't need it."

Gaynell got in her truck and took off. She left Maggie standing in the decomposed granite parking lot, trying to decide whom she despised more: manipulative Tammy or her lecherous manager, Pony.

* * *

The meadow that abutted St. Pierre Parish Airfield buzzed with activity as workers rushed to finish transforming it into festival fairgrounds. Maggie, still fuming about how Pony Pickner had treated Gaynell, unloaded boxes from the trunk of her car. She then loaded the boxes onto a hand-cart and pushed them through the temporary encampment behind the scenes of the festival where craftspeople and musicians housed themselves in tents and trailers. She reached the fairgrounds, passing an army of porta-potties and washing stations. A large stage was set up at one end of the field; wooden booths painted in purple, green, and gold ringed the field, each booth decorated with colorful illustrations of musical instruments.

The festive atmosphere lifted Maggie's mood. As she walked past Kyle Bruner, who was married to her cousin

Lia, she waved to him. Pregnant with triplets, Lia had been put on bed rest by her ob-gyn, so Kyle was manning the booths for her bakery and candy businesses, Fais Dough Dough and Bon Bon Sweets. At the moment, he was setting up the Bon Bon booth. "Your booth is next to Fais Dough Dough," Kyle said. "If you need extra hands, let me know. I'll share Clinton and Brianna with you." The two teenagers were siblings who held part-time jobs at Lia's shops.

"Thanks, I may take you up on that."

Maggie continued on her way. "Hey, Maggie, you and Bo set a date yet?" Lucinda Hebert called to her from the Hebert's Sno-ball stand.

"Working on it," Maggie said. A few minutes later, she gave the same answer to Winnie Garvois, who was manning a po' boy booth. Maggie had come to accept that a Crozat-Durand marriage was the Pelican equivalent of a royal wedding. Not for the first time, she wished she had a sibling. At least Princes William and Harry got to take turns being the center of attention.

* * *

Maggie retreated to the Crozats' booth and began unpacking her boxes. She arranged a stack of souvenir mugs and mouse pads and hung two of her paintings on either side of the booth's PELICAN PRALINES sign. As she laid out an array of pralines, Eula Banks, the town's seventy-something new mayor, waddled by. Eula used her cane to wave at a well-wisher and then addressed Maggie. "Hey there, Magnolia Marie. You and Bo set a wedding date yet?"

"No. And you're only the third person today to ask me that question."

"It's a natural question to ask. You're not getting any younger."

"I'm only thirty-two! Would you like a praline? On the house?" Maggie hoped this deflection would end the conversation, but no such luck.

"Thank you, chère." Eula took the praline. "By the time I was thirty-two, my oldest was thirteen. I was a grandma seven years later. I'm just saying, ticktock." She eyed the stacks of pralines. "Wouldn't mind one to grow on. Maybe rum?"

"Of course," Maggie said through gritted teeth, handing over the second praline. Eula thanked her and sauntered off. *After this festival's over, Bo and I are locking down a wedding date so I can avoid these annoying conversations,* Maggie thought to herself.

"I'd like three pecan pralines, ma'am."

She looked up and saw her fiancé grinning at her. It was the rare time he was in his police officer uniform, and the sight made her heart flip-flop. He held his seven-year-old son Xander's hand. Maggie handed Bo two pralines. "I'm giving you the friends-and-family discount. You owe me zero dollars."

"Considering my Pelican PD salary, I'll take that discount."

Xander's eyes caught sight of something, and he wiggled free of Bo. "Friends." He grabbed his praline and took off. The adults watched with affection.

"He has friends, Maggie," his father said, a catch in his

voice. Xander had been friendless and lonely before moving to Pelican, bringing about a case of selective mutism he'd only recently conquered. "A 'posse.' That's what he calls them. My son has a posse."

Bo said this with such pride that Maggie felt herself choke up. She glanced over at Xander, who was listening intently to something a young girl was telling him. She was tiny and whisper-thin. Her pale, almost-white hair was held in place by a headband made of glittery pink butterflies. Xander never took his eyes off the girl, and when she finished talking, he smiled. Maggie was struck by this, since he rarely made eye contact *or* smiled. "I think Xander's got more than a posse. I think he's got a crush."

Bo followed Maggie's gaze. He broke into a grin. "That's Esme. She's new to his school. And yup. Looks like my kid's got his first case of puppy love. Speaking of love . . ." Bo leaned in through the booth opening and kissed Maggie.

"Hey, you two, what you got going there, a kissing booth?" This came from Vanessa Fleer, over in the Fais Dough Dough booth. Vanessa, once a candidate for Doucet Slacker Tour Guide of the Year, had found her métier helping to run Lia's businesses while the mom-to-be was laid up.

Before Maggie could respond to Vanessa, a loud screech came over the PA system. She and Bo covered their ears. Although the sun was still high in the sky, floodlights meant to illuminate the festival at night flickered on and off. "They've been having some problems with the electrical system," Bo said. "I better get to work. Cal, Artie, and I are doing security tonight."

He leaned in for another kiss.

"Maggie, you gotta start charging for those smooches," Vanessa called to her. "I bet you'd make more money than selling pralines."

Maggie's retort was drowned out by more ear-piercing squeals from the PA system. This was followed by an equally ear-piercing squeal, but this one was from a "giggle" of girls who ran past her booth. Maggie leaned out and saw the cause of the teen stampede.

Tammy Barker and her entourage had arrived.

Chapter 5

Gigi, Tammy's cousin, and Sara, the singer's manager, jostled each other as they competed to push back the crowd. Tammy sauntered down a row of booths, oohing and aahing at each one, taking the occasional sample but passing on anything seafood related, which ruled out an entire subgroup. "If it comes from the sea, I don't eat it," Maggie heard her tell a vendor. "I'm super allergic. Makes my throat close up, which is not exactly prime for a singer."

Tammy chuckled as if she'd made a joke, eliciting an obsequious guffaw from Little Earlie Waddell, who was recording her every move on his phone. Little Earlie, the editor and publisher of the *Pelican Penny Clipper*, was determined to turn his freebie handout into the town's paper of note. He was equally determined to nudge it into the digital age and had recently started an online channel. Tammy's story was his biggest to date, beating out the sow who gave birth to a record-setting twenty-seven piglets.

Maggie noticed the Gator Girls were mixed in with Tammy's band of man buns, but she didn't see her friend.

"Where's Gaynell?" she asked Pixie, the Gator Girls' drummer.

"Tammy wanted to come to the festival early but told us not to bother Gaynell. Said she needed her rest or something. She'll be by later, I guess."

Maggie's bad mood returned as Pixie scurried away to catch up with the singing star. Tammy had opted to isolate Gaynell—it was right out of Stealth Bullying 101.

* * *

After Mayor Eula Banks cut a large ribbon and declared *Cajun Country Live!* up and running, Maggie became too busy to brood about Gaynell's mistreatment. After several hours of selling pralines and souvenirs, she took Kyle up on his offer of help. The Poche siblings manned the booth while she made a porta-potty run. She passed the backstage area, where Pony Pickner was barking out instructions to the roadies. "We don't need a music tech. The band does its own thing. I'll be the sound tech. And nobody touches Tammy's mic but me. Got it? Nobody, no-*body*."

The roadies, imported from New Orleans and used to working for the biggest acts at Jazz Fest, didn't bother hiding their annoyance at being addressed like amateurs. "We know the drill," a guy with a big gut and long white ponytail said. "Nobody touches the kid's mic. No-*body*." His mimicry brought a few snickers from the other roadies, as well as Maggie.

She held her nose and hopped into a porta-potty, hopping out as quickly as possible. She washed up, then returned to the Crozat booth. She saw Rufus sauntering down the grass midway, scanning the crowd for potential troublemakers. He wore a tight, ill-fitting Pelican PD uniform she'd never seen before. "Hey, Ru. Is that a new uniform?"

"Nah, it's our dress uniform. Haven't worn it in years but figured I should fancy things up for the Hollywood crowd. I'll take a traditional." He plunked down a dollar in change.

"On the house," Maggie said, handing over the praline and his change. "I heard about the mayor campaign. Sorry you had to drop out."

"Yeah, thanks," Ru said, his expression wry. "If you know anyone who needs a hundred pennants that say I'M ROOTING FOR RUFUS FOR MAYOR, lemme know." He dropped the wax paper bag holding his praline and bent from the knees to pick it up.

"I hear a lot of creaking and groaning," Maggie said. "You might want to bend from the waist."

"Can't. Ain't worn this thing in years. My pants'll split." The festival floodlights blazed on, sputtered, blazed off, and then blazed on again. "Electrical problems. I better see what's up."

Rufus headed off. Maggie used the lull in customers to check out the crowd. Night had fallen; families with younger children headed home, replaced by hordes of teenagers and young adults just getting off work and ready to party. Uffen, Tammy's handsome British bass player, walked by, examining the license of the besotted young girl who clung to his arm. "You're way prettier than your license photo." She giggled, and Maggie rolled her eyes.

"You got any rum pralines left?"

"Gaynell, there you are." Maggie reached through the booth opening to hug her friend and hand her a praline. "Tonight's almost over. Why'd you come so late?"

"Pixie told me she and the others wouldn't be here until late, so I didn't hurry."

Maggie gritted her teeth to keep herself from revealing that Gaynell's bandmate lied to her. "Tammy's about to close the night," Gaynell continued. "I should go look for the others."

She joined the festivalgoers heading for the stage. Gran wandered over to the Crozat booth and plopped down on a folding chair. "Lee started dozing off on his feet, so I sent him home." Gran and Lee Bertrand had been "courting," as she liked to call it, for months. The town doyenne and service station owner made an odd match that somehow worked. "I can cover the booth if you want to go watch the prodigal daughter of Pelican strut her stuff."

"I'm fine listening from here."

"You're 'not a fan,' as they say?"

Maggie made a face. "If you want to put it politely."

The Crozats' booth gave Maggie a well-angled view of the performance area. She watched as Eula Banks made her way back onto the stage. "Oh dear, my age is showing," the pushing-seventy civil servant said between deep breaths. "All righty, Pelican, it's time for the big event. Join me in welcoming our li'l town's very own TV and recording star . . . Tammy Barker!"

Tammy and her band took the stage to wild cheers. Tammy clutched the mic Pony had so vehemently insisted on handling. "Hello, Pelican! I can't tell you how good it is to be home. Let me sing it to you . . ."

Tammy pulled the mic from its stand and launched into her biggest hit, a song unimaginatively titled "Home." It was a crowd-pleaser, though. She followed it with several more songs off her debut album. Maggie grudgingly got what Pony meant when he told Gaynell that performers needed sex appeal. Tammy rocked the stage in her Daisy Dukes, tight tee, and high-heeled, sparkly cowboy boots. She wore her hair in a loose braid that swung back and forth as she shimmied and body-rolled. To Maggie's ears, the songs all sounded alike, bland country songs designed to appeal to the most common denominator with lyrics either moaning about heartbreak or celebrating pickup trucks. The material lacked the exuberance of the Cajun and zydeco tunes Maggie loved, and her attention drifted. *Why exactly did Tammy have Gaynell meet with Pony? Was it a setup to damage Gaynell's self-confidence? Was it to humiliate her? If I lost five pounds, could I get back into my Daisy Dukes?*

Tammy's introduction to the final song of the evening shook Maggie out of her fog. "This is a new song. We're playing it for the first time ever right here, and I really hope you like it. It's called 'Forget the Past.'"

Maggie gasped as Tammy's band began an up-tempo

version of Gaynell's lovely song. *"Forget the past, just clear your mind, forget the past, let me be kind."* Tammy did a double dose of stage gyrations as she belted out the words, ending the song with a jump in the air.

"That was awfully peppy for a sad song," Gran yelled to be heard over the cheers and foot stomping.

"It's not supposed to be peppy; it's supposed to be a ballad," Maggie yelled back. "Watch the booth for me; I have to find Gaynell."

Maggie rocketed away from the booth and elbowed her way through the crowd. She found Gaynell standing near the stage's edge. The young musician started when Maggie touched her shoulder. "Why did you let Tammy sing your song? And in that way? I thought you were saving it for your Jazz Fest set."

"I didn't. I was." Gaynell looked like she was in shock.

Maggie put her hands to her head, trying to comprehend what had happened. "Are you saying she just did the song without asking? She stole it?"

Gaynell nodded. Her face flushed red and her eyes flamed. She pushed past autograph seekers to a cordoned-off area. A sign reading PASSES ONLY hung above it. Maggie followed her. Narcisse put out a hand to stop them and pointed to the sign. "You see the sign. It says passes only. That means you need a pass."

"It's me, Narcisse," Maggie said. "I'm hosting your cousin-in-law, remember?"

This threw the bodyguard, who seemed slow on the uptake in general. "Oh. Then I guess it's okay."

Gaynell and Maggie maneuvered through well-wishers. The floodlights flickered on and off again. Tammy was just coming off the stage, followed by her band and the Gator Girls. "Hey, what's the deal with the electrical system at this thing?" she demanded from a crew technician. "It's freaky dangerous. If they don't fix it by closing night, I ain't going on." She saw Gaynell and Maggie and plastered on a big smile. "Heeeey. Did you like your song? I wanted to surprise you."

"Oh, you surprised me all right." Gaynell was furious. "You stole my song."

Tammy's mouth gaped open. "*What?* You think I stole it?"

"It ain't what I think, it's what I know. You've had it in for me ever since high school. Lord knows why, since I'm here"—Gaynell held a hand low to the ground—"and you're here." Gaynell stood on her tippy-toes and held a hand as high as she could.

Tammy shook her head in disbelief. "Okay, this is nuts. I was trying to do something good, I swear."

"You didn't even give Gaynell credit for writing the song," Maggie jumped in.

Gaynell turned to Maggie. "Please, let me." She turned back to Tammy. "What Maggie said."

The country star affected a sheepish look. "Oh no, I totally forgot. I'm so sorry."

Pony approached his client. He put an arm around Tammy's waist and gave her a squeeze. "The new song sounded great."

"That was Gaynell's song." Maggie couldn't keep herself from standing up for her friend. "It's supposed to be a ballad. It was supposed to be her big audition song for Jazz Fest."

The manager shook his head. "Not a great idea. Tammy sang the hell out of it. She made it her own." He faced Gaynell. "You're going to suffer by comparison, trust me. People who heard Tammy sing it will talk. And what they say won't be nice."

Tammy bit on the knuckle of her index finger. "I feel so bad about this. I wish there was a way to make it up to you. Maybe I can put the song on my next album or something. At least you'd make some money off it."

Pony grunted, annoyed. "Seriously? Tammy, you know that's not gonna happen. The album list is set. You've got tracks by . . ." He rattled off names of some of the most famous names in country music. "You want me to call one of them and say we're cutting their song for some neophyte?"

The blank look on Tammy's face told Maggie she had no idea what the word *neophyte* meant. But the singer faced Gaynell and said, "I'm sorry. He's right. I can't tick off all those big stars. I have to think about my future."

"While you're busy ruining mine."

Gaynell's tone was biting. Pony stepped between the women. "Whoa, let's all take a breath. Gay, remember our conversation this afternoon. You've got a long way to go before you can think about a future in this business. And if you need help, my offer still stands." He winked at her.

Maggie was appalled. "If that's your way of lightening things up, it's disgusting."

Gaynell took a step toward Pony. Maggie had never seen her friend so angry. "Nobody but my family and friends get to call me *Gay*." She poked the manager in his chest with her finger. "And if you ever flutter an eyelid at me again, the next thing you'll be winking at is a gator at the bottom of the bayou."

Gaynell stormed off. Maggie followed her. "Gaynell—"

Her friend stopped. She was in tears. "I need to be alone for a bit."

"Okay. If you need me, I'll be at our booth packing things up."

Gaynell nodded and walked away from Maggie, who marched back to Pelican Pralines. Kyle looked up as she stormed past. "Whoa, you look madder than a box of hornets."

"There are horrible people in this world. That's all I'm gonna say."

Maggie pulled out a box and slammed a praline inside. It shattered into crumbs, and she gave an exasperated groan. "Angry packing's just gonna make more work for you," Vanessa called over from the Fais Dough Dough booth. "You'll feel better if you talk to someone."

"I know you, Vanessa," Maggie called back to her often-annoying frenemy. "You're just looking for gossip."

"You get something off your chest and I get the 411. It's win-win."

Maggie ignored Vanessa but forced herself to calm

down and pack away the sweets more carefully. There was an electrical sputter and the floodlights blinked on and off and stayed off. "Just what I need," Maggie muttered to the darkness. She was distracted by shouting coming from the performance area just as the lights blinked on again. She saw Pony yelling at a stagehand.

"What did I tell you? Nobody touches Tammy's mic but me."

The stagehand held up his hands. "Dude, relax. All I did was bump the stand."

Maggie couldn't hear Pony's response. He strode over to the stand and grabbed the mic. It was stuck. He put one foot on the stand and both hands on the mic to dislodge it. There was a buzz and then a crackle loud as lightning. Maggie started and shuddered. Suddenly there was an explosive, sizzling sound. Pony Pickner let out a scream. His body vibrated, then flew into the back wall. He fell to the ground, where he lay still as death as the floodlights went off, plunging the festival grounds into total darkness.

Chapter 6

The festival grounds were silent for a moment. Then the floodlights blinked on and stayed on, bathing Pony's body in bright light. The silence turned to screams. People ran for the exits. Gran watched in dismay. "What's wrong? What happened?"

Maggie placed a comforting hand on Gran's shoulder. "There was an accident. You head home; I'll check and see what's going on."

Gran, still upset, nodded. The two women looked toward the stage, where Bo and his Pelican PD officers raced to clear the area as an ambulance pulled onto the field. EMTs jumped out and ran to Pony. Within minutes, they were treating the prostrate manager with defibrillator paddles. "That poor man," Gran said. "My poor festival."

Maggie bucked the fleeing fairgoers and ran to the stage. Officer Cal Vichet lifted the police tape he was stringing to let her duck underneath. Bo was in the middle of an intense conversation with the potbellied roadie who'd mocked

Pony's obsession with Tammy's mic. She heard hysterical weeping and saw Tammy surrounded by members of her band, who seemed to be in shock. Valeria, Tammy's backup singer, also in tears, was being comforted by Bokie, the band's drummer. Sara, the superstar's assistant, stood planted in place, a stunned expression on her face. The Gator Girls, looking lost, had formed their own huddle. "I told you the electrical system was messed up," Tammy yelled to the roadie.

"And as I'm telling this officer here, the stage was on a different circuit than the lights," the roadie yelled back at her. "No way they caused this."

The EMTs gave up on the defibrillator and placed a sheet over Pony Pickner's body. Tammy saw this and screamed. Her knees buckled, but Sara caught her before she hit the ground. Tammy's assistant waved to the paramedics. "Over here, we need help!"

Curious but not wanting to interrupt the investigation, Maggie moved closer to the stage. The electricity powering the festival had been turned off. Artie and Cal were directing underlings on where to set up the police department's own floodlights. Bo, Rufus, and the roadie were examining the area around Tammy's mic stand.

"It's wet," the roadie said.

Bo bent down and touched the mat under the stand. He pressed down on it and water squirted up.

Rufus frowned. "Water and electricity. Not a good match."

"Nope," the roadie said, shaking his head. "It couldn't

have been there before the chick's set. My guys would've checked for it."

Bo and Rufus conferred. Bo nodded and headed toward the knot of musicians. He stopped when he saw Maggie.

"Hey," she said. "This is awful. Do you need me? Can I do anything?"

Bo gestured with his head toward Tammy and the others. "I need to ask some questions. You hover and watch. Let me know if you pick up any reactions I should know about. I can't look at everyone at the same time."

Maggie nodded. Her intuition and artist's eagle eye for details had proved useful to Pelican PD's cash-strapped, undermanned department, helping them solve several recent murder cases. She followed Bo to the VIP area but hung back to get a full view of the group. Tammy pulled away from her assistant. She stood up to her full height of five feet plus six-inch heels and got in Bo's face. "I don't care what that guy says, the system here is effed up. You need to arrest someone for malpractice."

"Okay, first of all, malpractice doesn't apply to this situation." Maggie admired Bo's calm tone. She would have instantly lost it with the singer. "And what Benny, that roadie, said is true. The stage's system was separate from the lights so that they wouldn't overload one circuit. But we did find water under the mic stand. Anyone spill something onstage?"

He directed this at all the musicians, who shook their heads as one. "Never," said East, Tammy's guitarist. "Too dangerous. If one of us had, we would've said something."

Tammy gasped. "Oh my God. I could have been killed. Do you think someone spilled it on purpose? Did someone want me dead?"

Bo's phone pinged a text. He read it and then looked up. He took a step away from the group, motioning for Tammy to follow him. Maggie took a discreet step closer to them while keeping an eye on the others. "That was the police chief. He talked to the roadie who moved your mic stand so you could prance around stage."

"It's not prancing," Tammy said, insulted. "We pay a choreographer buckets of money to come up with those moves."

"Whatever. The guy swears there was no water on the stage when you were performing. He would have felt it under his feet."

"So what are you saying, no one was after me?" Tammy sounded disappointed. Apparently, an attempt on a star's life was the ultimate badge of honor.

"Was it well known that your manager was in charge of your mic?"

"I guess, I mean, at least in the music business. We get very attached to our microphones. We develop a relationship with them. It's like . . . what's that thing where people think of animals or other stuff like people?"

"Anthropomorphic."

"Yeah. It's like that." Tammy furrowed her brow. "Wait. Are you saying you think someone wanted to kill Pony?" Bo didn't respond. Tammy's brow cleared. Her eyes widened. "Oh my. Oh my, oh my, oh my."

"Someone come to mind?"

Tammy nodded, her expression grave. She wrung her hands nervously. "I don't want to get anyone in trouble." Maggie tensed. Then Tammy said exactly what she feared the singer would. "There's this girl I know from high school. Her name is Gaynell Bourgeois. I had her meet with Pony because she's so talented. But Pony's kind of a dog when it comes to girls, even though he's like fifty or something." Tammy said this as if fifty was a hundred. "He kind of hit on her, and she did *not* take it well. She threatened to feed him to the gators. It's not just me; we all heard it. Even her."

Maggie froze as Tammy wheeled around and pointed at her.

"I'm not talking to her right now, I'm talking to you," Bo said, rescuing his fiancée. "Why don't you tell me exactly what happened?"

Bo put a hand under Tammy's elbow and guided her toward a chair. As he did, he glanced back at Maggie and mouthed the word *Go*.

She followed his instructions and hurried away from the stage, back to the Crozats' booth. She sunk below the window so no one could see her and sent a text to Gaynell: WHERE ARE U?

HOME, Gaynell wrote back. WHY?

THINK PONY PICKNER WAS MURDERED, Maggie texted. TAMMY TOLD BO ABOUT YOUR FIGHT W HIM.

Gaynell responded with a line of shocked emoji faces and exclamation marks, followed by a plaintive question: WHAT SHOULD I DO???

Maggie felt for her friend. She texted back: NOTHING NOW. BE HONEST IF THEY TALK 2 U.

Gaynell sent back a thumbs-up emoji followed by several sad faces. Maggie retrieved her purse from the box where the Crozats stored valuables during the festival and put away her phone. She pulled out her car keys, and then hesitated. Tammy had basically accused one of Maggie's best friends of murder. There was no way sweet, kindhearted Gaynell could be pushed to that extreme, even by a lecher like Pony.

Maggie stuck the keys back in her purse and stood up. Contrary to Bo's instructions, this wasn't the time to go. It was the time to start figuring out, if Gaynell didn't kill Pony . . . who did?

* * *

Maggie texted Bo to let him know she was sticking around but planned on maintaining a low profile. She needn't have worried. The Pelican PD's mobile evidence van, usually relegated to hauling floats during Mardi Gras, was parked on the field, its crime scene technicians scouring the stage for evidence. All the available officers had been drafted to interview anyone around who was affiliated with the festival, be they guest, roadie, or band member.

Except for the area lit up by police lights, most of the grounds were dark, making it easy for Maggie to wander around unnoticed. Unfortunately, the moonless, cloud-filled night made it tough to find clues. Maggie gave up looking for them. Instead she eavesdropped on a few police interviews until Rufus, who was taking notes while talking to a Tammy fangirl, caught her in the act. "You need something, Magnolia Marie?" His tone told her he knew darn well she didn't.

"No, I'm good. I'm just, you know, poking around." Maggie cringed at her lame response and tried to cover. "And looking for Bo. Mostly that. If you see him, tell him I took off."

Rufus tapped on his pad. "Little busy. I hear there's an invention where you can type out a message and it flies through the air to a person. Might wanna try that."

"Will do." Embarrassed, Maggie fled. She glanced around and saw Bo finish an interview with Tammy's band-member, Toulouse. As soon as the redheaded fiddler and accordionist left Bo's company, a roadie replaced him. It was going to be a long night for the force.

* * *

Maggie took Ru's advice and messaged Bo she was leaving. By the time she got home, it was three AM. She fell into bed with her clothes on, and woke up four hours later feeling like she hadn't slept at all. Maggie went into the living room, where she was surprised to find Little Earlie Waddell video-ing her grandmother with his cell phone. "Is there anything else you'd like to share about the tragic events of last night?"

"Yes." Gran spoke to the phone. "Again, our hearts go out to Mr. Pickner's friends and family. We've hired the best commercial electricians in the state to check and double-check the festival electrical system. They were there at dawn this morning and have assured me that the problem with the lighting equipment has been solved and this awful accident had absolutely nothing to do with it. The accident was the result of human error."

"Error?" Little Earlie flipped the video so it recorded him instead of Grand-mère. "Or intentional? Station PPC will keep you up to date, live-streaming what will surely be an interesting investigation by the Pelican Police Department." He turned off the phone. "Thank you, ma'am."

Maggie folded her arms across her chest. "Going the sensationalism route as always, Little E."

"Hey, it's what sells. You like my call letters?"

He was so proud of having utilized the *Pelican Penny Clipper* for his online channel that Maggie's annoyance faded. "Very clever. But I hope Station PPC keeps bringing us human-interest stories. Those twenty-seven piglets were adorable."

Little Earlie packed up and headed out to search for more scoops. Maggie collapsed onto the antique, velvet-covered sofa next to Grand-mère. "How are you doing this morning? Are you okay?"

"*Comme ci, comme ça.*" Gran picked up a mug from the coffee table and took a sip. "So-so. Not exactly how I envisioned the kickoff to our little shindig. But as Oscar Wilde so famously said, the only thing worse than being talked about is not being talked about. And Lordy, are we being talked about. It's just a bit after seven AM and I got a text that ticket sales are through the roof." She took another sip of her coffee. "Lee was so sweet. He stayed outside the cottage in his car most of the night to make sure I was all right."

"He adores you."

"Adore is a strong word. Especially for two geriatrics like us." Gran drained her mug. "What about you? What happened after I left?"

"Nothing good," Maggie said, her tone grim. "Little E will be happy to know that it doesn't look like this was an accident."

"Oh dear."

"Worse than that, Tammy pointed a finger at Gaynell."

"*What?* That's absolutely ludicrous."

"You and I know that, but Gaynell had a run-in with Pony right before the show. Hopefully she has an alibi for where she was after that." Maggie stood up. "I need to get ready. I have to make a boatload of pralines for the booth."

Gran handed Maggie her coffee mug. "Would you mind getting me a refill first?"

Maggie sniffed the cup. "This isn't just coffee, is it?"

Gran patted her perfectly coifed silver hair. "A bit of bourbon happened to fall in. And I wouldn't mind at all if that happened again."

* * *

Maggie sent Gaynell a message, then prepared for the day. She checked her phone; there was no reply. She left the cottage for the manor house, where she discovered her mother knee-deep in a variety of breakfast meals. "Not to be callous or anything, but I thought with Pony's diet off the table—literally and figuratively—you'd have less to do."

Ninette shook a frying pan with one hand and flipped pancakes bubbling on a skillet with the other. "Oh, how I wish. Tammy insisted on Gigi and Narcisse spending the night, which of course I understand. She's been through something very traumatic and needs her family around. They requested Cajun comfort food. So, my banana pancakes with brown sugar butter for Gigi, cheese grits and boudin for Narcisse, shrimp and grits for that Sara girl, and a veggie omelet for our resident celebrity." She pointed to the broiler. "And your father's making himself a steak. He's gonna be on the Paleo-whatever diet until we use up all that food."

Maggie began pulling praline ingredients out of the B and B's large pantry. "Unfortunately, I need to commandeer a burner. I have to make more pralines." She placed containers of baking soda and brown sugar on the counter, then retrieved buttermilk and two sticks of butter from the refrigerator. She took a large copper pot off the hanging rack and placed it on the stove. She measured out milk and poured it into the pot, then dropped in the butter and added a spoonful of baking soda. "Were you up when Tammy and her group came home last night?"

"Yes," Ninette said, trying not to elbow her daughter, which was impossible since Maggie was left-handed and her mother right-handed. "That's how I learned about what happened. Terrible." Ninette turned the heat off under the frying pan and negotiated the narrow space between the stove and the kitchen table. "According to Gigi, Tammy was an absolute wreck at the festival. But she calmed down by the time they got back here. It was pretty late. They may not even be up for breakfast. All this may be a waste of time and food."

"I wouldn't worry about Gigi and Narcisse missing out on free eats." Maggie had pegged the two as a couple of moochers especially after learning that Gigi had convinced her husband he should adopt her surname of Barker as an "homage" to Tammy. *More like an opportunity to name-drop and get freebies*, Maggie groused to herself.

Her mixture came to a boil. She inserted a candy thermometer to make sure it had reached the firm-ball stage. It had, so Maggie took it off the stove, added vanilla, and beat the ingredients until they were a creamy beige. She added cups of pecans, then searched for an empty spot of counter where she could roll out parchment paper. "You'll have to do that in the dining room," Ninette said. "There's not a bit of room left in here. And chère, I love you more than life itself and I know you're doing us a big favor taking over the praline sales, but you're gonna have to make those somewhere else next time. I need every spare inch of space for as long as our guests are here. If the cottage kitchen is too small, ask a friend."

"Got it."

Maggie retreated to the dining room with her pot and a roll of parchment paper. As she dropped spoonfuls of the praline mixture onto the paper to harden, she thought about Tammy and her entourage. Any number of people—music pros, hangers-on, and fairgoers—had probably heard Pony insist that no one except him touch Tammy's mic. But how many held a grudge against the manager? Maggie was sure that limited the field of suspects to Tammy's immediate circle.

There was a knock at Crozat's massive oak front door. Maggie covered the drying pralines with a second sheet of parchment paper. She strode down the hall and opened the door. Bo stood there, dressed in his standard detecting outfit of jeans, jacket, white button-down shirt, and cowboy boots. "I have to say, I miss the uniform a little."

"I don't. That thing's uncomfortable."

"You sure looked better in it than Ru did in his dress uniform."

Bo gave her a blank look. "We have a dress uniform?"

"Apparently." Maggie held the door open, and Bo followed her into the high-ceilinged, wide front hallway of the manor house. "You haven't kissed me."

"This is business."

Maggie got a knot in her stomach. "I was afraid of that."

"Can we talk somewhere private?"

She nodded and led her fiancé to the front parlor. She sat on the room's Victorian-era black walnut settee, upholstered in a rich rose damask. Bo sat opposite her in a chair that was the settee's mate.

"Well, this isn't too awkward," Maggie said.

Bo snorted. "Tell me about it." He pulled out a small pad and pencil. "I need you to tell me everything you saw last night regarding Pony Pickner's interaction with anyone."

"Is this now an official murder investigation?"

Bo gave a grave nod. "Ben, the head roadie, noticed someone removed the safety ground connection from the sound system. This energized the mic shell. Pony, standing in water, pulling the mic out of the stand with both hands . . . you couldn't ask for a better electrocution setup."

"That would take someone who really knows how you set up for a concert."

"Maggie, come on."

"What?" she said, feigning innocence.

Bo pulled his chair toward her. He rested his hands on his knees. His look bore into Maggie; she could have sworn he didn't blink once. She'd never felt so nervous and uncomfortable. *He's* really *good at his job*, she thought.

"I heard Pony order the crew not to touch Tammy's mic" Maggie crossed one leg over the other, trying to affect a casual pose. "Pretty much everyone who was there at the time heard that."

"But not everyone had a motive."

"He wasn't a nice guy. I'm sure he ticked off a lot of people." She had a brainstorm. "Maybe someone who came to the festival just to get rid of Pony. That really widens the field of suspects. Y'all are gonna be working hard."

Bo ignored her attempt to sidetrack him. "Tell me about the dustup between Pony and Gaynell."

"I wouldn't call it a dustup. Just some words. Which he deserved, by the way. But nothing happened that would make Gaynell a suspect, believe me."

Bo sighed and sat back. "Chère, I know you're trying to

protect your friend. But right now, not only is Gaynell a suspect, she's *the* suspect."

Maggie balled up her fists. "It's because of Tammy. She's trying to get Gaynell arrested; it's part of her crazy jealous vendetta. I told you she had it in for her, I told you, I—"

Bo interrupted her. "It's not because of Tammy. Gaynell's the number-one suspect because of this." Bo took out his cell phone. "Little Earlie sent it to me." Bo opened the photos on his phone and played a video clip of Gaynell's heated exchange with Pony.

"So? I saw that, and it wasn't anything."

"But you didn't see this." Bo fast-forwarded.

The video showed a tearful Gaynell storming past. Little Earlie wasn't on the screen, but his voice could be heard calling to her. "I heard there was an incident between you and Pony Pickner, Tammy's manager. Can you tell us what happened?"

"Absolutely not." Gaynell stopped and looked straight at Little Earlie's phone. Fury had replaced the tears. "But I'll tell you this. If that SOB ever bothers me again, he'll be leaving Pelican in a pine box."

Chapter 7

For a moment, Maggie was speechless. Then she recovered. "Oh, come on. Those are just words. It's an expression. I've said it myself. You've said it. Remember how mad you were at Rufus when you were stuck living with him after the great flood? I heard all kinds of threats coming out of your mouth. Some of them were pretty creative. And a little scary."

Bo put away the phone. "Look, this is all circumstantial. We don't know if she left, if she stayed. And we haven't uncovered any evidence linking her to Pony past that fight. I'm as fond of Gaynell as you are. But until there's evidence pointing to someone else, she's going to be in our crosshairs."

"What about Pony's phone and computer? The guy was a total sleaze. There has to incriminating stuff on all his electronics."

"They're gone. Tammy's assistant Sara said he took everything with him to the festival. The crime unit searched there, searched his digs here . . . Nothing."

Maggie leaned forward. "Sara. I could tell she couldn't stand Pony. I bet they have a history. You need to look into that."

Bo gave his fiancée a look of reproach. "Of course we will. We'll look into every single potential clue, Magnolia. Now, can you find a way of defending our friend without insulting my intelligence or professionalism?"

"I'm sorry, cher." Maggie said, abashed. She released an exasperated grunt. "I wish Chret was in town." Chret Bertrand, Gaynell's boyfriend and Lee's great-nephew, was a Marine vet who'd started a successful construction business that employed fellow veterans. He'd been invited to share his experience at a career symposium in Washington, DC, sponsored by a veterans-affairs nonprofit organization. "Gaynell would've told him what Pony said to her, Chret would've decked him, and we wouldn't be having this conversation. Tammy wouldn't have had any ammunition against Gaynell."

"You can't just lay this on Tammy. She didn't see what Little E recorded."

Maggie scowled. "Figures Little Earlie would find his way to the middle of this."

Tug, who was walking down the hallway with a newspaper under his arm and a juicy piece of steak on a plate, walked backward and came into the parlor. "Did you say Little Earlie? Take a look at this."

He dropped the *Pelican Penny Clipper* on the parlor coffee table. Bo sniffed the air. "Man, does that smell good."

"Tastes good, too. I could get used to this Paleo thing. Long as I didn't have to give up sugar and bourbon."

"I think that defeats the purpose, Dad." Maggie picked up the paper. She read the headline and let loose enough epithets to make both Bo and Tug raise their eyebrows. She held up the *Penny Clipper*. The entire cover was one headline: Suspicious Fest Death. Maggie opened the paper and skimmed the story. "Music manager ... Tammy Barker ... electrocution ... suspicious circumstances ... blah blah—oh. Oh, here we go." She read from the story. "Country and television superstar Tammy Barker witnessed local resident Gaynell Bourgeois exchange angry words with the victim. 'I can't imagine anyone as nice as Gaynell doing this,' Tammy said. 'At least, without a good reason. Everyone knows Pony Pickner had a reputation for being what my grandmère would call a "handsy guy." If his behavior pushed some poor, innocent girl like Gaynell to take drastic action, I will not only provide emotional support, I will pay all her legal costs. Hashtag me too!'"

Maggie threw down the paper. "She's using a national movement to give Gaynell a motive for murder. That's despicable."

Bo picked up the paper and took a moment to read the article. "Good, Little E didn't mention the video he sent to me. I told him not to; it's evidence."

Maggie stood up and glared at her fiancé. "Of what, Gaynell losing patience with a sexual predator?"

Tug cleared his throat. "Uh, I'll leave you two be," he said. He scurried away, holding tight to his steak.

Maggie paced the room. "My friend—*our* friend—is

totally being set up. And if this guy was so 'handsy,' why was he even Tammy's manager?"

"Because he's a hitmaker and starmaker. I did a little research." Bo opened an app on his phone and showed Maggie. "These are just a few of the acts he's launched."

Maggie glanced at the list, which included some of the most famous pop and country singers in the country. "Okay, impressive. But are any of them still his clients?"

"I haven't gotten that far. But I did find out that he's famous for putting up-and-comers on the map. Which is exactly what he did for our li'l country girl, Tammy. Whose big smile and aw-shucksin' are clearly an act."

Maggie heard the disgust in Bo's voice and calmed down. "I'm sorry," she said in a quiet tone. "I shouldn't have overreacted like that. I'm just so mad and frustrated. But I shouldn't take it out on you."

"It's okay. You just had a bad case of shoot-the-messenger-itis." Bo put an arm around Maggie's waist and pulled her to him. "Any chance we can kiss it out?"

Maggie shook her head. "It doesn't feel right." "But I could really use a hug."

Bo wrapped his arms around his bride-to-be. She responded in kind, and the two held on to each other.

* * *

As soon as Bo left, Maggie texted Gaynell. She received a quick response: RUFUS HERE. INTERVIEW. GETTING CALLS FROM MAGS AND WEBSITE FOR MY 'STORY,' SO LAYING LOW. LOVE U.

Maggie stuck her cell in her jeans pocket and left the parlor for the dining room. She bagged the pralines. The batch only half-filled a box. "Great," Maggie muttered. She pulled out her phone and sent a text to her bedridden cousin Lia.

Half an hour later, Maggie was installed in Lia and Kyle's spacious new kitchen at Grove Hall, the gracious plantation home they'd brought back from the brink of dereliction. Lia lay on a hospital bed that could be rolled around the home's beautifully restored first floor. She watched as Maggie mixed together the ingredients for rum pralines, filling the room with the scent of butter, brown sugar, and the liquor. "How can Gaynell be the primary suspect?" she wondered. The cousins had exchanged updates. Lia was equally upset about the cloud of suspicion hanging over their mutual friend.

Maggie gave her copper pot an angry stir. "I don't care what Bo says, I blame that Tammy chick. She's a flat-out horror of a human being."

"Is she ever. I'm deleting her album from my playlist." Lia held up her phone, then hesitated. "After I listen to it one more time. It's really good. I love that song 'Home.' Oof."

Lia flinched. She put her hands on her large belly. Maggie dropped her wooden spoon into the pot. "What, is it the babies? Do we need to go to the hospital? Should I call Kyle? Should I boil water? Please, please, please, do not have those babies here!"

Lia laughed at the panic in her cousin's voice. "Relax, I'm fine."

"You're sure?"

"Yes. It's just the critters duking it out in here. I hope they get along better once they're released into the world."

"Okay then. Phew." Relieved, Maggie returned to her stirring.

Lia patted her stomach. "You'll see what it's like when it's your turn."

"I think with Bo and me, it's going to be one and done."

"We'll see about that," Lia said with a sly smile.

"Xander will have a new sibling in a few months, anyway. He'll need some time to adjust to that."

"The adoption is moving along?"

"It's settled, and everyone couldn't be more thrilled—including Xander." When teenager Belle Tremblay, the town's Miss Pelican Mardi Gras Gumbo Queen, revealed she was in the family way, Maggie introduced her to Bo's ex-wife Whitney and her second husband Zach. The couple, who longed for a second child, were unable to conceive, and instantly agreed to adopt Belle's baby when she gave birth.

"Happy to hear that. Now, what about you? What's going on with wedding plans? Fill me in. Save me from dying of boredom."

"Oooh, tough order. Especially since we haven't figured out anything yet. We can't even decide on a date. We do know it won't be a summer wedding. I don't want to be the first family bride to sweat through my ancestor's gorgeous old dress. Consider yourself filled in. Now let's talk about your baby—*babies*—shower."

Maggie's Trombone Shorty ringtone interrupted the conversation. She looked at her phone. "It's Gaynell." She lowered the flame on her pot and took the call. "Hey, I'm with Lia. We were just talking about you." Concerned, Maggie mouthed the words *She's crying* to Lia. "Gay, chère, what's wrong?"

"It's the folks from Jazz Fest." A teary hiccup came from the singer. "They're not coming to hear our set."

"Oh, no. You know what, just forget them. Your set is going to be so great that they'll hear about it in New Orleans and kick themselves for missing it."

"I'm not going to do the set, Maggie. I can't perform with the Gator Girls right now. It's not fair to them. I don't want the group associated with my problem. We'll never come back from that."

"Gaynell—" She said this to a dial tone. Her friend had ended the call. Maggie cursed and slapped her hands on the counter.

"That sounded bad," Lia said, worried.

"It is." Maggie relayed the conversation to her cousin. "I can't just sit around making pralines while a friend's looking at going to jail." An expression of stony determination crossed Maggie's face. "I think it's time I get to know the musicians in Tammy's band a whole lot better."

Chapter 8

Belle Vista, the largest extant plantation home in St. Pierre Parish, had been turned into a luxe resort and Crozat Plantation B and B's stiffest competition. The main house, a combination Greek Revival/Italianate confection built in the 1850s, held court in the middle of additional guest housing, tennis courts, gardens, and a pool. The place was a wedding location magnet. Even the story of its dual-lingual name was romantic. The plantation was originally called Belle Vue. When the owner fell madly in love with an Italian opera singer who became his second wife, he renamed it Belle Vista, changing the second word to the woman's native language in her honor. She left him and the plantation for a riverboat captain, hence a local joke that, instead of Bella Vista or Belle Vue, the place should be called Rear View.

Maggie parked between a Tesla and a Bentley in the resort's capacious lot. She stuffed down the pang of competitive jealousy she always felt when visiting Belle Vista and made her way to the front desk. Kaity Bertrand, Lee's nineteen-year-old great-granddaughter, was manning it. The girl's lightly freckled face lit up when she saw Maggie, and she came out from behind the desk to give her a hug. "It's so good to see you."

"You too, Kaity. How's the job going?"

"*So* great. After I'm done at Coastal Community, I'm gonna transfer to LSU. I totally wanna work in the hospitality industry."

Maggie grinned at the bubbly teen's enthusiasm. "That's one lucky industry. Hey, do you know where I can find Tammy's musicians?" She held up a box. "I thought I'd bring them a few treats. I figure they can use some sugar comfort after what happened."

Kaity grew serious. "I know. How awful was that? Poor man dying that way. Ugh. Not to be selfish, but I'm glad I wasn't there to see it." She brightened again. "I'm going to the fest when the Gator Girls play. I *love* them. Gaynell is awesome."

Maggie forced a smile. Better not to mention Gaynell's plan to cancel; hopefully, she'd change her mind. Or better yet, the real killer would be in custody by then. "The musicians?" she prompted.

"Right. Sorry. They're by the pool. I saw them hanging out there a little while ago."

Maggie thanked Kaity, eliciting a hug goodbye. She navigated the resort's maze of paths, all lined with lush foliage and perfumed with the sweet scent of magnolias and gardenias. *Even the air here smells expensive*, Maggie thought as she trudged along. She located the pool, where the musicians were parked on chaise lounges shaded by large beige umbrellas on the pool's far side.

Only Louisiana native Toulouse and backup singer Valeria wore bathing suits, hers an orange one-piece with sexy cutouts that accentuated her voluptuous figure. A laptop rested on her stomach. The Sound wore what appeared to be his uniform, a knee-length white cotton tunic over jeans. His feet were bare, his light-brown hair pulled into a tight man bun. The others, dressed in a variety of ripped jeans and tees, heavy boots, and piercings, looked completely incongruous. Maggie was struck by the fact that although each of them had so much presence onstage, several were slight in person. Bokie, the drummer, was the only band member with some height and heft. *Maybe because he's a drummer*, Maggie thought. *Pounding a drum kit is probably a great bicep workout. Maybe I should take it up.*

A friendly greeting from Toulouse interrupted Maggie's off-topic musings. "Hey there," he said, waving to her. "Maggie, right?"

"Right." Maggie walked past a nineteenth-century statue of a Greek goddess to where the band was hanging out. "I'm so sorry about what happened to your manager last night."

"Wasn't *my* manager," Valeria said, not hiding her resentment.

"He was only Tammy's," Toulouse explained. "Rest of us were hired on for the tour."

"Ah. I don't know much about the music business." *Boy, is that an understatement.*

"Is Gaynell okay?" Toulouse asked with genuine concern.

"I saw her for a minute after the show, but she didn't want to talk."

Don't reveal too much. "She's upset about what happened, like everyone."

"Well, tell her I'm thinking of her."

"I will. I made more pralines for our booth and thought I'd bring some by for y'all. Thought you could use a treat."

Toulouse brightened. "Homemade pralines? Talk about good." He called to the other musicians, who were either playing with their phones or listening to music through headphones. "Y'all, ya gotta have a fresh, homemade praline. Best candy ever."

The others separated themselves from their electronics and wandered over. "I'm so sorry about Mr. Pickner," she repeated as she handed out the pralines. The musicians mumbled replies as they examined the pralines as if they'd been delivered from space. The Sound, Tammy's keyboardist, took a wary bite. "Good stuff. Thanks." Praline in hand, he headed back to his chaise lounge. The other musicians, minus Valeria, followed.

Maggie couldn't tell if the band members were generally sanguine or not that broken up about Pickner's sign-off. She noted that no one of them seemed curious about the suspicious nature of his death. "I have to say, I'm surprised y'all are still here. I figured Tammy might want to cancel her dates after Mr. Pickner's death."

Valeria responded with a snort. "Give up her first slot at Jazz Fest? Like that would ever happen. There'll be some kind of memorial for Pony when we get back to LA, I guess.

I won't be there. I'm still waiting for the solo career he promised me."

There's one new suspect, Maggie thought. Valeria was bitter, to be sure. Whether she was bitter enough to kill was the question.

Maggie debated her next move. She noticed Uffen, the group playboy, checking out the license of a giggling, pretty young girl. "He's got a type. And a go-to line."

Valeria guffawed. "He's not looking at their pictures. He's checking their birth dates to make sure they're legal."

"Oh," Maggie said, embarrassed by her naïveté. But Valeria was proving to be a good source of information. *Maybe coming off dim and starstruck will work for me*, she thought. She sat down on the chaise next to the backup singer. "I've never been around professional musicians before. It's so exciting."

Valeria lifted the corner of her mouth in a half smile. "What's the old expression . . . how ya gonna keep 'em down on the farm once they seen Paree? Paree here being some cool dudes that played with the biggest singers on the planet."

"They seem really different offstage. I'm so curious about what they're like, you know, in real life." *God help me, I sound like a total idiot.*

Luckily, Valeria didn't seem put off by Maggie's guilelessness. The backup singer was the only woman on the tour besides Tammy, who treated her like a subordinate— the music business equivalent of a waitress or housekeeper. Maggie got the impression that Valeria welcomed the opportunity for a little girly gossip. Valeria leaned forward, and Maggie followed her lead. "Over there, that's East MacLeod," Valeria said in a low voice. "He played with a one-hit wonder group, Bright Sky."

"'Not the One,'" Maggie said, recalling the name of the group's only big song.

"Yup. They broke up right after, your basic battle-of-the-bandmates ego trips. East got a chip on his shoulder and a drinking problem. No one would hire him for the longest time. I couldn't believe it when I found out he was on this tour."

Maggie subtly checked out East. He was probably close to her own age, but the deep lines and crevasses on his face spoke to some hard living. Sun glinted off sparks of silver in the tight curls of his brown hair. He'd replaced the phone in his hand with a cigarette that was almost out. He pulled a fresh cigarette out of a pack and used the dying embers of the first to light the second. Everything about the musician radiated tension.

"Then there's Uffen." Valeria was on a roll. "Talk about a dog. That man's sown his seed worldwide. He's the male version of open for business." Maggie tried not to flinch at the singer's coarse language. "And he likes 'em young as he can get 'em."

Maggie couldn't hide her reaction to this nasty piece of gossip. "Ew," she said, crinkling her nose. She surveyed the group and noticed The Sound had left his lounge chair. He'd pulled off his jeans, revealing bicycle shorts underneath, and was doing yoga on the resort's verdant lawn.

"What about The Sound? What's he like? And why does he have a such a weird name? What's his real one?"

"If anyone knows, they don't remember," Valeria said. "This is the first time I've toured with him. So far, he's pretty chill. I tease him sometimes and call him Mr. Namaste. He owns a piece of this yoga chain, Piloga. It's a mash-up of Pilates and yoga. A big thing with the LA celebrities right now, and I think he wants to expand to other cities. Not a big talker, kind of keeps to himself. Like, he rented his own car while he's here. He's a pot smoker, but who isn't?"

Me, Maggie thought. *Or anyone I know.*

Valeria gave the musicians a once-over to determine whom she'd missed. "I don't know much about Toulouse. Pony hired him out of Nashville, not LA. He's kinda weird. I mean, he's real enthusiastic and super into God. But there's something off about him. Like he's faking it or something. I don't know. I can't explain it."

"He's younger than the other musicians. Maybe he's got a different energy because he's new to your world."

"Maybe."

Maggie eyed the last musician, Bokie, who'd resumed listening to music. He drummed on his knees, eyes closed, occasionally singing a snippet of whatever song he was listening to, loudly and off-key. "What about him? He seems nice."

Valeria looked toward where Maggie was pointing. "Who, Bokie? He is. Real nice guy. He's on the deaf side because he got stubborn about wearing earplugs when he played. Said only wimps wear them. He eventually got on board, but not before some damage was done. He was heavy into drugs for a long time, but now he's in recovery. He's got a solid good heart, that I can tell you."

"I'm getting the impression you wouldn't say the same about Pony Pickner."

A look of disgust crossed Valeria's face. "If they opened him up and looked inside, they'd probably find a hole where his heart should be. He took advantage of people. You wanna hear something wild?"

Oh boy, do I, Maggie thought, her adrenaline racing at the thought of a possible clue to the manager's murder. But she chose to play it casual with Valeria, tossing out an off-hand, "Okay."

The singer looked around and then whispered, "I heard Pony hired a PI, who was trolling for his old flames so he could pay them off before they sued him. That's a big thing right now. It's taken down a lot of guys like him."

"I've read about that."

This salacious bit of dirt was followed by a lull in the conversation. Valeria looked down at her laptop and Maggie took the hint. "This has been so cool," she said, sounding as starstruck as she could. "But I better go. See you later."

Valeria had started typing and didn't look up. "Uh-huh, later."

Maggie stood and stretched, a subterfuge move that allowed her to evaluate the musicians a final time before leaving. Toulouse was reading the Bible; Maggie figured that alone made his jaded bandmates mark him as a weirdo. East, looking lost in dark thoughts, lit yet another cigarette, while Uffen hit on yet another young girl. The Sound had twisted himself into a yoga position that only a contortionist could copy; Bokie was sound asleep under his headphones. With nothing more to be learned from the group, Maggie left them to their various forms of relaxation.

She wanted to say goodbye to Kaity on her way out, but the young desk clerk was on her lunch break, so Maggie returned to her car. She tried to call Bo and report the possible connection between Pony and a private investigator, but her Bluetooth wouldn't behave. Instead, she texted him to meet at Crozat in half an hour.

Parched, Maggie made a pit stop at Park 'n Shop. Her grumbling stomach alerted her that it was also lunchtime. She picked up a container of prepackaged California roll. Then, hearing Ninette's voice in her head cry out, *Convenience-store sushi? What are you thinking?* She put it back. Maggie saw Kaity, who was in the midst of a conversation with her grandmother, Gin Bertrand. Kaity and Gin stopped talking the minute they saw Maggie. "Hey, you two." She took a bottle of water from the refrigerator case and brought it to the checkout stand. Gin made no move to help her. "Gin? Could you ring me up?"

Gin and Kaity exchanged a look, then Gin came to the register. She scanned Maggie's bottle. "One dollar and twelve cents."

Gin's cold tone puzzled Maggie. "I have exact change." She counted it out. "Everything okay?"

"Fine. Absolutely fine." Gin's frosty tone belied her words, but Maggie didn't have time to find out what was bothering the older woman. She took her water and left the store. She was about to get in her car when Kaity came out of the store and ran up to her. "Hi, sorry about that. Grammy's so old-fashioned about some things."

"No problem," Maggie said, still wondering what was going on.

"I don't care what anyone says, I think dating a musician would be awesome." Kaity's strawberry-blonde ponytail bounced back and forth as the animated girl spoke. "I mean, Mr. Durand is hot and all, but still. Any chance you can get me VIP tickets for Tammy's closing set at the festival?"

"*What?*" Maggie said, stunned. "No, no, no. I'm not dating one of those musicians. I'm engaged." As proof, she held up her left hand, where a bejeweled gumbo pot decorated her ring finger. This was Bo's idea of an engagement ring, and Maggie loved him for it.

But Kaity wasn't to be swayed. "I read about this girl who was married for about six weeks, met a guy at the gym, and dumped her new husband for him. I'm just sayin', stuff happens."

Kaity winked at her, then scurried back into the store. Maggie started to follow the girl to set her and her judgy grandmother straight, but she stopped.

The misunderstanding had given her an idea.

Chapter 9

Bo arrived at Crozat moments after Maggie. She waited for him on the manor house's wide, airy veranda. "I hear you've been stepping out on me," he said with a grin as he came up the centuries-old cypress steps.

"You heard the rumor already? Wow, that must set a record in this town. But I think I know a way to make it work for your investigation." Maggie sat on the porch swing and motioned for Bo to join her, which he did. "Before I get to that, Valeria, Tammy's backup singer who's my new BFF, told me Pony had a PI hunting down women he was inappropriate with. The goal was to pay them off so that they never went public with sexual misconduct accusations."

Bo frowned. "That's good, but she might have mentioned it when we interviewed her. It would help if people shared intel like that with those of us who can actually do something about it."

"I know. Honestly, if I hadn't played dumb and pushed her to gossip, she probably wouldn't have told me either. And speaking of gossip, here's my idea. I think we should pretend we broke up." Bo raised an eyebrow. "Or pretend we're taking a break. Basically, we act like there are problems in our relationship. That way I can spend more time with the musicians under the cover of being the heartbroken ex-fiancée looking to soothe my wounds with a rebound romance, and I can pick up possible clues from them." She stopped to take a breath.

Bo made a face. "Oh, boy. I don't know, chère."

"It's a good plan."

"You know I've never been one to wag a finger and say don't get involved. You're smart and have great instincts. You dig up valuable stuff—case in point, what the backup singer told you. But it's one thing when you're using your connections and status in town to get info from locals. These are Hollywood people."

"What makes them more dangerous? Our guests are always from out of town, and once one of them was a murderer."

Bo rubbed his forehead. "I'm thinking maybe we should go a little more by the book here."

"It's Louisiana. When do we ever go 'by the book'?"

Bo had to laugh at this. "True dat. And we are short-handed at the station, as usual."

"With Tammy and Sara staying here, plus Gigi and Narcisse now glomming on as guests on Tammy's dime, I have great access to those four. Our little white lie would let me cover the whole crew. The only thing is, I don't want to lie to my parents or Gran. They'll have to know the truth. Xander, too."

"Xander absolutely. He can't be lying to his mom and stepdad, which means Whitney and Zach will have to know. That's a lot of people who'll know the truth."

"And we can trust every one of them. They may not love the plan, but they know we're doing it for Gaynell." Maggie threaded her fingers through Bo's. She gave him an impish smile. "Sounds like you're on board."

"Reluctantly. And I'm putting a clock on it. Three days. Seventy-two hours. I'm not thrilled about being broken up even that long."

"I promise I'll make it up to you when we get back together."

Bo raised an eyebrow. "Now *that* I like the sound of."

The two rocked back and forth for a moment, hands still entwined. "Us having relationship problems may not seem too farfetched to people," Maggie said. "I keep getting asked why we haven't set a wedding date. The 'we're not in any hurry and haven't had time' excuse is getting old. I think they'll buy the 'we got cold feet so we're taking a break' excuse. That may be why the rumor traveled so fast. People were already wondering what's going on." Maggie shook her head, bemused. "Only in a town this small could the relationship between an artist and a cop be the lead local story."

"You do know Ru will be onto us in a heartbeat."

"Doesn't worry me at all. Remember his favorite saying . . ."

"In Louisiana, we only follow the rules we like," the couple said simultaneously.

Bo's coal-black eyes flashed concern. "Just be careful."

"I will be. Frankly, the musicians all have such big egos that I don't think it would occur to them I'm there for any other reason than being a groupie. Except for Toulouse. He's got a thing for Gaynell. Not in a bad way, in a sweet way."

An alarm on Bo's smart watch dinged and he checked it. "I gotta get ready for my shift at the festival. But before I go, I'm giving you three days' worth of kisses."

And he did.

*　*　*

After Bo left, Maggie retreated to the shotgun cottage to research Tammy's band members. She sat down at the antique desk that served as her mini-office, turned on her laptop, and typed in Uffen's name. His sketchy sexual pro-clivities made him number one on her list. Although there were no indications that private-eye-hiring Pony's tastes in women skewed as young as the bassist's, it was a link worth searching for.

Maggie scanned the list of references to Uffen that popped up on her screen. Most related to various tours he'd signed on for. But a couple sparked interest. Posts on two music blogs shared the story of a threatened lawsuit in a case where Uffen had been dating both a mother and her seventeen-year-old daughter. Quotes from the aggrieved mother indicated she was more concerned about Uffen two-timing her than about him dating her underage daughter. The charges against the musician were dropped when the girl recanted her story about their affair. The post concluded with the catty observation that the teenager and her mother were later seen driving brand-new, matching candy-apple-red Corvettes. Maggie leaned back in her chair and considered this. Uffen obviously paid off the duo. Did Pony have anything to do with this? Had the manager used his own experiences and legal counsel to get Uffen off the hook? If so, did Uffen owe him? And resent it?

Her musings were interrupted by a knock at the door. Maggie rose and went to answer it. Gigi, looking tired and harried, stood there, her arms filled with clothing and folders she struggled not to drop. Perspiration dripped off her forehead onto the bundles she carried. "You need some help?" Maggie asked.

Gigi shook her head. "Not with this. But I need the key for Mr. Pickner's room. I looked for your parents and can't find them."

"They're probably resting. It's exhausting making individual special meal orders for four different people."

The hint of admonishment sailed over Gigi's head. "I just need the key. The crime people are done looking for whatever it was they were looking for and Tammy needs anything related to the tour that they didn't take, like her backup mic. She's never gonna use the one that killed Pony again, that's for sure. Pee-yew."

Maggie saw an opportunity. "Gigi, you look like you have a lot to do. Why don't I go through Mr. Pickner's room?"

Gigi hesitated. "Well . . . you do have experience going

through murdered people's rooms. Crozat must have the highest death rate of any B and B in the state. Maybe in the world."

"I wouldn't go *that* far," Maggie said, bristling.

"It would be a help. I could do the"—Gigi glanced at a sticky note attached to one of the folders in her arms—"nine other things Tammy wants me to do now that I'm her assistant on top of being her fan club president." Gigi shared the news of her promotion with pride.

"Congratulations on the new job. But what about Sara?"

"She got promoted to Tammy's manager for the rest of the tour and maybe after that. She's the one who's been handling most of the day-to-day stuff for Pony. At least, according to her."

Gigi didn't bother to hide the bitterness she felt toward her rival for Tammy's attention and affection. Maggie didn't care. Where Gigi saw an enemy, Maggie now saw Sara as someone whose step up the music business career ladder was a potential motive for murder. She motioned to Gigi's list. "You go take care of those nine other things. I'll clean out Pony's room and organize everything for Tammy."

"That would be great. Except . . ." Gigi's brow creased with worry. "Could we kinda keep it between us? I don't want Tammy to feel like I can't do the job. I'm thinking if it goes well, she'll take us to California with her. I'm so over Pelican. Pee-yew." In Gigi's vernacular, "pee-yew" covered everything from murder to small-town living.

"No worries," Maggie said, quelling her annoyance at

the Pelican diss. "I won't tell anyone." A thought occurred to her. "Sad as Pony's death is, I guess it makes things a little easier for you and Narcisse."

Maggie's hope that guileless Gigi might respond in a way that incriminated her was dashed by the woman's wary response. "How so?"

"I got the impression he'd try to fire Narcisse as soon as he could, and maybe even keep you away from Tammy."

"Tammy's the star," Gigi said, her tone even. "Pony worked for her, not the other way around. Thank you for your help; I truly appreciate it." Gigi took off, her exit bumpy as she dropped and picked up various items from her load. Maggie closed her computer and stole a couple of Gran's empty death-cleaning boxes. Then she headed over to the manor house, where she pulled a key for Pony's room from the B and B's box of spares. She walked over to the carriage house, which was located behind the beautifully manicured bushes of Crozat's parterre garden. Maggie opened the carriage house's main door and walked into a small hallway. She used the key she'd retrieved to enter a room on the left.

The carriage house lodgings were suites. A small living room decorated with Crozat family antiques abutted a bedroom with a king-size bed and more lovely furniture. The suite, sans an occupant, smelled musty. Maggie opened the large front window, and the scent of almond verbena wafted in. Then she circled the room, hoping to find a clue among the former music manager's belongings.

But either the crime scene technicians had removed

anything that might provide insight into Pony's murder, or he lived a sparse life. Aside from a small stack of papers on the suite's antique walnut desk, there was no sign of the late guest. Maggie picked up the stack, which proved to be handouts from the *Cajun Country Live!* planning committee. She thumbed through the pages to see if Pony had annotated them. He hadn't, so she placed the stack in a box. She lapped the room, getting on her hands and knees to look in every nook and cranny, then picked up the sofa pillows. There wasn't even loose change to be found, thanks to the efforts of the B and B's part-time housekeeper.

Coming up empty from the living room search, Maggie moved on to the bedroom. There she saw more signs of life. Pony's carry-on sat on the suitcase stand. She looked through it but found nothing. Next, she examined every pants and jacket pocket. She recognized the names of several high-end clothing lines, which only proved the late manager had pricey tastes. In addition to clues, Tammy's backup mic was nowhere to be found. She texted the news to Gigi, who responded, NVM THAT. POLICE HAVE IT. WILL GET IT FROM THEM.

"Would have been nice to know that sooner," Maggie griped to the empty room. She stepped into the bathroom, which was empty of sundries. She assumed they were currently the property of Pelican PD, along with the errant mic. About to give up, Maggie picked up the bathroom trash can, just for the comfort of knowing she'd looked everywhere. She noticed a piece of paper stuck to the bottom of the can and peeled it off. It was a prescription for something called abiraterone. Maggie returned to the bedroom, pulled out her phone, and typed the drug's name into a search engine. She read the results, which showed abiraterone was a hormone therapy used to treat prostate cancer.

The prescription was made out to Pony Pickner.

Chapter 10

Maggie packed Pony's belongings into his suitcase and one of the boxes she'd brought with her but kept the prescription to give to Bo. Then she remembered they'd "broken up." She took a photo of it and texted it to him. He texted back a thumbs-up emoji, followed by a broken heart and a wink.

Her phone showed that she was due at the festival in fifteen minutes. Maggie loaded pralines into her car and then returned to the shotgun cottage, where she retrieved a small box from the far edge of her lingerie drawer. She took off her engagement ring, placed it in the box's satin cushion, and made her way to the large old black safe in the manor house. "It's not forever, my friend," she said as she put the ring inside the safe next to family heirlooms like jewelry, deeds, and a gumbo recipe handed down through generations of Crozats. Then she left for the festival.

Maggie had accepted Kyle's offer to lend her some members of his sales team, and high school students Clinton and Brianna Poche were now helping her man the Crozats' booth. "These are good," Clinton acknowledged as he snacked on a sweet potato praline. "But my grand-mère's sweet potato pralines are better, no offense or anything. Her recipe's super awesome. And they taste just as good when *I* make them." Clinton, a budding confectioner, said this with pride.

"Why don't you make a batch and sell them here?" Maggie said, seizing an opportunity to lighten her workload while encouraging a bit of entrepreneurship. "You can keep the proceeds from your sales."

"Really? Sure." Excited, Clinton took out his phone and started writing a list of ingredients he'd need.

"People's coming," his sister said, gesturing to the entrance gate.

As they waited for customers, Maggie unconsciously reached for her engagement ring. Then she remembered it wasn't there. She'd developed a habit of playing with it, and not wearing the ring felt disconcerting.

"Where's your ring?" Brianna said, noticing Maggie's bare hand.

"Home. I just thought I'd leave it there today." She lied as badly as possible, throwing in a sad face as a punctuation mark. Clinton and Brianna exchanged a knowing look. Then Brianna pulled out her phone and began texting, sending the rumor engine into first gear.

Maggie saw Xander and his friends strolling up the grass midway and waved. The "posse" steered itself in the praline booth's direction, and soon she, Clinton, and Brianna were busy selling the group pralines. "Two, please," Xander said, holding up two fingers.

"These are on the house," Maggie said, handing them to him.

Xander thanked her, then turned to Esme, the girl Maggie had noticed before. "Here," Xander said, offering her a praline.

Esme shook her head. "No thank you."

She walked away, leaving a crestfallen Xander. Maggie's heart broke for the boy. "Hey, buddy, it's okay. Lots of kids don't like nuts. No big deal. Now you get two pralines." Xander didn't respond. "Tell you what. For tomorrow, I'll make my dad's recipe for Chulanes. They're chewy chocolate pralines. Kids love chocolate. How does that sound?"

Xander brightened and nodded, then ran to rejoin his friends.

"Bet she'd like my grand-mère's sweet potato pralines," Clinton said. "Just sayin'."

This drew a groan from his sister and a laugh from Maggie. "I'm going to take a break," she told her helpers. "If you need me, text me."

Maggie left the booth and wandered around the festival grounds. With Pelican Pralines in the capable hands of the Poche teens, she debated her next move. She intended to use her newly "single" status as a way of cozying up to Tammy's musicians. Maggie doubted they'd make an appearance at the festival this early in the afternoon, but on the off chance one of them was an early riser—meaning they got out of bed before four in the afternoon—she headed down to the performance area. As predicted, there wasn't a musician to be found. Maggie was about to return to her booth when she saw Sara, Tammy's ersatz manager, deep in conversation with a roadie, who was taking notes as she spoke. Maggie made her way toward them in time to hear the roadie say, "But—" and Sara respond, "I don't care what Pony wanted. He was wrong and I'm right. If he was still with us, he would've eventually come around on this, trust me."

"Fine, we'll do it your way," the roadie said, looking unhappy as he turned to go.

Sara noticed Maggie and pointed to the departing roadie. "You see what women in this business have to put up with? He'd do anything Pony asked without saying a word about it. But I tell him to set up the stage with Uffen on Tammy's right instead of her left because they have great onstage chemistry—plus she's a righty so she naturally gravitates in that direction—and I get pushback. It makes me *furious*."

Maggie noted that Sara didn't sound furious. She sounded downright exuberant. "You handled it really well. If Pony was still here, he would have been impressed."

Sara made a wry face. She pulled off the shirt she'd wrapped around her waist and blotted the back of her neck with it. "I doubt it. I don't know what would have impressed Pony. I tried pretty much everything and never got a single positive response from him."

Maggie took a delicate approach to her next question.

"Did he ever try to . . . ?" She purposefully left the sentence unfinished.

"Hit on me?" Sara chortled. "Even me being gay didn't put him off. I think it turned him on more. But I always circled back to business, and the thing with him was that he'd eventually get bored and move on." Sara turned and gazed toward the stage. "He was a genius, you know. Like, no joke. A true legend. I learned a ton from him. But . . . what's that old saying? When the student knows more than the master?"

"The student has become the master."

"Pony was old. And this isn't a business for old people. You've got to know when to get out or you wind up getting pushed out. Anyway, I've gotta run; I have to Skype with the Jazz Fest people in ten."

The young manager took off for the VIP trailer, her strides long, her posture confident. "Get out or pushed out," Maggie murmured. Pony hadn't given off any sense of wanting to retire from his prominent position, leaving "pushed out" as the only option for someone with ambitions to replace him. Someone like Sara.

*　*　*

Maggie mulled this over on her walk back to Pelican Pralines. She spent the next few hours selling sweets and souvenirs, which proved to be a welcome respite from worrying about Gaynell facing a murder rap. A couple of twenty-something hippie wannabes approached the booth. One was short with a potbelly that stuck out from under his faded T-shirt, the other gangly and dreadlocked. Their glazed eyes indicated they'd been partying with more than liquor. They eyed the pralines with longing and a dose of suspicion. "These look good, but are they made from pelicans?"

"What? No." Maggie made a discreet gesture to quiet Brianna and Clinton's giggles. "They're made *in* Pelican, not *of* pelicans."

The ganglier of the two looked skeptical. "You sure?"

"So very, very sure."

"Might I step in?" The British accent belonged to Uffen, Tammy's bassist, who emerged between the stoners. "Allow me to be your taste tester." He chose a praline piece from the sample bowl of broken bits, sniffed it, then ate it. "Oh my. An almond praline. Unique and absolutely delicious. I'll take ten. No, make it twenty. And you know what? Make it an assortment, please."

"Sure, of course." Maggie handed Uffen a premade box of assorted pralines.

He pulled a twenty-dollar bill out of his pocket and exchanged it for the box. "Gentlemen, these are for you."

Maggie hid her own giggles as Uffen passed the box of pralines to the stoners and was rewarded with a chorus of "Dude!" and "Awesome!"

"Thank you for that," she said to the bassist as the men departed with their prize.

Uffen flashed a dimpled smile. He released his hair from its man bun prison. It hung past his shoulders, curly and golden. "My pleasure. I just dropped by the fair to pick up some barbecue for the group back at the B and B. Why don't you stop by later?"

"Sure, if I'm free."

"Oh, you're free."

The rumor engine had shifted from first gear straight into fifth. But Maggie played dumb. "How do you know?"

"A little birdie told me. A birdie who's only sixteen, unfortunately."

"I'm surprised you didn't ask to see my license before inviting me over."

The bassist favored Maggie with his most sultry look. "I don't need to see your license to know you're legal."

"You do realize that's not a compliment."

For a moment, the musician looked flustered. "Oh. Right." He quickly regrouped. "The invitation still stands."

"And is accepted." Maggie hated her own flirty response. She could feel the disapproval as Clinton and Brianna whispered to each other. She knew her plan was a good one but hadn't counted on how difficult it would be to execute.

"See you later, then," Uffen said. "And feel free to bring some of those delicious sweets of yours."

He crooked his lips in a half smile, added a dose of bedroom eyes, and departed for the barbecue booth. Maggie and the Poches watched him go. "He's a lot," Brianna said.

"Yes, he is," Maggie responded. *And I hope I can handle him.*

* * *

By the time Maggie closed the praline booth, it was past ten PM and she was exhausted. She texted Uffen, hoping the musicians had called it a night while knowing in her heart they hadn't. Uffen confirmed this and included an order for more barbecue. Maggie steeled herself for a round of flirting, then bought out the last of the Pigalicious BBQ booth's chicken, ribs, and pulled pork. She drove up the River Road to Belle Vista, where she was hailed as a hero by the musicians, who descended upon the buckets of food she carried. "The ribs are mine," Tammy said, snatching the container from Maggie.

"I thought you were a vegetarian," Maggie said as she joined the others at a picnic table on BV's wide green lawn.

"Pony had me on that stupid diet. He said it was better for my voice. And my weight. He was always on my case about that. Not anymore. May he rest in peace, amen." Tammy added the last as an afterthought. "Ooh, Zapp's Voodoo Chips. My favorite." She tore open a bag of the spicy potato chips, then alternated between crunching chips and stuffing down ribs. Maggie noted this benefit of Pony's death, although it was hard to envision freedom to eat ribs as a motive for murder, even for someone as self-involved as Tammy.

Gigi and Narcisse appeared on the lawn's horizon. Gigi trudged up the slight incline, Narcisse loping behind her. "Hey, coz," Gigi said, addressing Tammy. "I got everything done on your list. I was wondering if I could wash your delicates tomorrow? I'm kinda worn out."

"I hear you." Tammy licked each finger, then cleaned

her hands with a wet wipe. "Except I really need that stuff washed. I don't have to tell you how easy it'd be to find an assistant who don't get wore out."

Gigi tried and failed to turn a grimace into a smile. "Message received. Narcisse?"

"You take the car." Narcisse said this with a mouth full of pulled-pork sandwich. "I'll catch a ride back with Tammy later."

Gigi stood immobile for a moment. "Okay then," she finally said, as brightly as possible. "See y'all back at Crozat."

Gigi left. Maggie was relieved to see Uffen had lost interest in hitting on her, instead choosing to recline on a chaise lounge and vape. The Sound and Valeria rose to take food back to their rooms. "I have to make some business calls to LA," The Sound said.

"Piloga biz, huh?" Valeria jokingly bowed to him. "Mah-nasty, my friend."

"It's *namaste* and you know that," The Sound responded, but he said it with a glimmer of amusement.

They took off, but the others stuck around. No one seemed to wonder why Maggie was there, which saved her from having to put on her rebound-romance act.

The musicians made small talk as they ate, referencing people and places that were alien to her. Although the general conversation was casual, she sensed an underlying tension. This was no surprise. The man who was the power behind the tour had been killed. Dispassionate as the performers appeared, the shocking death affected them, especially since the murderer was still at large and the police were targeting an unlikely suspect with the flimsiest of evidence.

"How's Miss Gaynell doing?" Toulouse asked, as if reading her mind.

"She's good," Maggie lied. She was torn between pretending Gaynell was in the clear and ramping up the fact that her friend was under suspicion. The first choice might make the real killer nervous enough to make a mistake; the second might relax them enough to get sloppy and slip up. But Toulouse saved Maggie from having to pick a path.

"I can't believe the police think she killed Pony." Angry, Toulouse turned to Tammy. "How could you do that to her?"

The singer held up her hands. "Hey, I only shared what I saw. I'm on her side. It's not my fault Pony messed with one woman too many."

Toulouse pointed a finger at her. "See? Talk like that's what got her into trouble."

"I'm not the only one who heard Gaynell be all nasty with him." Tammy turned to Maggie, who was hanging back, letting Toulouse fight the fight for her. "You heard her, too."

Cornered, Maggie bit back the urge to attack the it-rhymes-with-witchy singer, instead opting for a passionate defense. "Gaynell is one of my closest friends in the world, and no matter what happened between her and Mr. Pickner, I can tell you that it would never drive her to violence."

"Agree a million percent," Toulouse said with a vigorous nod.

"Somebody's crushing on Miss Gaynell." Uffen called this in a singsongy voice from his chaise.

Toulouse's face flamed. "It ain't that. I just think she's a good person."

"Uh-huh."

"Leave me alone."

"Somebody's also quite sensitive."

Uffen's taunts upped the level of tension, and the air crackled. "Get off his back, Uffen," East said through gritted teeth. Uffen responded with a derisive laugh, and East clenched his fists. "I'm sick of you picking on people and thinking it's funny." Maggie held her breath.

"Whoa." Bokie, the good-natured drummer, patted one of East's fists. "Take a breath, dude. Let go, let God."

Uffen groaned theatrically. "Oh please, spare me the twelve-step BS."

"It's not BS; it helps me."

Bokie sounded wounded, and Maggie felt for him. "I think everyone's a little touchy right now, which is totally understandable."

"They're always like this. Ignore them." Tammy weighed in without looking up from her cell phone. Narcisse lolled next to her, headphones on, oblivious to the drama.

East released his fists, but his mood remained dark. "It would've been great if Pony had controlled himself for a change. What an idiot."

Uffen snorted as he refilled his vape cartridge. "There's gratitude for you. That 'idiot' saved your career and probably your life. If it weren't for Pony, you'd be playing bar mitzvahs and weddings. Or dead."

East slammed his fists on the table, startling the others and even rousing Narcisse from his stupor. "I know that, okay? Stop reminding me."

The guitarist kicked over his chair, unleashed a flood of foul language, and stormed off. No one spoke for a moment.

"You shouldn't upset him like that," Toulouse said. "It's not nice."

Maggie coughed, fighting back hysterical giggles induced by the Cajun musician's massive understatement. Pushing the volatile East's buttons was more than "not nice."

It was dangerous.

Chapter 11

East's explosion ended the evening. Maggie was loopy with fatigue by the time she got home, but that didn't stop her from powering on her laptop and searching for East MacLeod. Music magazine articles and blog posts detailed a past littered with drunken rants, missed tour dates, and a couple of arrests for disorderly conduct—then a long career lull until his name appeared in the lineup for Tammy's band. Why would he resent Pony, the man who resuscitated his career? Had Pony insisted on something untenable in exchange for the job? Maggie pulled out a Post-it pad and wrote down, *See if Pelican PD researched musicians' contracts*. Then she stumbled into bed and a dreamless sleep.

A morning shower followed by black coffee rejuvenated Maggie. She slid on jeans and her *Cajun Country Live!* T-shirt, then joined her grandmother in the living room, stepping around three piles of the older woman's belongings that were taking up most of the floor. What little space remained had been commandeered by Gopher, who was splayed out to his full basset length and width. Jolie was on the couch, her little body tucked next to Gran's side. "Do you want to come to the festival with me later?" Maggie asked.

"Do you need me to help out?"

"No, I've got the booth covered."

"Then I'll pass," Gran said. "While I pat myself on the back for coming up with this idea, music festivals are a young person's game. I'll show up at some point, if they want me there, and wave like a royal . . ." She mimed the queen of England's wave. "But I think today I'll take Lee up on his offer of lunch in Breaux Bridge."

"No worries, I get it." Maggie motioned to the piles on the floor. "What are those for?"

"*Keep, discard, maybe.* Emphasis on the *discard* pile."

Maggie picked up a worn cardboard frame decorated with elbow macaroni spray-painted gold. "I made this for you in kindergarten. Please tell me it's in the *keep* pile."

"I'm afraid not. It's lost half its macaroni. But no worries, I've kept several of the treasures you made me over the years. Like this." Gran held up a glazed clay alligator. "I've always loved this little fellow. If you don't mind, I'd like to be buried with it."

Maggie made a sour face. "Oh, dear Lord, let's talk about anything else. Even murder."

"Speaking of which, your mother told me about your faux breakup with Bo. She and your father aren't too happy about it, but they know you see it as a way to help Gaynell."

"What do you think?"

"I'm all in, as they say in the military. However, if my

grief about the breakup is to be believable, I'll have to dust off the old acting chops. I took an acting course at Newcomb back in the day." Gran held a hand to her lightly wrinkled forehead, affected an anguished expression, and quintupled her Louisiana accent. "I'm bereft over the dissolution of my beloved granddaughter's betrothal. Is she destined for life as an old maid? I cannot bear the thought."

Maggie raised her eyebrows. "Simmer down, Blanche. Leave the acting to me and Bo. If anyone asks, go with a nice, simple 'No comment.'"

"Fine," Gran said with a pout. "But you're wasting my talents. Did you know I was able to cry on cue? There are Oscar winners who'd kill for that skill." She picked up a stack of faded letters tied together with a fraying pink ribbon. "Oh my. Love letters from your grandfather. I haven't looked at these in years."

"Aw. Those are a *keep forever and ever*." Maggie stood up and stretched. "Time to go make yet more pralines. Kyle and Lia are having Grove Hall baby-proofed today, so I'm candy-making at Vanessa and Quentin's. I'll see you later."

Gran, absorbed by a letter she'd removed from its envelope, didn't respond.

"Gran?"

The octogenarian looked up. Her eyes glistened. "I'm sorry. This is bringing back so many memories." Her lip quivered.

Moved, Maggie hugged her grandmother, who wiped

tears from her eyes. Gran pulled away from her grand-daughter and flashed an impish smile. "Told you I could cry on cue."

Maggie, bemused, shook her head, and Gran returned to reading the letter.

* * *

Vanessa and Quentin lived in a McMansion subdivision midway between Pelican and the neighboring town of Ville Blanc. The large home was designed to look exactly like the manor home it wasn't. As Vanessa so aptly put it, "This place is just like a plantation house but without all that icky old stuff."

The Fleer-MacIlhoney kitchen was gigantic, equaled only by the size of the great room attached to it, which was indeed a "great" room with its 75-inch television screen, L-shaped taupe leather couch, and ornate pool table. Charli, Vanessa's almost-one-year-old daughter by ex-fiancé Rufus, bounced up and down in a door jumper, cooing and occasionally throwing cereal at Vanessa's miniature poodle, Princess Meghan.

Vanessa perched on a barstool, sneaking chocolate chips from Maggie's stash of ingredients. She wore a "Mac" PELI-CAN GREAT AGAIN, VOTE FOR MACILHONEY T-shirt that was so tight her ample chest threatened to escape from it. "That shirt's a little out of date," Maggie pointed out.

"Yeah, it's pretty much a collector's item. But it was either wear it or cut it up for rags, and it fits too good for rags." Vanessa emptied a handful of chocolate chips into her mouth. "I'm sorry about you and Bo breaking up, but I have to say, I am not at all surprised. Rufus and I never thought you two would make it to the altar."

"Really." Maggie gritted her teeth and gave the Chulane mixture bubbling on the top-of-the-line, six-burner stove a hard stir.

"Oh, yeah. We would've put money on it, but Ru was too cheap. You're lucky you got out before you got married. The divorce attorney in Quenty's practice is price-*y*. Hey, he just got out of his third marriage. I can set you up. If it don't work out, at least the divorce'd be free."

"I'm not looking for a serious relationship right now. I need to grieve the last one."

Vanessa eyed her suspiciously. "You don't look that sad."

Oh boy, I'm a worse actress than Gran. "It's what they call denial, I guess. I still can't believe Bo and I are over."

"Well, the sooner you do, the sooner you can move on. And the best way to get over one relationship is to jump into a new one."

Maggie couldn't have disagreed with Vanessa's philosophy more, but she saw an opportunity to justify her socializing with Tammy's musicians. "You have a point. A little rebound thing might help me get past the breakup. Not with anyone local who might get hurt, though. With someone passing through. Like someone in Tammy Barker's band. They're all pretty cute." With that seed sown, Maggie steered the conversation in a different direction. "Van, you used to be a bully." The future Mrs. MacIlhoney didn't deny this. "I'm trying to get inside Tammy's head to see why she's still so mean to Gaynell. Where do you think that's coming from?"

"Looking for an expert opinion, huh? Charli, darlin', let go of Princess Meghan." Vanessa pried her baby's fingers off the stoic dog's tail. "I'm thinking if I were Tammy, rolling in money and fans, pretty much nothing about some Podunk singer in a Podunk town would get to me."

Maggie retrieved the bag of chocolate chips from Vanessa and dumped them in the praline mixture. "Not really loving that description of Gaynell or Pelican."

"You want to get in that girl's head, and that's what I'm trying to do." Vanessa closed her eyes and scrunched up her face as she concentrated. "If I were Tammy and high school was in the rearview mirror, why would I still be so mean to Gaynell? I guess if I was insecure and knew she was more talented than me."

"Which Gaynell is."

"But also, if she'd done something to me in the past that hurt so bad that no matter how much success I have, I won't be happy until I get her back for it." Vanessa's eyes popped open and she folded her arms across her chest, her exploration into the psyche of a bully complete.

"That's good," Maggie acknowledged. "Very good. I'll tell Gaynell to go deep into their high school history and see if there was some problem between her and Tammy that she's forgotten about but Tammy hasn't. Thanks for a little insight into the dark art of bullying."

"You're welcome." Vanessa jumped off the barstool and pulled at her jeans, which, like her tops, she always wore a size too small. "I gotta go doll up my little dolly. They're having a baby beauty contest over in Ville Blanc and Charli's dying to enter." Ignoring Maggie's skeptical glance, Vanessa lifted Charli out of the door jumper, deftly dodging the baby's attempts to grab on to her hair. "When you're done, lock up after yourself. I'll see you at the festival later."

"I'll be there eventually. I may stop by Belle Vista first."

"Belle Vista." Vanessa gave Maggie the knowing look she was fishing for. "Home to some hottie musicians. Rebound away, girlfriend."

Vanessa held up her hand for a high-five that Maggie returned, albeit with discomfort. Much as she hated her new persona as a relationship loser trolling for a little somethin' somethin', the conversation with Van had been useful. Tammy Barker might offer only circumstantial evidence against Gaynell, but it was all Pelican PD had, and Maggie feared the department would contort themselves in an effort to nail a suspect. As soon as Vanessa and Charli departed, Maggie texted Gaynell to search her past for any dustup that could be fueling the star's vendetta.

* * *

Maggie's optimism about this new direction faded when Gaynell wrote back to her, STILL NO IDEA WHY TAMMY HATES ME. STAYED OUT OF HER WAY AS MUCH AS POSSIBLE.

Maggie pulled into the Belle Vista parking lot around one PM, figuring the musicians would be up by then— which showed how little she knew about musicians. Only East was awake. She found him pacing the plantation's

English garden, his tattoos and body piercings making him an anomaly among the lavender and rose bushes.

The guitarist noted the box Maggie carried. "More pralines, huh? Those could be my next addiction," he said with a dry smile.

"Maybe I better hide them from you."

"No, I'll take a couple. I haven't eaten yet."

Maggie, who occasionally made a meal of pralines herself, didn't judge. She handed him two, then joined him on his walk, which was simultaneously aimless and tense. East scarfed down the first praline, then nibbled on the second, his attitude pensive. "I'm glad you came by. I wanted to say sorry about my rant yesterday. I always tell myself, *Don't let that idiot Uffen get to you.* And then I let him get to me."

"He seems like a button-pusher."

East gave a mirthless chortle and used a few more colorful words to describe the bassist, then said, "I heard you and that detective guy broke up."

Way to go, Pelican gossip hotline, Maggie thought to herself. Rather than speak, she responded with a sad nod.

"I saw Uffen checking you out. Whatever you do, don't rebound with that man-whore. God knows what STDs he's picked up."

Maggie wrinkled her nose. "Pee-yew, as Gigi would say."

This earned a real smile from the guitarist. "She's a major case. And that husband of hers. What's the word for someone who's a user?"

"Parasite."

"Right, that's it. And that's what he is. Big time." They

passed through BV's parterre garden, a sculpted wonderland of meticulously pruned bushes twice the size of Crozat's humble parterre. "You're good people, Maggie. Do yourself a favor and don't get sucked into our world."

Their stroll had brought them to the resort's pool. Steam rose from the water, a result of a hot afternoon sun mixing it up with high humidity. East's forehead was dotted with beads of sweat. He stopped at a poolside table and cranked open its umbrella, then dropped into a chair, pulled out a cigarette, and lit it. Maggie instinctively waved the smoke away from her face. "Sorry," East said. "My last vice. I'll have to stop when the baby comes."

Baby? This was an unexpected development. "Your wife is expecting? Congratulations."

"Not wife yet. We're waiting until after he comes and then we're going to have a kick-ass wedding. And yeah, I know it's a *he*. Look." East reached into the back pocket of his jeans and pulled out a small, frayed photo. "Our ultrasound. That's my boy."

The pride in the weary man's voice almost brought Maggie to tears. "East, that's wonderful. Congratulations."

"Took me years, but I finally got something right. Her." East pulled another, equally frayed photo from his pocket. Maggie got the feeling he used both pictures as worry beads, talismans to calm himself or prevent a relapse. This photo showed a stunning young black woman resting her hands on her swollen belly, her smile beatific. "She's beautiful."

"Janeece. She's a singer. Pony was gonna hire her for the

tour, but we didn't want her stressing anything in the last trimester. I miss her. A lot."

The mention of Pony offered Maggie a segue to the late manager. She spoke in a tone that was curious yet sympathetic, which she hoped would draw East out. "It's none of my business, but you seem to have had a complicated relationship with Mr. Pickner. I mean, he gave you a job, he was going to give your girlfriend a job . . ."

She let the sentence hang unfinished. East gave a slight nod. He took a deep drag on his cigarette and blew the smoke away from Maggie. "Pony gave me my first break. He managed Bright Sky, this band I was with. After Bright Sky broke up, I fell down the rabbit hole and lived in that space for a long time. And then he hired me again. The only one who would. Oh man, he made me pay for it. Drug tests, Breathalyzer tests, bottom-rung pay. I hated him for that. It was some major tough love, lemme tell you. But the thing is, love was part of it. I wouldn't be here without him. He was kind of like a dad to me. If my own dad cared as much, maybe I wouldn't have bottomed out in the first place." East gave an embarrassed grin. "Pretty insightful for a high school dropout, huh? Janeece got me into therapy. Wouldn't sign on to me without it. No fool, that girl."

"I thought you hated Mr. Pickner—Pony. When you kicked over the chair yesterday, you looked so angry."

"I was. I am. Pony's gone. He'll never meet my kid."

East turned away from Maggie. He dropped his cigarette butt on the cement, tamping it out with the toe of his boot, then picked up the butt and tossed it in a nearby garbage can. The break in the conversation gave Maggie time to think. "Did Pony ever have children of his own?"

East shook his head. "None that he knew about." He reached for another cigarette, then pushed away the pack. "In a way, we're all his children. He gave second chances to a lot of us." The guitarist stood up. "I didn't mean to talk so much. But I appreciate you listening."

"Sure. I'm glad I got to hear some nice things about Pony."

"You were right when you said our relationship was complicated. Pony was a complicated guy." East's phone sang out the song "Not the One," which Maggie recognized as Bright Sky's only hit. "That's Janeece. I need to take it."

"Of course."

East walked off to take the call. Maggie sat back in her chair, thinking. The conversation with East forced a recalibration of her attitude toward Pony Pickner. He wasn't the cartoon villain she'd imagined. And while East's hairtrigger temper was worrisome, his emotional attachment to the music manager made him an unlikely killer.

Unfortunately, this also meant there was one less suspect to take the heat off Gaynell.

Chapter 12

The combination of praline-making, clue-hunting, and a warm, moist afternoon left Maggie fighting to keep her eyes open. She decided to rest on a poolside chaise lounge for a few minutes before driving back to Crozat. Resting turned into dozing until a persistent tapping woke her up. She opened one eye and saw Valeria writing on a laptop. "Hey," the backup singer said. "You were really out."

Maggie yawned. "What time is it?"

"Two o'clock."

Maggie bolted upright. "Seriously? I've been asleep for almost an hour."

"Did you have to be somewhere?"

"No." Maggie leaned back in the chaise. Bokie rested on a lounge chair on the other side of the pool, eyes closed and his ubiquitous headphones in place. Tammy sat at a café table, texting. She was clad in giant black sunglasses, a hot-pink string bikini, and platform sandals. Maggie realized her nap offered an unexpected opportunity to ferret information out of a few more band members, and she was determined to take advantage of it.

"How're you doing?" Valeria asked this with a compassion that mystified Maggie. Then she remembered that the news of her breakup had traveled with warp speed.

"Okay, I guess." Maggie sighed and gave a lifeless shoulder shrug.

"I've been there. Breakups suck. Especially when they're with a piece of man candy like that detective of yours."

Maggie managed not to succumb to the jealousy she felt hearing another woman call her fake ex-fiancé *man candy*. "I'm trying not to bottom out about the whole thing. It's so hard. I need distractions. And I mean more than making buttloads of pralines." Maggie gestured toward Bokie, who, still wearing his headphones, was singing a song Maggie recognized from Tammy's set. "What's his story? Is he seeing anyone?"

"Bokie?" Valeria chuckled. "No, he's single. If you like your men hot and on the dim side, he's your guy."

The drummer opened his eyes and noticed the two women staring at him. His face lit up and he waved. "Hey, Val."

"Hey, honey."

Valeria blew him a kiss, and Maggie gave her a look. "He likes you."

"I know. But it's not like that. At least not for me. Too much baggage."

Maggie studied Bokie. She thought of East's past

tailspin. "It seems like all these musicians come with baggage."

"Now that being healthy's a thing, it's way better than it used to be. But when you're on tour, not much to do when you're not playing. Easy to get in trouble, especially if you're young and good-looking."

Maggie appraised Valeria, an attractive woman who exuded self-confidence and sexuality. She understood her appeal to Bokie—or any man. Yet the singer radiated a warmth and morality that made her likable to women as well. "How do *you* stay out of trouble?"

Valeria gave a sly smile and tapped her laptop with a red-lacquered fingernail. "I channel my energy into this baby. I'm writing a memoir. I have a lotta stories to tell and they're all in here." She then tapped her forehead. "And here. Just call me keeper of the secrets."

A frisson of fear shot through Maggie. If there was one thing she'd learned from the spate of recent murders, it was that secrets could be deadly. However, she'd also learned they often held clues. "I'm curious about something East told me. He said he was being underpaid."

"Oh honey, they all are. I'm the only one who's getting my quote. When East's girlfriend Janeece decided not to do the tour, Pony needed someone quick, so he couldn't low-ball me." Valeria leaned forward toward Maggie, her voice low. "I can trust you, right? I mean, who you gonna tell out here in wherever we are? Pony Pickner's thing was to scrounge for talented guys who needed a break. He had a stable of them that he underpaid, which kept costs down on the tours but earned him big fat bonuses if none of the guys went south on him. And they almost never did because then their careers would be over forever."

"I got exactly that impression from East."

"But . . ." The singer moved closer. "There's something extra weird about this tour. None of these guys are from his stable. He'd never worked with any of them before except East. I mean, they're all effed up like the others. But I got no idea why he'd bring together a bunch of Pony Pickner first-timers." Valeria sat back. "Makes you think, doesn't it?"

Does it ever, Maggie thought. Before she could respond, she was distracted by Tammy. The singer marched over to Bokie. She pulled up one side of his headphones, startling him. "Stop singing that flippin' song," she yelled into his ear. "We're cutting it from the set."

She released the headphone, which snapped back against Bokie's ear. "Ow." He removed the headphones and rubbed his ear. "Whaddya mean, we're cutting it? Why?"

"Good question." This came from Valeria, who was also surprised by Tammy's announcement.

"I'm sick of singing it. Pony always made me because it's a 'fan favorite.'" Tammy made derisive air quotes. "Well, he's gone, rest in peace"—again, this came across as an afterthought—"and I'm in charge of my own career now."

"I thought Sara was your new manager." Maggie couldn't resist throwing this in, earning a glare from Tammy.

"She's handling the day-to-day stuff—"

"Meaning grunt work," Valeria muttered under her breath.

"But I'm making the big decisions. We'll be giving the fans some new favorites, and I'm gonna make the album *I* wanna make." Tammy grabbed her cell phone from the café table and tromped off.

"Any chance one of the secrets in your book is that Tammy murdered Pony and could be put away for life?" Maggie asked.

Valeria pursed her lips and shook her head. "I wish."

* * *

As she drove to the festival, Maggie replayed her talk with Valeria as well as East's comment that Pony gave second chances to many musicians. Did all his hires see it that way? Or did some see it as strong-arm tactics bordering on blackmail? Take the lowball deal or really be out of the business? Bo once told her that humiliation was the main motivation behind most murders. A musician practically having to beg for a job was certainly humiliating. Was that enough to drive someone to kill?

Trombone Shorty sang out from her cell phone. She smiled when she saw the caller was Bo and pressed the receive button on her Bluetooth earbud. "We're broken up, remember?"

"I know, but it turns out I'm the codependent one in our relationship, so I had to touch base."

"I'm glad you did. Aside from missing your voice, I have

some updates." She filled him in on her conversations with East and Valeria, as well as on Tammy's newfound freedom to run her own career. "If Pelican PD found any contracts among Pony's belongings, it might be a good idea to see if one of the musicians was being paid way less than the others. Did you find out anything about that prescription I sent you? And I know that this is Murder Investigation 101, but did Pony have a will? I'm just curious."

"You and me both. Get this. His lawyer is in rehab and can't be reached for a week. He's a one-man operation, so it's not like a firm where we can hit up a different lawyer in the practice for the info. Pony's LA assistant won't talk to us without a lawyer, but she can't afford one because she's out of work thanks to his murder, so she won't talk to us at all. LAPD got a warrant to search Pickner's work computer, but the one thing Sunrise—yes, that's her actual name— did tell us is that he kept all his personal documents on his own laptop, which I'm guessing is gator feed by now, along with his phone and tablet."

"Obstacle after obstacle."

"Yup." There was a pause in the conversation. "So . . ."

"So . . ."

"I don't want to hang up," Bo said.

"Me neither. But . . ."

"I know. I do have to get to the festival."

"I'll be there for a little while," Maggie said. If we run into each other, make sure you act all awkward. And I'll be cold."

"Wait, so you're implying I'm the one who called us off? No fair."

"We have to. No one will believe that I'm the one who broke up with the town hunk-a-doodle-do."

"Chère, you're selling yourself short. You could do way better than me. Not that I want to give you any ideas."

"If there's one thing I know in this world, it's that I could never, ever do better than you, Beauregard Durand."

"Right back at ya, Magnolia Marie Crozat."

After a few more affectionate exchanges, the couple ended the call. Maggie parked in the festival vendors' lot and carried her praline stash to the Crozats' booth. Brianna Poche applauded as Maggie approached. "Yay, I can get me some pralines that aren't sweet potato." She cast a baleful glance at her brother.

"I've been experimenting with my recipe," Clinton explained. "I want it to be perfect so's I get repeat customers. And they do that thing where they tell other people how good my pralines are."

"Word of mouth."

"Yeah, that." Clinton stood up, He twerked and gyrated in an energetic dance move. "From my mouth to your mouth to everyone's mouth, oh yeah!"

Brianna groaned. "Why couldn't I be an only child?"

"You're not, and someday you'll be thankful for that," Maggie said. "I have to leave in an hour. When my friends get off work, we're shopping for a baby shower we're throwing. If you have any problems, call me, but I'm sure you'll be fine."

"We be more than fine, we be so fine."

Clinton accentuated this with a few more dance moves,

earning a chuckle from Maggie and a desperate plea from his sister to stop embarrassing her. The three then focused on preparing to open the booth for festivalgoers, who were beginning to straggle in. Maggie saw Uffen and The Sound browsing a few of the other stalls. Uffen waved to her, but she pretended not to see him. She sensed that if the bassist got the smallest whiff of a chance to score, his pursuit would be relentless.

"Hey, Maggie. Y'all open?" The booth's first customer of the day was Pixie, the Gator Girls' drummer.

"Sure, what can I get you?"

"Two pecans and a coconut."

Maggie exchanged the pralines for Pixie's cash. "I thought y'all canceled your set."

"Gaynell did, but Tammy said she'd sing with us, so we didn't have to. It's the most awesome opportunity."

Maggie felt hot with anger. "Auditioning for Jazz Fest with Gaynell would have been equally awesome," she said, fighting to keep her tone even.

"Oh, this is way better. Tammy may even take us on tour with her." Pixie waved at a cluster of girls Maggie recognized as her other bandmates. "Gotta go. 'Bye."

Maggie hadn't noticed Uffen hovering on the periphery. He sauntered over and rested his elbows on the booth's counter. "Ah, the unbridled enthusiasm of the amateur. Adorable."

Loath as she was to defend Gaynell's self-involved bandmates, Maggie found Uffen's superior attitude too annoying to ignore. "The Gator Girls are talented, and audiences love them. Sounds like someone's threatened by the competition."

"Hardly. Tammy's over country music. She wants to cross over to pop."

"I doubt her country fans will cross over with her."

"That's always the catch, isn't it? Lucky for me, I won't be around to find out. Once I'm done with this gig, I've got sessions and tours lined up for the next two years."

Uffen rattled off a list of the world's biggest rock and pop stars. Maggie had to admit it was impressive. "Would any of those jobs come up if Pony hadn't hired you for Tammy's tour?"

Uffen helped himself to a handful of praline pieces from the samples bowl. "Pony liked to take all the credit for my rebirth. But when a singer or a band needs a great guitarist, they have very short memories. Plus, there's the whole 'he without sin' angle. We're a motley crew, we musicians. Why, that would make a great band name."

He smirked at his own joke and strolled off, checking out every pretty teenager he passed. Maggie watched, repulsed. "I need a little air," she told Brianna and Clinton. "I'll be back in a minute."

She left from the back of the booth, walking away from the crowds perusing the stalls to a less populated area by the parking lot. Maggie leaned against a brand-new, tricked-out black pickup truck with gold spinners. She enjoyed a brief moment of quiet, then noticed The Sound making his way through tall grass toward the lot. He was holding a bag of groceries. "Hello." His tone was polite yet measured, as always. He pulled car keys out of his pants pocket. "Are you waiting for me?"

"No." Maggie pulled away from the truck. "Is this yours?"

"My rental."

"Sorry, I didn't know."

"Not a problem."

"I see you discovered our local organic farmer," she said, referencing the keyboardist's bag. "They have excellent produce."

"We'll see." The Sound studied her. Maggie felt acutely uncomfortable. "Do you know the definition of a third eye?"

"Not the literal definition. I know it's spiritual."

"It's a speculative invisible eye that provides perception beyond ordinary sight."

"Interesting." *Where, oh where, is this conversation going?*

The keyboardist continued to stare at her. Maggie could have sworn he didn't blink. "I've been in this business for twenty years. Since I was sixteen. I know what groupies look like. How they act. What they want. I know enough to know that you're no groupie. So the question is—what do you want?"

Maggie didn't respond. She stepped back. The Sound walked past her and got into the truck. He powered up the engine and drove off, leaving Maggie feeling unnerved.

Chapter 13

When Maggie returned to the Crozats' booth, she saw her friend Ione waiting to meet her for their baby shower shopping excursion. "What's wrong?" Ione asked. "You look like my mama did after my late uncle Claude showed up in a dream to tell her that she forgot to put shoes on him when he was buried, and she should send a pair up to him in the coffin of the next kin who passed."

"That makes no sense," Brianna said, wrinkling her nose. "Why would you need shoes if you're walking on clouds? They're soft."

"Okay, before this conversation gets any more surreal," Maggie said, "I'll tell you why I look the way I do, which has nothing to do with shoes or kin or clouds." She pulled Ione away from the curious teens and relayed her conversation with The Sound. "It left me with this uncomfortable feeling."

"His name alone is enough to make a person uncomfortable. I think you're spending way too much time around these musicians. There's something not right about their world."

"I know. But it gets my mind off my breakup with Bo. It's been so hard." Maggie grabbed a fistful of praline samples. "Look at me, I'm stress-eating."

Ione gave her a doubtful look. "Right. We better get going. Vanessa and Sandy are waiting on us in the parking lot."

Maggie followed Ione to the older woman's van. Vanessa and Sandy were already there. The friends all greeted each other warmly, but Maggie made sure to sit between Vanessa and Sandy as insurance against any leftover ill will from their men running against each other for mayor.

"We're picking up a surprise guest along the way," Ione told them.

She made a right off the River Road onto a street Maggie was happy to recognize. "You talked Gaynell into coming with us? That's fantastic."

"I promised her a Tammy-free zone and she caved."

Ione pulled up in front of a small creole cottage and honked the van horn. There was a brief pause, and then Gaynell emerged. Maggie's heart sank when she saw her. Only a few days had passed since Pony's murder, but Gaynell looked like she'd lost ten pounds. Her face was drawn, her eyes tired and hooded. The musician's bouncy blonde curls were hidden under a head kerchief.

"I almost don't recognize her," Vanessa whispered.

Maggie felt the same way but didn't articulate it. Instead, she waved to her wan friend. "Hey, Gay! We missed you."

Gaynell reached for the door. She hesitated. "Are you sure it's okay if I come?"

Ione crossed her arms and give her a look. "Seriously? You have to ask? Get in."

Gaynell jumped into the front seat and the friends cheered. As they traveled I-10 to the local party store, located in a mall on the outskirts of Baton Rouge, they kept the conversation generic, careful to avoid the topic of Pony's murder. Maggie did some sighing and staring out the window to reinforce her status as a heartbroken ex-fiancée. Ione parked in the party store's lot, and the women disembarked. Maggie noticed a text from Bo. "It's from one of the kids managing our booth," she lied. "You go ahead; I'll catch up."

The women entered the store and Maggie rang Bo back. "I walked by Pelican Pralines acting like I was ignoring you," he said, "and then I realized you weren't there to ignore."

"We're at Party Hearty picking up supplies for Lia's baby shower. I've been acting up a storm myself. I hope my friends don't kill me when I tell them the truth. Ouch, poor choice of words."

"I'll let you get back to your performance in a minute. I wanted to let you know that I checked out the hard copies of Pony's contracts with the musicians and didn't pick up any big discrepancies. The salaries sure seem high to a small-town detective, but not exorbitant, except for Tammy's. Man, is she making bank. Too bad I can't carry a tune. Bottom line, nobody's pulling down much more than anyone else, including Valeria who's only getting a couple of hundred bucks a week over the others. I'm going to do a little research into the usual rate for musicians on tour to see if Pony was really lowballing these guys. If he was, maybe they all got together and offed him."

"Do you think that could have happened?" said Maggie, hopeful for any scenario that might shift Pelican PD's attention to a different suspect.

"To be honest, I'm reaching."

"Oh," she said, disappointed. "I better get inside. They're going to wonder why I'm spending so much time talking about candy."

"I love you."

Maggie turned her back to the store in case one of her friends happened to glance out the store window. "I love you more."

Bo's voice was low and sexy. "Impossible."

He hung up before she could disagree.

*   *   *

Baby shower decorations and paraphernalia took up an entire aisle of Party Hearty, making the selection process laborious. Since Lia and Kyle had opted not to learn the sex of their triplets, Maggie chose yellow as the party's color scheme. Vanessa pouted as they loaded up a cart. "This makes me sad I never got a shower for Charli."

"Sorry, but we didn't like you then," was Ione's blunt response. This elicited a smile from Gaynell, who'd seemed distracted during the shopping expedition.

"Well, you better like me enough to do it when the next one comes along."

Ione raised an eyebrow. "Somethin' you're telling us?"

Van waved her hands in the air. "Oh, no. No, no, no. No babies until MacIlhoney puts a ring on it."

"You're living with him and a baby you had with another man. Little late for putting a ring on it to be an issue."

"I'm trying to make up for past mistakes." Vanessa swiped a candy from the ten-cent candy bin. "I think if Quentin hadn't come along, I still would've bailed on Rufus at the altar. It wasn't meant to be. A gal's better off being a single mom than being in the wrong relationship. The kid's better off, too. Oh Maggie, I'm so sorry." She flung an arm around Maggie's shoulder. "All this relationship and baby talk must be hard on you with the breakup and all. Especially at your age."

"I'm thirty-two, not eighty-two," Maggie felt compelled to point out.

"It's all my fault." Gaynell said this so quietly Maggie wouldn't have heard it if she wasn't standing right next to her.

"My breakup? Gaynell, no. It had nothing to do with you."

"You two were getting along fine until you started arguing about whether or not I was a suspect."

Gaynell's self-flagellation upset Maggie. She hugged her friend. "Bo and I broke up because we were on different pages about having kids. I want them. He's got Xander and thinks that's enough." This was a half-lie. The issue *had* almost broken up the couple, but they'd resolved it and were now looking forward to eventually giving Xander a sibling. "You have to believe me when I say if there's one thing that still binds Bo and me, it's believing you're totally innocent. The fact anyone would think otherwise is insane."

The other women seconded Maggie's comments. "Thank you," Gaynell said with a catch in her voice. "I wish I could do something to prove it to everyone else."

"Don't worry, we're working on it." Maggie caught herself. "Separately. Bo's working on it. And I'm working on it. Boy, does shower shopping make me tired. I'm ready to check out."

Ione shot Maggie another skeptical glance but wheeled one of the two carts the women had filled toward the checkout line. Maggie followed. Vanessa spotted a bin of tiny American flags at the checkout counter. "How cute are these? Too bad Quenty dropped out of the mayor race. I could've tied them to our VOTE FOR MAC pencils and handed 'em out at the festival."

Sandy pursed her lips. "Rufus and I had decided not to spend any more money on swag."

"Meaning you didn't have any more money to spend," Vanessa retorted.

"Unlike you, I didn't need to bribe people into voting for my boyfriend. His record spoke for itself."

Vanessa guffawed. "Oh chère, you do *not* want to look under the rock of Rufus's record. He's like to wind up arresting himself."

"Balloons. We need a balloon bouquet," Maggie said, interrupting the tart exchange before it devolved into a catfight.

"Ooh, me, me!" Van waved her hand in the air. "I love

putting together balloon bouquets. Should we do ten or twenty? Never mind, I'll figure it out." The other women hid their smiles as Vanessa ran off to pick out balloons.

"Nice save," Ione said to Maggie.

"If there are two things Vanessa's an expert on," Maggie said, watching Vanessa toss a pile of uninflated balloons at a beleaguered sales clerk, "it's hair dye and balloon bouquets."

* * *

The balloon bouquet proved so massive that it took up the whole back of the van, leaving no room for Sandy, Maggie, and Gaynell, who called for a ride share. The car dropped Gaynell off first. "Thank you for this afternoon," she told her friends. "It was a nice break from worrying. I think I may have come up with an idea for my next step."

A feeling of apprehension overcame Maggie. "Be careful, Gay. You're better off doing nothing than something that might get you into trouble."

Gaynell nodded but said nothing. She disappeared into her house.

The ride share dropped Sandy off at DanceBod, her dance studio in the center of Pelican, and then brought Maggie back to the festival. It was nine PM, an hour before closing. The crowd, packed with local college students, was raucous. Maggie sent the Poche siblings home and ran the booth by herself until closing. She tallied the sales results, then packed up unsold pralines and carted them back to her car. She was about to drive home when her cell rang. It was an unfamiliar number, but she recognized the Los Angeles area code and answered the call. "Hello?"

"Maggie? Oh, thank God."

The caller was a woman; she sounded hysterical. "I'm sorry, who is this?"

"It's me. Valeria."

The singer began weeping. Maggie's heart raced. "Valeria, you sound terrible. What's wrong?"

"Someone attacked Bokie." For a moment, Maggie heard nothing but gulping sobs. Then Valeria said, "He's in a coma. The doctors think he may die."

Chapter 14

Maggie raced to St. Pierre Parish Hospital. She found Valeria in the ICU waiting room. The singer paced by herself, away from East, Uffen, and The Sound, who huddled together in a corner of the room. Relief replaced anxiety when Valeria saw Maggie. "Thank you so much for coming." She hugged her.

Maggie returned the hug, then pulled Valeria further away from the others. "What happened?" she asked in a low voice.

"It was awful. We were at the pool. I said I was going inside to take a nap. Bokie said he was going to come by later with some dirt for my book. Really good stuff. Someone must have heard him. Poor baby doesn't know how loud he is because of his hearing loss. He never showed, so I just did my thing, hung out, had dinner. And on the way back . . ." Valeria's lower lip quivered. "I saw him lying in the bushes on the side of the building where my room is. Blood was on the back of his head, all in his hair." Tears began rolling down her cheeks. "He cared about me. More than anyone. And now I almost got him killed."

"Did you call the police?"

"Right after I called 911. The police came and talked to all of us already. I waited until they were gone to call you. I needed a friend, and you're as close to one as I have here." Maggie would have found this surprising if she hadn't picked up on the negative undercurrent infecting Tammy's entourage.

"What in the name of the Almighty is going on around here?" The angry voice belonged to the star herself, who marched into the room flanked by her shadows, Gigi and Narcisse. Manager Sara brought up the rear.

The musicians all exchanged looks but none responded, so Maggie spoke up. "Bokie's been seriously injured. And it doesn't appear to be an accident."

This news evoked a torrent of foul language from Tammy. "Let's find Bokie's doctor," Sara interjected. "He can tell us what's really going on. The rest of you should go back to the resort."

"You're high if you think I'm leaving," Valeria declared. "I'm not going nowhere. I'm quitting the tour and staying right here with Bokie. If you got problems with that, feel free to sue me." She put her hands on her hips and took a defiant stance.

Tammy threw her hands up in the air. "Great. I don't have a manager, a drummer, and now a backup singer." She waved a fist at the other musicians. "If anyone else gets attacked or murdered on this tour, I'm firing all of you!"

She turned and stormed out of the room, Gigi and Narcisse on her heels. Sara ran behind them. "I'll make some calls to LA. We should be able to get replacements at least in time for the Jazz Fest set." Her voice faded as the foursome disappeared down the hospital hall.

East and The Sound glared at Valeria. Uffen hung back but didn't look much happier. The expression on Toulouse's face, sadness with a hint of empathy, was what Maggie expected from the kindhearted Cajun.

"You and that stupid book of yours," The Sound spat at Valeria.

East jumped in. "Really. You think your effing memoir's some big secret, Val? It ain't. Everyone knows about it. And nobody cares."

Uffen spoke up. "Not true. Somebody cared enough to try and kill Bokie, possibly the only decent human being in this nauseating business."

"No one has to worry about my book anymore," Valeria said, her voice quiet, the defiant attitude gone. "I deleted the file. Emptied the trash bin. It's gone."

"Too little, too late, love," Uffen said. "I don't know about anyone else, but I could use a stiff, strong shot of something. Anyone not in recovery or interested in falling off the wagon, come with me."

Uffen left by himself. Toulouse took Valeria's hands in his own. "I'm praying on Bokie. Isaiah 41:10. 'Fear not, for I am with you; be not dismayed, for I am your God; I will strengthen you, I will help you, I will uphold you with my righteous right hand.'"

"Amen," Valeria responded.

East put a hand on Toulouse's shoulder. "We best get going, brother."

"Let us know if there's any change," The Sound said to Valeria.

She nodded, and the three men left. A thought occurred to Maggie. "It's interesting. If whoever attacked Bokie was worried he'd reveal something damaging for your book, the most logical suspect would be someone in the business. And on this tour. But I don't get that any of them suspect each other."

Valeria snorted. "Because they're all part of an elitists' boys club. Yeah, even in the music business, there's rank. These guys probably think some crazy roadie went after Bokie, because anyone on their level is way too cool to be bothered by some dirt in my book. They're all angry at me now, but if my book ever got published, they'd be way madder if they *weren't* in it."

"That book is dangerous. You could have been next on the killer's list. I think you were smart to delete it."

"The thing is . . ." Valeria poked her head out the waiting room door, looking in both directions to make sure she and Maggie were alone. "I kept one copy." She dug through her large black leather purse and pulled out a flash drive. "I didn't want to say anything in front of the guys when the police were here, but the file's on this. It's just called STUFF, in case anyone found the drive. They wouldn't think it was important." Valeria pressed the drive into Maggie's hand. "Give this to your ex, the detective. See if he can find anything on it that could help find whoever tried to kill Bokie. And probably killed Pony. Let's get the sucker."

Only Valeria used a much more colorful word than *sucker*.

*   *   *

Maggie sat by the edge of Bayou Beurre behind Crozat. The water was still as always; the only sound came from a great horned owl perched somewhere in a nearby tree. A full moon reflected in the slow-moving stream, the image occasionally disrupted by bubbles from the bayou's fish. Maggie closed her eyes and breathed in the scent of moss and banana shrubs.

She heard the sound of twigs cracking under the pressure of footsteps. The branches of a sweet olive tree parted, and Bo emerged. Maggie stood up and they went to each other. "Sorry I'm late," he said. "Took us forever to interview everyone who was at Belle Vista when Tammy's drummer was attacked. The place is sold out, thanks to the festival."

"I'll tell Gran. She feels responsible for the whole thing, so she'll take some comfort from that. She was worried that this second attack would drive people away for sure. There's a little positive news about Bokie. Valeria texted me that she talked to his doctor and he's more optimistic about his recovery."

"Glad to hear it. So, what's going on? Or is this a booty call? I don't see an open spot of land that could hide us, though."

"I wish." Maggie gave Bo the flash drive. "Valeria's been writing a tell-all book. The file's on here under STUFF. She wants you to take a look and see if any clues jump out at you."

"Got it. Thanks." Bo pocketed the drive.

"But this is good for Gaynell. There's no way she'd be fodder for this book."

"And lucky for Gay, we've yet to come up with any physical evidence tying her to Pony's murder. Or tie anyone else to it, which is frustrating."

"Do you have any leads on the weapon Bokie's attacker used to knock him out?"

"We found fragments of cement on the ground. Kaity Bertrand said a statue of a small cherub was missing from the grounds near his room. Cal and Artie are on the hunt for it, but most likely it's in the bayou along with Pony's electronics. I did dig up a little on that Narcisse nimrod. Arrested twice, once for a DUI, once for a fight over a girl. Not his wife, someone before her."

"Yeah, I don't get that he'd clock anyone over Gigi. You know, I remember Pony wasn't at all happy when Tammy said she was hiring Narcisse. He threatened to ax him. Maybe Narcisse got rid of Pony before Pony could get rid of him. Or Gigi. She's on a mission to follow Tammy back to Los Angeles and knew Pony was an obstacle to that. They both had motives. It might even have been a joint effort."

"Who knew I'd find a murder theory so sexy?" Bo pulled Maggie toward him. After a moment, they broke apart. "I really can't wait until our little scam's over. I don't like thinking about you and those musicians. I can tell that skinny Brit's got an eye on you."

Maggie shuddered. "So not my type. None of them are. They pretty much all look like they could use a shower, and I'm guessing more than one of them has a venereal disease."

Bo laughed. "One thing I've learned is that I would've been hard up for dates in this town if I hadn't met you. Not one woman who's come on to me has been *my* type."

Maggie frowned and pulled away. "Exactly how many women would that be?"

"Who cares? It could be a thousand. None of them is you."

Feeling a little better, Maggie responded when Bo bent his head down to kiss her. They were interrupted by excited dog barks. Gopher and Jolie came bounding through the brush toward the couple. Both dogs leapt on Bo, yapping for joy. "I'm not the only one who's glad to see you," she said.

"Hey, little buddies." Bo fake-tussled with both dogs. "I better go before they give me away. 'Night, chère."

"'Night."

Bo left the way he'd come, and Maggie followed the path from the bayou back home to the shotgun cottage.

Maggie got a decent night's sleep, the first in a few days. She decided to put murder out of her mind and start the morning with a run. She pulled on black bicycle shorts and a patterned purple top that wicked moisture, then headed out. Her route went up a dirt road, past the old lodge that Chret Bertrand and his crew of veterans were rehabbing into housing for servicemen and servicewomen. The vets who were there working on the place waved and shouted greetings to her, which she returned. The restoration of the stone-and-log lodge was almost complete, and Maggie looked forward to her new neighbors.

She jogged along the River Road, where only a few cars passed by, then down the decomposed granite driveway that ended at the Crozat manor house, eventually completing her run by circling back to the shotgun. Maggie went inside, making sure to pull the screen door shut behind her as an extra precaution against a spring swarm of mosquitoes. She got a towel from the bathroom, a bottle of water from the kitchen, and then took a seat on the living room couch next to Grand-mère. Maggie motioned to a bundle of old letters her grandmother was sorting through. "More love letters from Grand-père?"

"Yes, the last batch. They're quite powerful. Listen." Gran picked one out of the bundle. A corner of the brittle paper disintegrated, sending small flakes to the floor. "'Every minute I don't see you feels like an hour, every hour a day, every week a month,'" she read. "'Try as I might, I cannot find words that express the depth of my love for you.'"

"That's so beautiful," Maggie said, touched by her grandfather's passion.

"It is, isn't? Except that your grandfather didn't write it to me." The letter fell from Gran's hands into her lap. "He wrote it to another woman."

Chapter 15

Maggie stared at her grandmother, not comprehending. "What do you mean, he wrote it to another woman? He only loved you."

"Apparently not. According to this particular batch of letters, he was also crazy about this Carina person."

"That's so weird." Maggie tried to process the unexpected development. "Grand-père always told me you were the love of his life. He talked about sneaking out of his dorm room at Tulane to visit you at Newcomb after curfew."

"Those were fun times." Gran held up a letter. "But apparently not as fun as the time he had with Carina at Pontchartrain Beach Amusement Park."

"Was he . . . could he have been . . . having an affair?"

Gran shook her head. "The letters are dated during the summer months of 1954. We met in fall of that year."

"Oh." Maggie's brow cleared. "He had a girlfriend before you. That's not so bad."

"Not just 'a girlfriend,' Magnolia. Someone who was his 'whole world, whole universe,' quote, unquote. And why does he have the letters he sent to her along with her letters to him?"

"She must have returned them to him."

"Which means I was his rebound relationship." Gran tugged at a rare errant curl. "Not exactly flattering." She frowned. "I know the past is the past, but what upsets me is that your grand-père never said a word about this girl to me. If I wasn't *Döstädning-ing*, I would have gone to my deathbed never knowing about her."

"I'm begging now, you *have* to stop using the word *death* in any form or language. You know, you're assuming she broke up with him. Maybe she did something terrible and Grand-père broke up with her and demanded she return his letters."

Gran brightened. "Well, that paints a much better picture. I need to find out more about this . . ." Gran looked down at an envelope. "Carina Albieri."

"Are you going to do a search?"

"Yes. If the Internet can steal our private information and throw it all over the place willy-nilly, I might as well take advantage of that. But first I'll finish reading all these letters." She picked up another and skimmed it. "How lovely," she said, her tone sarcastic. "Now they're tasting each other's ice cream cones at Brocato's in the Quarter."

"If you need any help—or a dish of self-soothing ice cream for yourself—let me know."

Maggie kissed Grand-mère on her soft, pale cheek. She retreated to the bathroom for a shower and then dressed for a humid day under the hot spring sun.

She left the cottage for the manor house, where she was surprised to see a group of extremely fit young women in leotards and dance skirts hanging out on Crozat's veranda. Some were lazily stretching, contorting their bodies into positions Maggie couldn't have dreamt of achieving at her youngest and slimmest. A few others smoked and chatted with each other.

Maggie circled around the house, entering the kitchen through the back door. Ninette was there, the tiny woman almost lost behind piles of vegetables, fruits, and meats crowding the table. "What's going on, Mom?" Maggie asked, helping herself to an apple from a bucket of them. "Who are those girls outside?"

"Dancers. Tammy imported them from New Orleans and Houston. She also ordered a wooden floor for the party tent so they can practice there. They're all staying with us because everywhere else in town is booked." Ninette held up a printout. "They also came with more dietary requests. Lots of them. When one girl said, 'Don't worry about me, I don't eat, I just smoke,' I was actually grateful."

Loud pop music blasted from outside the house, then stopped. This happened three times in short succession. Maggie flinched. "I better check that out."

"Thank you. I don't have time. I need to figure out the difference between vegan, vegetarian, and raw food."

Maggie left for the B and B's party tent, located in its large side yard. The dancers she'd seen on the veranda had moved their stretching into the tent, adding a few leaps and pirouettes along with hip-hop moves. "Front and center, ladies," an androgynous-looking man wearing a headset barked at them. "We're running the routine again."

The women took their positions as Tammy sashayed to a spot in front of them. Maggie almost jumped out of her skin as the music she'd heard before came blasting out of a speaker behind her. Tammy sang as she and her dancers launched into a complex dance number. They finished, and Narcisse, who was lolling around, applauded. So did Tammy's manager, Sara, who was operating the sound system. "Wasn't that awesome?" Sara said to Maggie, her enthusiasm indicating it was a rhetorical question.

"It's certainly different from Tammy's usual music." Maggie, unimpressed, chose her words carefully.

"That's the whole point," Sara said, impatience in her voice. "Tammy's crossing over into pop. Pony didn't want her to; he said the field was too competitive and she risked losing her base, but I totally support her."

"I guess Tammy's lucky you're running the show now," Maggie said. She indicated the performers. "Literally."

"Yup, so lucky. She's going to debut the new material at Jazz Fest. Captive audience, big press buzz. Tammy's gonna kill it." Realizing her poor choice of words, Sara hastened to add, "Of course, Pony was the master of what he did, and I'll always be grateful to him. Sorry, I need to get back to work. We're paying these dancers by the hour." She turned away and manipulated a lever on the system, then pressed a button. The music roared on. "Let's run it again," she called to the performers.

Having been dismissed by Sara, Maggie left Tammy

and her dancers to their gyrations. She walked back to the shotgun cottage, where Gran was still ensconced on the couch, reading a letter from the shrinking packet on her lap. "Have you moved since I left here?" Maggie asked.

"No. I can't put these letters down."

Maggie went into the kitchen and came out with two bottles of sparkling water. She handed one to Gran. "Did you discover anything else about the mysterious Carina?"

"She had flowing black hair and olive skin that made her blue eyes stand out like"—Gran read from the letter—"*the Star of India sapphire.*"

"Whoa. I had no idea Grand-père was so poetic."

"Nor did I," Gran said with asperity.

Maggie took a sip of her sparkling water to hide a smile. "You sound jealous."

"I am, a bit. I'm getting the impression that your grandfather wore himself out in the romance department with this Carina woman. He was wonderful to me, but a bit less starry-eyed." Gran's cell phone pinged a text. She picked up the phone and read it. "Lee's been badgering me to go to the festival so he can 'show me off.' After the bruising my ego's taken from these love letters, that sounds like a good idea."

"I need to be there with pralines by three. Luckily, I stored a bunch in the freezer so I don't have to make any today." Maggie held up her hands. "I've got calluses from stirring."

"You're a trooper for manning the praline fort. I've been so absorbed in your grandfather's romance, I've barely thought about what's going on outside this room. How's that poor boy who was attacked at Belle Vista?"

"His prognosis has improved, but he's in for a long recovery."

"That's terrible. Is Pelican PD eyeing any suspects?"

Maggie shook her head. "Not that I know of. But it makes Gaynell much less of a suspect. Pony's murder has to be linked to the attack on Bokie, and I've spent more time with that drummer than Gaynell has."

"Ah yes, your faux breakup. I'll have to remember that at the festival if anyone asks about it. How's that little scam going?"

"Harder than I thought," Maggie admitted. "Flirting with other guys feels really uncomfortable. But it's worse knowing women are into Bo. Like, big time."

"No surprise there."

Maggie pulled away from her grandmother and shot her a look. "Way to make me not feel better."

"I'm sorry, chère. I'm a little edgy right now. Trust that Bo is yours and you are his."

"That's beautiful, Gran."

Gran held up a letter. "I'm paraphrasing your grandfather, who wrote to Carina, *Trust that I am yours and you are mine.*" She put down the letter and picked up a tall glass. "Do your grand-mère a favor and doctor up this Coke."

Maggie did so, then retired to her bedroom. She lay on the bed, eyes closed, clearing her mind of all thoughts. The women in her family possessed a well-developed sense of intuition, but tapping into it took intense focus. Maggie ran through a list of potential suspects: conflicted East, smarmy Uffen, weirdo The Sound, user Narcisse, clingy Gigi, ambitious Sara, ruthless Tammy. *Am I missing anyone or anything?* she thought.

Maggie woke up from a deep sleep an hour later. She jumped out of bed, then took a quick shower and threw on jeans and a fresh *Cajun Country Live!* T-shirt. "Ugh," she muttered at her reflection in the bathroom mirror. Her hazel eyes were shadowed underneath, her pale skin slightly paler. She gently patted concealer under her eyes, then applied foundation, blush, and mascara. "Much better," she told her reflection. Maggie wasn't one to obsess about her looks, but with Bo "available" and single women swarming him, she wasn't taking any chances.

She went over to the manor house kitchen, where Ninette was supervising her husband as he packed up a dozen to-go lunches. "Chère, can you help your father deliver these to Tammy and her crew?" Ninette asked. "They're all individually labeled, so it shouldn't be confusing."

"Sure." Maggie opened the freezer. "I just need to take out today's batch of Pelican pralines." She removed a few boxes and placed them on the counter to defrost, then stacked her arms with the lunch boxes.

"*Allons-y*," Tug said.

They left the kitchen for the party tent, where Tammy's band members had joined the others. The dancers were milling about aimlessly while East and the other musicians set up a drum kit. "We're auditioning drummers to replace

Bokie," East explained. "A couple of the girls can sing, so they'll cover for Val."

"How's he doing? Any word?"

"A little better. But wow. It's just . . . wow."

Maggie gave a sympathetic nod.

The day was relatively comfortable for south Louisiana, with the humidity index on the lower side. Tug had turned on the tent's modular cooling system to help cool it off, but the combined body heat of a dozen performers was giving the machine a workout.

"Lunch," Maggie called to the group. The dancers responded with cheers and abandoned their positions to grab the boxes. The musicians followed suit. Gigi, who was working a sewing machine in the corner, jumped up and ran over. "I'll get mine and Tammy's." But Sara beat her to Maggie, grabbing her lunch and the singer's.

"Get mine while you're there," Narcisse called to Gigi without looking up from his phone. She scowled but did as she was told.

Maggie helped her father set up ten-gallon coolers of water and sweet tea for the assemblage. Tammy, clad in a multicolored sequined bodysuit that was a far cry from her folksy Daisy Dukes look, waved a hand to get everyone's attention. "Y'all, Gigi's going on a coffee run if anyone wants something."

Gigi looked up from her lunch. "I am?"

"Just give her your orders," Tammy continued.

"But . . . I'm supposed to finish mending your practice dance skirt."

"No worries, coz; you can do that when you get back. Or tonight."

The dancers and a few of the musicians surrounded a nonplussed Gigi, peppering her with a list of complicated coffee drinks. Once they placed their orders, the crowd dissipated. Gigi, a furious look on her face, held up a middle finger to Tammy's back. Maggie was surprised by the venomous gesture but had a little more respect for the superstar's put-upon cousin.

Toulouse poured himself an iced tea, then lingered by Maggie. She wondered why, but simply asked, "Can I get you anything else?"

Toulouse shook his head. "I was just wondering if there were any updates with Miss Gaynell?"

"She's okay. Toulouse . . . just so you know, she and her boyfriend are pretty serious."

"Everything is in the Lord's hands." Toulouse looked upward. "I give my life to Him and let Him show me the path." He returned his gaze to Maggie. "Let Gaynell know I'm thinking about her and praying on everything."

The ginger-haired accordionist left the tent to join the other musicians at a picnic table. Maggie poured herself a cup of tea. She was tempted to doctor it up with a splash of Gran's bourbon. The interaction with Toulouse disturbed her. Was he simply a kindhearted, God-fearing country boy? Or was he a zealot?

Maggie checked the time on her cell phone. Not due at the Crozats' festival booth for two more hours, she decided to treat herself to a stint of painting. Losing herself in a new piece of artwork always had a calming effect. She left the tent, passing by a few dancers who were sunning themselves on the B and B's lawn while eyeing the musicians at the nearby picnic table. "I'm so over dating guys in the business," a thin, stunning blonde said to an equally thin, stunning brunette. The other thin, stunning girls nodded vigorously in agreement.

"Tammy said there's a detective in town who just broke up with his girlfriend," the brunette said to a chorus of lascivious *ooohs*. "I know, right? If he's as hot as she says he is, he can handcuff me and read me my rights, uh-huh!" She jumped up and twerked to screams of laughter.

Maggie bit her lip to keep from blowing up and stomped through the woods to her art studio, housed in the plantation's former schoolhouse. A murderer had once set fire to the place with Maggie in it, but locals had donated their time and services to repair the quaint old building. Now it sparkled with new paint and gleaming windows that allowed natural light to pour into the room. Paintings in various stages of creation rested against the walls. On a small easel sat a half-finished painting of a kitten that combined childlike innocence with a mature eye for detail. The artist behind the painting was Bo's son Xander, not Maggie. He came to her for weekly art lessons. Teaching the seven-year-old prodigy was one of the great joys of her life.

Maggie took out her cell phone, pulled up her playlist of favorite Cajun and zydeco tunes and pressed the PLAY arrow. C.J. Chenier and the Red Hot Louisiana Band's "Zydeco Cha Cha" blasted out of her wireless speaker in all its rambunctious glory. Chenier—the son of the king of zydeco himself, Clifton Chenier—worked his accordion magic, and the tune's blend of African Creole, Cajun, funk, and rhythm and blues filled the room with up-tempo energy. Maggie put an apron over her clothes and dabbed paint onto a palette. Then she got to work on the portrait she was painting of Gaynell in her outfit as *capitaine* of a Courir de Mardi Gras, the traditional Cajun Mardi Gras run. Behind Gaynell were Mardi Gras—in Cajun Country, the term was a proper noun as well as a noun—dressed in costumes and masks that were a riot of colors and textures.

As usual when she painted, Maggie forgot the world around her and lost track of time. Luckily, she'd set an alarm. As soon as it dinged, she cleaned up, turned off the music, and headed to the manor house to retrieve the batch of defrosted pralines. The party tent was empty and the B and B quiet. Maggie breathed in the warm-but-not-too-warm late-afternoon air, feeling relaxed for the first time in days. Lee's pickup was parked next to the shotgun cottage. Maggie hoped his affection for Gran would help her get past her late husband's love letters to another woman.

She grabbed the boxes of pralines from the kitchen and strode to her car, where she balanced the boxes on one knee as she pulled car keys from her pocket. She noticed some scratches she'd never seen before on the car door around the key area. *That's strange*, she thought. Then she saw the door was unlocked and her nerves tingled. She peered through the driver's-side window, pressing her face against the glass to get a better view of the car's interior.

Suddenly, a large snake on the driver's seat uncoiled. It reared its head, hissing and baring its fangs as it attacked the window. Maggie shrieked and fell backward. The boxes of pralines fell with her, their contents shattering as they hit the ground.

"Snake," she screamed to anyone who could hear her. "*Snake!*"

Chapter 16

Maggie's screams brought her family running. Tug and Ninette burst out of the manor house while Gran ran from the cottage, Lee on her heels. "Maggie, what happened; are you okay?" Tug, winded from running, gasped for breath at the end of the sentence.

Maggie, heart racing, pointed inside her car. Tug peered through the window, and the snake reared its head with an angry hiss. Ninette and Gran shrieked as Tug stumbled away from the creature.

Lee strode over to the car. "Lemme take a look and see what we got." He rapped on the window, eliciting fury from the snake.

"For the love of God, Lee, be careful," Gran cried out.

"It's all right, Charlotte. Our friend here can hiss all he wants, but he can't break through the window." The eighty-something mechanic studied the reptile. "My family had some land where we farmed sugar cane. Think it was part of Belle Vista way back in the day. When I was a kid, I'd help my great-uncles harvest, and they trained me on what critters to watch out for. This fella's not a copperhead or a cottonmouth, which you're most likely to find around here. Doesn't look like any kind of rattler either." He turned back to the others. "I think he's an import."

Maggie stared at him, not comprehending. "What do you mean? Like, he's from another country?"

Lee nodded.

"Then what's he doing here? And in my car?"

The look on Lee's weathered face was grim. "That, chère, is a good question. Someone best give Pelican PD a call. And Animal Control. Make sure they send a snake wrangler, not a dogcatcher."

*　*　*

A half hour later, officers Artie Belloise and Cal Vichet had joined the Crozats and Lee in the family's parking area. The group watched as a snake-removal expert coaxed the unwanted guest into a trap. "Maggie, you sure you didn't leave a window open?" Artie asked. He stood a safe distance from her car.

"Positive. Also, I keep my car locked, but the driver's-side door was unlocked."

"Downside of a vintage auto like yours. I could pick that lock with my pinky nail."

The snake expert, a tattooed man in his fifties who looked straight out of a wildlife reality TV show, held up the trap. "Got him." The others gave him a wide berth as he sauntered over to his van and secured the trap inside. "Love to know how a Mexican pit viper made its way to these parts."

"Could it have gotten here by itself?" Cal asked.

The expert shook his head. "Not likely. Probably smuggled across the border by an exotic animal dealer to sell in the States."

Maggie put her head in her hands, trying to make sense of what was happening. "So, someone put a venomous snake in my car. To scare me? To kill me?"

The man shrugged. "Maybe both."

After a brief confab with Artie and Cal, the snake handler took off. "We need to interview all of you and whoever else is here," Cal said. "Find out if anyone saw anything suspicious."

Artie pointed to the ground. "That's a sad, sad sight."

Maggie's box of pralines lay where she'd dropped it, littering the ground with broken sweets. Gopher and Jolie were investigating the candy with interest, but Maggie shooed them away. "Chocolate's not good for dogs, you two." She bent down and began picking up the candy, now ruined. The others helped. "I guess I'll be closing the booth early tonight. Like that's my biggest problem."

"I'll throw these out, chère," Ninette said, taking the box from Maggie. "Don't give the booth a thought. You had a scare, a bad one. We all did." She shuddered.

Artie crooked a finger at Maggie. "A minute?" She followed him away from the others. "I know you and Bo broke up, but I texted him the details of what all happened. He's handling security at the festival today, but I thought he'd want to know. I'm sure you two still have some kind of connection."

Given her run-in with a deadly animal, Maggie didn't have to fake being overwrought. "We do. It's been a rough day, and I appreciate you getting in touch with him."

Artie hiked up his pants, which would never be in danger of falling off given a girth born from a love of all things edible. "We need to interview everyone at Crozat, starting with y'all. Cal, why don't you hunt around for guests and I take the family?" Artie called this to his partner, then addressed Ninette. "Ma'am, what would be a comfortable location? I'm thinking maybe the kitchen?"

Ninette knew the drill. "Good idea, Artie. I can put together a plate of some afternoon snacks."

Artie beamed. "Sounds like a plan."

"Artie, do you mind starting with me?" Maggie asked. "And can we do it here? I need to get to the festival."

Artie frowned but nodded. The others traipsed toward the manor house with Cal behind them. "All righty, Magnolia," he said, taking out a pad and pencil, "walk me through your day so far."

"I went for a jog, met our new guests, napped for an hour, then served our guests lunch. After that, I went to my studio and painted for a while, then got the pralines and went to my car. I didn't see or hear anything unusual."

"So between eleven and now, your car was unattended, just sitting parked here in the way back."

"Yes."

Artie furrowed his brow and tapped his pencil against it. "This'll take some work. You can go to the festival. Let me know if you think of anything else."

"For sure."

Artie took off for the manor house kitchen at a fast clip. Maggie circled the Falcon warily, then ran into the shotgun cottage, emerging with her set of keys to the B and B minivan. She adored "Vince," as she'd once nicknamed the convertible, but needed a day or so to put the image of the snake out of her mind before driving the car again. She climbed in the van, but checked her phone before starting the engine. Bo had sent a barrage of text messages. She responded: I'M OKAY. CAL AND ARTIE WILL FILL YOU IN. Maggie hesitated, then added a string of x's and o's.

* * *

Maggie was still on edge when she showed up at the festival booth. She deposited a small box of pralines in front of Clinton and Brianna. "There was an accident with the bigger batch," she told them, "and these aren't fully defrosted. We'll sell the few we have left from yesterday, and if these aren't ready to go by then, we'll close early."

Clinton flashed a wide grin. "Or not." He reached down and pulled up a basket filled with individually wrapped pralines the color of burnt umber. Each displayed a label featuring a smiling sweet potato holding a sign that said POCHE SWEET POTATO PRALINES.

"Clinton, this is fantastic," Maggie said. "They're adorable. And look delicious."

"He was up real late making the labels. He said they had to look fancy." This came from his unimpressed sister. "You're such a girl."

"Shut up; you are."

"Well, *yeah*, I'm *supposed* to be."

Maggie held up her hands to referee. "Enough. Clinton, great job. Brianna, lay off him. Both of you—move the goods."

Since the Chulane pralines hadn't survived the fall from her arms, Maggie put aside two extra-large sweet potato ones for Xander. But she knew in her heart that potatoes were no substitute for chocolate with the under-ten crowd and was relieved when Whitney texted that Xander was skipping that night's festival.

Clinton's pralines did prove to be a big hit with the over-ten crowd. Maggie stepped back to let the teen enjoy his success. She chatted with customers browsing her souvenirs and even sold two paintings, but found it hard to focus. Her mind kept wandering back to the pit viper in her car. Wrangling a poisonous snake had to require some experience. Rock stars sometimes used snakes in their live performances, albeit the less lethal kind. She pulled out her cell phone and texted Bo: CHECK MUSICIANS FOR SNAKE EXPERIENCE.

A middle-aged woman wearing a T-shirt that read BOURBON STREET BABE in bedazzled lettering approached Maggie. "Excuse me; that girl says you're the artist who did this drawing." She held up a mouse pad decorated with an illustration of the Doucet's manor house. "Would you autograph it for me?"

"Of course. Thank you so much for asking."

"It'll make it worth more when I sell it online. Autographs really boost the price."

"Really?" Maggie said. "Too bad I'm not a dead artist. The price would skyrocket."

Oblivious to the sarcasm in Maggie's voice, the woman gave a vigorous nod, which sent her large shelf of a chest bouncing up and down. "Good point. I'll hold on to it for a little while. Ya never know what could happen, right?"

She chortled, gave Maggie a thumbs-up, and moved on to another booth. Maggie tamped down her annoyance and checked her cell. No response from Bo. She scanned the festival grounds, then scowled when she realized why he hadn't gotten back to her. Her "hot detective" was surrounded by Tammy's dancers. Even from a distance, Maggie could tell they were in a contest to out-flirt each other. She sucked in a breath, then exhaled, trying to blow the jealousy out of her system.

Bo pulled his cell phone from a pocket and answered a call, then politely disengaged from the fawning performers. His face darkened, and he strode off the field, still on the call. His walk turned into a run.

Maggie considered a course of action. She punched in the numbers for Cal Vichet's cell. He answered on the first ring. "Cal, hi. I just saw Bo take a call and then go running off. Did something happen? Was there a break in Pony's case, or Bokie's?"

"Yeah, something happened." Cal's tone was terse. "Gaynell Bourgeois was just arrested for murder and attempted murder."

Chapter 17

"*What?*" Maggie said, her emotions vacillating between shock and fury. "Bo's the lead detective on those cases. Did he give the go-ahead to arrest her?"

Cal sounded nervous. "I really don't wanna say too much, but I can answer that with one word. No."

"Rufus." Maggie spat out the name like it was poison.

"I need to go now."

Cal ended the call. Maggie let loose a string of epithets that brought forth some shocked gasps and a few *tsk-tsk*s as she stormed past festivalgoers. She threw herself into the B and B van and rocketed out of the parking lot to the Pelican PD station. The spots in front of the building were taken up by a couple of news vans. Reporters were already in position on the building's steps. She saw Little Earlie, a small man, maneuver his way around the others and score the prime position outside the front door.

Maggie parked a block down from the station and hurried over, dodging the reporters as she took the stairs two at a time.

"Hey, Maggie," Earlie called to her. She whipped around, and before she could unload on the pushy journalist, he shrank back, turning from pit bull to puppy. "Never mind."

She threw open the heavy glass front door and marched into the station just as Rufus came out of the hallway that led to offices, interrogation rooms, and a holding cell. With him was a plainclothes officer in his late twenties. Maggie planted her fists on her hips and glared at the police chief. "What do you think you're doing having Gaynell arrested?"

"My job."

"Since when is your job throwing innocent people in jail? Or did you have Bo do your dirty work?"

"No, I had Rogert here do it."

"I just got promoted to grade-one detective," Rogert, now ID'd as the plainclothes officer, said. "This was my first assignment post-promotion." The sandy-haired newbie didn't look happy about it.

"Magnolia, why don't we talk in private?"

Rufus beckoned to her. She followed him down the hallway to his office, a dreary room populated with beat-up, circa-1950s metal office furniture. He sat down behind his desk. She remained standing. "Let me give you a little backstory," Rufus said. "That's what they say in the movies, right? Anyhoo, the ADA on the Pickner case is Jace Jerierre, which rhymes with *derriere*, which is what he is. I'm sharing his nickname with you because it'd chap his actual derriere, which gives me much pleasure. The reason for Gaynell's arrest is that there was an unexpected development in the drummer's case. Security footage from Belle Vista puts Gaynell at the resort within the time frame that Bokie guy was attacked."

Now Maggie sat down. Or more like fell into a rickety metal chair. "Why? Why was she there?"

Rufus gave an *I dunno* shrug. "All she told Rogert is that she wanted to talk to the guy. Then she stopped talking and started crying."

"No. Poor Gaynell."

"That, coupled with her activities concerning Pickner, amounted to strong circumstantial evidence according to Derriere, I mean Jerierre. He accused me of showing favoritism to Gaynell and went and got an arrest warrant."

Maggie crossed her arms in front of her chest. "You know she didn't do this, Rufus."

Rufus leaned back in his chair. The shirt of his uniform strained at the buttons. "Here's the thing, Maggie. I *don't* know that. I know I like Gaynell. I know she and her family are good people. I know it's hard to *imagine* her doing this. But I don't know that she didn't. I've arrested a lot of people I never would have suspected of doing bad things. And they were flat-out guilty. You don't know what's going to push someone over the edge. Even a nice person like Gaynell."

Maggie searched for a response. Then she said, "I want to argue with you. But I can't. If there's one thing these last few months—and murders—have taught me, it's that people can surprise you in horrible ways. Still, every fiber in my being tells me Gaynell didn't kill or attack a soul."

"Believe me, I'd love to pin this murder on anyone else.

That's why Bo's out there chasing down clues about who put that snake in your car. I'm really hoping it's one of those musician man buns. I wish I could arrest guys just for that butt-ugly hairstyle. But until there's evidence, them and their hideous hair is free."

Maggie managed a slight smile. "At least we're on the same page when it comes to man buns. You're sure the security cameras didn't reveal anything else? Or anyone?"

"Give us a little credit for knowing how to do our jobs, Magnolia. There was no camera where this Bokie guy got conked. Either the perp did some homework or got lucky."

Maggie looked contrite. "I didn't mean to offend you. I'm grabbing at anything. Can I talk to Gaynell? Maybe I can get some new information out of her."

Another voice answered Maggie's question. "I'd have to say no to that."

Maggie turned around and saw Quentin MacIlhoney standing in the doorway. He was dressed in a bespoke charcoal suit, crisp white shirt, and red tie with dark-blue stripes. Maggie scrunched her eyes and saw that the stripes comprised a sentence: VOTE FOR QUENTIN MACILHONEY. "Tie's a little out of date, Quentin."

"I spent a fortune having my tailor make it for me. I figure I'll run again for office sometime and it doesn't hurt to start building brand awareness with the general public. To quote the late governor, Earl Long, when I die I'm going to be buried in Louisiana so I can stay active in politics." He removed a folder from his genuine-alligator briefcase. "Back to your question. Nobody talks to my client before I do."

Rufus glowered at his former mayoral competition. "Figures she'd hired you."

"Ms. Bourgeois won't be paying me a dime. This is a pro bono case. Let's go, Rufus."

Rufus grudgingly got up and went to the door. Maggie stopped the defense attorney before he followed the police chief out. "Thank you, Quentin."

"This one's a gimme. The whole town's pretty much behind her. I'll look like a hero for a change."

"Tell me that's not why you're doing it," Maggie said. Quentin's unabashedly selfish motives exasperated her.

"Who cares why I'm doing it? Point is, it's getting done. And by the best defense lawyer in the state, if I do say so myself. Which I do." Quentin handed her a gold metal pen. "Press the top; it lights up."

He took off after Rufus, leaving Maggie with the pen. She pressed the top and the barrel lit up with yet another slogan: 'Mac' A DIFFERENCE. VOTE MACILHONEY.

* * *

Maggie dodged the reporters on her way out of the station. Little Earlie managed to stop a few who pursued her. "She's a scary one," he warned them. "You push her, she might get violent." His assessment was overly dramatic, but it allowed Maggie to drive away in peace.

She took a few detours in case all the reporters hadn't

been intimidated. While she drove, she tried to understand why Gaynell would have gone to Belle Vista to talk to Bokie, a man she barely knew. Maggie couldn't come up with a scenario that made sense.

By the time she got home, Crozat was dark. The B and B's guests were either asleep or out. Maggie guessed it was the latter. Relieved that she could avoid dancing around the hot topic of Gaynell's arrest, she slipped into the shotgun cottage and crawled under the covers of her bed.

She felt like she'd barely fallen asleep when her alarm shrieked a wake-up call. Maggie stumbled out of bed, showered, and put on black leggings. She was about to throw on an extra-large *Cajun Country Live!* T-shirt, then changed her mind. She pulled a man's denim button-down shirt from her closet. It belonged to Bo; he'd lent it to her one night when she was wearing a summer dress and the evening temperature suddenly dropped. Whether unintentional or unconsciously, she'd yet to return it. She held the shirt to her face and breathed in Bo's scent. Then she put it on, rolled up the sleeves, and left the cottage for the manor house.

Ninette and Tug were leaving the house as Maggie approached. "I was going to help you with breakfast for the guests."

"Not necessary," Ninette said. "None of the dancers eat it, and the others just wanted coffee and croissants, except for that Narcisse fellow, who's eating like a bear going into hibernation."

"Or a cheapskate trying to load up on free eats while he

can," Tug grumbled. "I was looking forward to some of that Paleo steak and eggs for my morning meal, but that mooch ate it all."

"He did us a favor," Ninette said. "The way you were plowing through all that red meat, your blood pressure was like to set off the kind of alarms you hear when a tornado's coming." She put on a light-pink cotton sweater as she addressed her daughter. "We heard about Gaynell and were on our way to the courthouse to support her during the arraignment. Your grand-mère left with Lee a little while ago. She wanted to make sure she got an up-front seat in the courtroom."

"That's where I'm headed too. I'll see you there."

Ninette and Tug left for the courthouse. Maggie retrieved a croissant and left the house for her car. She circled the convertible before getting inside, examining it for unwanted visitors. She yanked open the driver's-side door and jumped backward in case she awakened an angry snake. Maggie used her key chain flashlight to carefully check under the car's bench seats, and then, confident that the car was empty of everything except Park 'n Shop burrito wrappers and empty sushi containers, she hopped in and headed for the courthouse.

The St. Pierre Parish clerk of court offices were housed in a gracious, white-columned Greek Revival edifice that dated back to the late 1800s. It was located on the far corner of the village square, and Maggie often wondered if Pelican's forefathers had positioned the building in a way that sent the message it was keeping an eye on the town.

She parked on a side street and kept her head down as she passed news vans and a knot of reporters surrounding Quentin MacIlhoney. The fact that Pickner and Bokie were attached to singing star Tammy made Gaynell's arrest a national story, which Maggie hated. Little Earlie and Rufus were engaged in a little dance on the courtroom steps, with the journalist trying to corner the police chief and the police chief trying to dodge him, which he finally did. Quentin, on the other hand, headed straight for the *Pelican Penny Clipper* editor and one-man publishing band. Little Earlie barely got out a question before Quentin launched into a spiel about the invaluable role a defense attorney played in society, ending with, "There are few crimes greater than sending an innocent man or woman to prison, and my life's mission is making sure that fate never befalls a Quentin MacIlhoney client." A journalist began to applaud, then remembering he was supposed to be impartial, stopped midclap.

The group moved en masse into the courthouse and then the courtroom, with Maggie bringing up the rear. She was moved to see that every spot on the worn wooden benches was claimed by Gaynell's friends and family, including Ione, Kyle, Vanessa, and Sandy. She knew the CLOSED sign must be hanging from Junie's Oyster Bar and Dance Hall front door, since JJ sat squeezed between several Doucet tour guides and an unexpected attendee—Toulouse from Tammy's band. *Then again*, Maggie thought, *given his feelings for Gaynell, why am I surprised he's here?*

The court bailiff entered the room from a side door. "All

rise," he announced, and everyone did so. "Court is now in session, the honorable Oliver Gaudet presiding." Judge Gaudet, whom Maggie recognized from her father's occasional Texas Hold'em parties, entered and took his seat. The attendees sat as well.

Maggie was too far back to hear much of what was going on, so she threaded her way through a clog of people on the far side of the room until she was closer to the lawyers. Gaynell sat on one side, next to Quentin, who was standing. A balding man in his forties with a skeletal build stood at a table on the other side of the aisle. Maggie assumed he was ADA Jace "Derriere" Jerriere. "The state believes this young woman purposely caused the death of an esteemed member of the music industry and caused grievous injury to a victim currently hospitalized in critical condition."

Quentin snorted. "I've been a defense attorney for thirty-five years, and I can say without any hesitation that the state's case is based on the most circumstantial evidence I've ever seen."

It was Jerriere's turn to snort. "You say that every time I bring a case against one of your clients, MacIlhoney. I believe a jury will disagree after assessing our evidence. State requests bail be set at one million dollars."

There was a collective gasp from the room. "Your honor, that's outrageous," Quentin protested. "If you put together all the salaries of everyone in this room, it wouldn't add up to a million dollars. Not including mine, of course."

"Considering the severity of the crimes, I think I'm being pretty generous," Jerriere shot back.

"I've known the defendant since she was a sprout," Judge Gaudet said. "So far in this young lady's life, her biggest crime is selling me too many Girl Scout cookies." He patted his portly belly. "Like to make me prediabetic. I tend to agree with MacIlhoney on this. It's a pretty flimsy case. You're lucky I'm not dismissing it entirely, Jerriere. Bail is set at fifty thousand dollars. The defendant is to remain within the county, stay in contact with law enforcement, and surrender her passport."

"I don't have a passport." Gaynell spoke up for the first time. "I've never even been out of the state."

"All the better."

"Wait, I lied." Gaynell said this with a note of panic. "When I was little, I went to Dallas for a great-uncle's funeral. Am I in trouble?"

"Only if you try to bribe me with a box of Thin Mints," Judge Gaudet responded with a chuckle.

The ADA, fuming, took a step toward the bench. "Your honor, we're talking about a second-degree murder charge. Fifty thousand dollars is loose change for a charge this serious."

"If you think fifty grand is loose change, maybe we're paying *you* too much," someone called from the back of the room, to a chorus of agreement and a smattering of laughs.

"For my client, fifty thousand dollars might as well be a million dollars," Quentin said. "But we'll work on making it."

"I'll post her bail."

The courtroom grew noisy with reactions to this

announcement. Everyone strained to see who had made it. People crowding the center aisle parted, revealing Tammy Barker. Behind her stood Gigi, Narcisse, and Sara. Tammy was dressed in a sleek black suit, white silk blouse, and black stiletto pumps. The outfit screamed expensive name brands. The singing star's hair was pulled back into her ubiquitous high ponytail; Maggie noticed no seams, indicating an extension touchup. "Your honor, it would be my honor and civic duty to put up the bail for Ms. Bourgeois. There is no price too high for freedom in these our United States."

Tammy delivered this odd speech with such commitment that Maggie wondered if the singer had confused her appearance in the courtroom with an audition for a TV procedural drama. Judge Gaudet seemed to feel the same way. "Is this being filmed or something?" he asked, looking around.

"It better not be," Jerriere said, annoyed. He thumbed in Quentin's direction. "But knowing this clown, I wouldn't be surprised."

The defense lawyer held up his hands. "I plead not guilty. But we will take Ms. Barker up on her generous offer. I'll make payment arrangements immediately."

Judge Gaudet brought an end to the proceedings, and the courtroom started to empty out. Maggie fought against the current and eventually wound up by Gaynell's side. Her friend's face lit up when she saw her. "You came," Gaynell said, and hugged her.

"Everyone came." Maggie gestured to the crowd. "I can

pretty much guarantee that there wouldn't be this kind of turnout for me if I was falsely arrested."

"Don't sell yourself short," Gaynell said. She managed a smile, but the traumatic events had taken a toll on the young woman. Her vibrant blue eyes had dulled and were encircled by dark shadows. She'd lost more weight. Her conservative outfit of beige skirt and bow-necked blouse, Quentin's obvious attempt to make her look as respectable and nonthreatening as possible, hung loosely.

Maggie spoke to her in a low voice. "Gay, I have to ask. What were you doing at Belle Vista? Why did you want to see Bokie?"

Gaynell's face colored with embarrassment. "I just wanted to talk to him and see if he could help me convince everyone I didn't kill Pony. He was the only one who was nice to me, and the only one Pony said anything nice about. It was stupid, but I was desperate."

Maggie put her hands on her friend's shoulders. "It was *not* stupid. You had no idea the real killer would go after Bokie."

"I guess. I need to find Tammy and thank her for what she's doing. Being mad at her cuz she sang my song seems like such small stuff now."

Maggie didn't respond. She distrusted Tammy to the point of wondering if the singer had staged an elaborate plot to ruin Gaynell. Then she shook off the farfetched idea. Tammy had been doing a perfectly good job of making Gaynell's life miserable before Pony's death. If she was the killer, taking control of her career made much more sense as a motive.

Gaynell went searching for her "savior," and Maggie left the courthouse. She texted Bo to meet her at their secret spot. Tomorrow was the final day of *Cajun Country Live!*, which meant Tammy and her entourage would be departing Pelican on Friday. Pelican PD—and Maggie—were running out of time to zero in on another suspect.

Chapter 18

Maggie once again waited for Bo at their meeting place on the marshy banks of Bayou Beurre. "Did you find out anything about snakes?" she called to him as he wended his way through the thick brush by the bayou.

"And hello to you, too."

"Sorry. Gaynell's arraignment—that's what it's called, isn't it? I've never been to one before. Whatever it is, it made me nervous. It's Wednesday, Bo. We don't even have two full days before Tammy and company head to New Orleans."

"I'm aware of that. The whole department is." Bo reached her side. He grimaced and used a leaf to blot a drop of blood from a cut on his arm where a branch had scratched him. "The snake investigation broke down on gender lines. The girls, aka the dancers, all went, 'Ew, we hate snakes.' They guys, which would be the musicians, showed some snake love. In East and The Sound's cases, literally. They both toured with a group called Snake Love, although not at the same time. Uffen had a pet boa constrictor a while. And Toulouse loves all God's creatures."

Bo wrapped his arms around Maggie. "It was pretty scary getting that call from Cal. You could have been killed, Maggie. I think that was the intention. Someone knows you're nosing around. I want to keep an eye on you, not be hunting for ways to avoid you. I'm calling off our breakup charade. It's too dangerous."

"Considering I have palpitations every time I even think of that snake, I'm not going to argue with you. We got as much as we could out of that scheme. I got insider intel about pretty much all the musicians and was able to limit my rebound flirting to Uffen, who lost interest so quickly it's a little insulting." Maggie brightened. "Oooh, I get to put my engagement ring back on. That'll get the gossip grapevine going. I'll find a way to clue in the boys in the band. And those dancers." She said the last with derision.

Bo laughed. "Was someone a *leeetle* jealous?"

"No, not at all."

Bo gave her a *You've got to be kidding* look.

"Maybe a little," she conceded. "They're so pretty. And that came out way whinier than I wanted it to."

"Yeah, they're pretty. But it would take all their brains put together to form one intelligent sentence."

Maggie pushed leaves around with the toe of her sneaker. "Were you ever jealous of any of the guys around me?" she said, trying and failing to sound casual.

"Every one of them. Especially that Uffen character. When I saw him coming on to you, I was close to doubling this week's murder rate."

"I feel a little guilty for finding that flattering."

"I'm glad." Bo bent down and kissed her. "The fact Gaynell was arrested isn't going to make our killer relax, especially since the judge was clear he thinks it's a weak case. Stay away from talk about Pony and Bokie. Let people think you're all about planning our wedding now."

"Oh, right, that."

"For your own safety, I'm going to share everything I learn with you. Forget department protocol."

"When has protocol ever mattered to Captain Rufus Durand? I've learned to see that as one of his great strengths."

Bo kissed her. "I gotta run. Keep an eye out wherever you go and check in with me regularly."

"Promise."

The two walked out of the woods together and went their separate ways. First stop for Maggie was the family safe in the manor house. She retrieved her engagement ring and placed it back on her finger. A ray of sunshine lit up the ring, making the topaz-and-chocolate diamond gumbo pot sparkle. "Welcome home," she said to it with fondness. Then she texted family and friends who were in on the fake breakup that she and Bo were officially "back together," resulting in a sea of happy faces and confetti emojis.

Next on the agenda was a new batch of pralines. Maggie would be making this round at Bon Bon Sweets, having run out of homes to impose upon. She was driving to the store when her cell rang. She pressed the button on her Bluetooth but couldn't connect with the call, and it dropped out. "Darn it," she muttered. She pulled over, took the earpiece off, shook it, then put it back on. Her cell rang again.

She saw it was Bo's ex-wife, Whitney, and pressed the button. This time it worked. "Sorry, I know you tried to reach me a minute ago. My Bluetooth is acting funky."

"No worries, hi. I wanted to let you know that the adoption is official. Belle and the baby's father just signed all the necessary paperwork."

"Whitney, that's wonderful. Congratulations!"

"It's an open adoption. Belle and the boy can go on and live their lives, but also have the comfort of knowing they can keep up with their child's life. I can't imagine how hard it would be to give up a baby and never know what happened to him or her." Whitney paused, overcome with emotion. She cleared her throat. "Zach and I can't find the words to thank you, Maggie. If you hadn't connected us to Belle, we wouldn't be sharing this news. So . . . you're going to be a stepmom to two kids now. That's something, huh?"

Maggie picked up the note of underlying concern in Whitney's voice. "Yes, and I couldn't be more excited about it."

"Oh, that's wonderful." The woman's relief was palpable. "And when you and Bo have your own kids, we'll all be one big happy, blended family."

"Until all the kids become teenagers and turn on us."

Whitney laughed. "Let's work together to make sure that *never* happens."

* * *

Whitney signed off, and Maggie continued driving. She thought about the conversation. The prescription she'd

found indicated that Pony Pickner had been battling prostate cancer. If that was the case, would it have caused him
to look back on his life and evaluate his legacy? Faced with
his own mortality, would he have been motivated to make
amends for his dodgy past? Who would inherit his estate,
which, given his success, must be substantial? She assumed
his will held the answers to some of these questions, but
with the manager's attorney still in rehab, Bo wasn't having
any luck producing the document.

Maggie latched on to an offhand comment from
Vanessa—that a child raised by a single mother was better
off than one being raised by two people who didn't belong
in a relationship. Had there been women in Pony's life who
would have cut him loose but kept a child their coupling
produced? Did he refute a paternity claim and then regret it?

Maggie pulled into the parking lot behind Bon Bon.
Instead of getting out of the car, she tapped a number into
her cell phone. "Hey, Maggie," Valeria said upon answering
the call.

"Hi. How's Bokie? Any progress?"

"The doctor says they're bringing him out of the medi-
cally induced coma tomorrow, hopefully. The swelling on
his brain's gone down."

"That's very good news. I have a question for you. It's
about Pony. Were there ever any rumors about him father-
ing a child?"

"Are you kidding? Sure. There are rumors about that for
pretty much everyone in the business. I left town for a few
months to take care of my mother in Puerto Rico when she

had pneumonia, and a rumor started that I'd gone there to have Prince's love child. I never even met the man. And leave town to give birth to an illegitimate kid? What is this, the eighteen hundreds? Wait . . . you think all that's happened, the murder, Bokie being attacked, has something to do with a Pony lovechild?"

"I don't know. Maybe. I'm just trying to look under every rock."

"Interesting. I'll see what I can find out here."

"*No.*" Maggie's response came out sharper than she intended. "Sorry, I didn't mean to snap at you. But please, don't do anything. One man's been murdered, another attacked. It's a very dangerous situation. In fact, don't tell anyone we had this conversation. Bokie needs you. You have to stay safe, if not for your sake, for his."

"Okay." Valeria sounded somber—even scared. "When will this be over, Maggie?"

"I wish I knew. All I can say is that Pelican PD may be small, but it's excellent. I can't imagine a better force."

"Or a cuter detective, huh? Too bad that ended. I sure would be sorry to see that one go."

"Actually, we got back together. The wedding is on again."

"Really? Congratulations."

Was it Maggie's imagination, or did Valeria sound less than enthusiastic? "Focus on helping Bokie recuperate. But if you do hear anything you think might be helpful, let the police know." *Although maybe not Bo.*

Maggie ended the call. She took the box of praline

ingredients from the back seat and carried them into Bon Bon's kitchen. Kyle, Lia's "tall drink of Texas water," as she affectionately called him, sat at the candy store's small office desk typing on a computer keyboard. "Filling online orders?" Maggie asked.

Kyle nodded. He pushed back from the desk, took off his black-rimmed glasses, and cleaned them with the shirt-tail of his plaid cotton button-down. "Business is pretty brisk, although I'd love to find a way to bring down shipping costs. But sending candy from Humid-siana is tricky. You can't cheap out on the ice packs."

He ran a hand through his salt-and-pepper hair, which was growing saltier by the day. Vanessa, who had a part-time job managing the Bruners' other shop, Fais Dough Dough, came in from the storefront. She wore an apron with the store's logo on it over her tight top and jeans. "Hey, Maggie, heard your voice. Your ring's back on. Y'all must be back together."

"Van, how did you even see my hand at the bottom of this box?"

"I've got jewelry radar. Jay-dar." Vanessa grinned, pleased with her response.

"Yes, Bo and I are back together. The break proved to us that we're meant to be together." Both Vanessa and Kyle snorted, annoying Maggie. "What?"

"I never believed you broke up in the first place," Kyle said. "You were definitely up to something, and I'm sure it has to do with the murder investigation."

"Oh, I snorted because I still don't see them making it

down the aisle," Vanessa said to Kyle. "But your idea's way better. So, Mags, what'd you find out?"

"First of all, a super hard pass on the nickname *Mags*. Also, I'm not going to gossip about an ongoing investigation." Maggie dropped her box on the counter with a thud. "I have pralines to make." Maggie pulled out ingredients, then the pots and bowls she'd need to make the candy. She poured sugar and buttermilk into a large Dutch oven on top of the stove, added butter and baking soda, then turned on the heat. She stirred the praline base. "As soon the festival is over, I'm putting all my attention on wedding plans."

"Have you picked a date?" Kyle asked.

"No," Maggie admitted.

"Quenty and I have. The twenty-first day of September. Cuz Quenty just *loves* that song. He loves it so much that he married his ex-wives on that day, too. I think we're gonna dance down the aisle to it, like people do in those videos." Vanessa began singing the song and dancing through the kitchen as if it were a church aisle, much to Kyle and Maggie's amusement. She suddenly stopped. "Ooh, I just had the best idea of my life. A double wedding."

"With what other couple?" Maggie asked, dreading the answer.

Vanessa gave her a poke in the ribs. "*You*, silly." She began jumping up and down. The old wooden floor vibrated so much, Maggie feared Van might bust through it into the basement. "Say yes, say yes, say yes, say yes . . ."

"Vanessa, I think that's something Maggie and Bo need

to decide on together," Kyle said, coming to Maggie's rescue. "Let her be."

Vanessa stopped jumping. "Fine," she said with a pout. "But think about it. Real hard."

She returned to work at the front of the store. "Thank you, thank you, thank you, thank you," Maggie said under her breath to Kyle. "I can't imagine anything I'd like less than sharing a wedding with Van. I still wake up in a cold sweat remembering the LSU pom-poms and hair bows I had to wear as the maid of honor for her nonwedding to Rufus. Now that she's marrying a man with a healthy bank account, I can't imagine her wedding will be *less* ostentatious. I'll say this for her, though; what she lacks in taste, she makes up for in enthusiasm."

"That's what makes her a surprisingly good store manager. For every ten over-the-top ideas she has, one will be a keeper."

Kyle went back to filling online orders, leaving Maggie to her candy-making. For the next two hours, she prepared a variety of pralines: plain, rum, traditional chocolate, coconut. Instead of finding the task annoying or a time suck, it provided a much-needed diversion from obsessing about murders and attempted murders. When the candies hardened, she slipped them into individual bags, then boxed them. She said goodbye to Kyle and slipped out the back door, careful to avoid Vanessa and her double-wedding dream.

Back home, she found Gran in the manor house office,

formerly the back parlor and gentlemen's smoking room. Centuries of Crozats had lounged on the ornately carved walnut furniture, discussing local economics and politics as they puffed cigars and swirled homemade brandy in crystal snifters. Although the current Crozats were nonsmokers, they'd kept up the tradition of painting the room in dark colors, maroon and forest green, to hide the tobacco stains of previous generations.

"Entering bookings?" Maggie asked her grand-mère, who was typing on the B and B's computer.

"No. I mapped the return address on some of the love letter envelopes, but the satellite image shows it's an empty lot. But I got a much better lead. I found Carina Albieri on Friendspace."

"Really?" Maggie peered over Gran's shoulder at a screen devoid of details. "Not much to go on."

"I know. A few photos, none of people, all of scenery. The only posts are from other people wishing her a happy birthday. It could be her page, it could be her daughter's, even a granddaughter's."

"Might not be a granddaughter's. The millennials have written off that site and moved on."

"Then there's an even better chance that it's her. I'll know more when she responds to my message."

Maggie pulled back. "You messaged her? Gran, are you sure you want to dig deeper into this?"

"Yes." Gran pushed back from the desk and faced her granddaughter, who saw determination in the older woman's pale-blue eyes. "Carina and your grandfather were madly in love. I was married to the man for fifty-one years. How could he never mention anything about this? I must find out what happened, why the relationship ended. I need to know. I can't explain why. I just do."

Maggie placed a hand on her grand-mère's shoulder. "You don't have to explain it. And if you need to talk about whatever you discover, I'm here for you."

"Thank you, chère. Now, back to death cleaning."

"Ugh." Maggie shuddered. "Let's go back to using the Swedish word for it, whatever that was."

She left for her bedroom, where she changed out of clothes marked with the detritus of praline prep. Her cell rang mid-outfit. Bo's name flashed on the screen, and she took the call. "Hey, fiancé. Yay, I get to call you that again!"

"I'm looking forward to celebrating our reconciliation." The sexy undercurrent in Bo's tone left no doubt of how he'd like to celebrate. "But let's get through the latest murder crisis first."

"You know, it just occurred to me that when it comes to the snake in my car, we left someone off the list—Narcisse. He's a local boy and used to whatever crawls out of the bayou. I know my snake wasn't native, but if he's comfortable with reptiles, he could have smuggled it in. Maybe with the help of Gigi, who's got one foot out the door of Pelican and is determined to complete the exit."

"I'll look into it. As long as we're on the topic of bayou boys, guess who was once arrested for assault?"

"Narcisse? I could see him getting drunk and doing something stupid."

"No, when it comes to the much more serious charge of domestic violence, we're talking about Mr. All God's Creatures himself . . . Toulouse Delaroux Caresmeadtrand."

Chapter 19

Maggie was silent for a moment. "Wow. That's a stunner."

"Yup," Bo said. "Four years ago, in Lafayette. The charges were eventually dropped. We tracked down the girl who filed them. Well, she was a girl then; now she's twenty-one. All she would say is that it was a misunderstanding, they were both drunk, he didn't mean it. What you sadly hear from a lot of domestic abuse cases. This girl had the good sense to end the relationship. And he moved to Nashville right after."

"Where he found God."

"Or appears to."

"That's the question."

Maggie's phone pinged a text. She checked and saw it was from Clinton Poche, who was at the festival manning Pelican Pralines: YOU COMING? BRIANNA CAN'T, FORGOT SHE HAS TEST TOMORROW.

"Shoot, I have to go. I'm late to the festival and short a teenager."

"Okay, I'll touch base with you later."

Maggie quickly finished dressing, then dashed to her car. She caught every green light and made it to the booth in ten minutes. She was surprised to see Gaynell helping Clinton sell his sweet potato pralines to enthusiastic customers. "Hey," her friend said. "Clinton was swamped. Hope you're okay with me pitching in."

"I'm thrilled," Maggie said. Concerned, she added, "But are you okay? I know you wanted to lay low."

"I did," Gaynell said. "But I'm feeling way braver after what all happened at the courthouse. I figure, if all those people can show up to support me, I can show my face around town."

"I'm so glad, Gay. For you and for me, because we could use the help tonight."

Maggie set out her boxes of fresh pralines. "We've got plain, chocolate, rum, and coconut. Let's sell these babies. And if you can move any of my art merchandise, even better."

The top of young Xander's head popped up in the booth opening. He placed his hands on the counter, stood on his toes, and the rest of his head appeared. "Hello."

"Hi, Xander," Maggie said with an affectionate smile. "What can I get you?"

"Two chocolate, please."

"Two, huh?" She saw Esme, Xander's crush, standing behind him with a small cluster of his classmates. "Here you go. On the house."

Xander grinned, showing newly missing upper and lower baby teeth. He took the pralines and offered one to

Esme. "No thank you," she said, then turned her back to him. The boy flushed and dropped his head, disconsolate. He dragged his feet to the nearest garbage can.

"Xander, no," Maggie called out as she ran from behind the booth. She took one of the pralines from Xander, then bent down so she was eye level with Esme. "Honey, are you sure don't want this? It's chocolate, not pecan, and it's pretty darn yummy."

The girl's brow creased; then she repeated what she'd said to Xander. "No thank you."

"But—"

A boy half a head taller than Esme, but with the same white-blonde hair, spoke up. "She can't. She's real allergic to nuts or anything that comes near 'em."

"She is?" Maggie said. "I'm so sorry." She felt foolish that this hadn't occurred to her. "Are you her brother?"

The older boy nodded. "Our mom taught her to say 'No thank you' whenever anyone offered her something that she didn't know where it came from. It's easier than explaining."

"Of course." She turned back to Esme. "You did the right thing, sweetie." Maggie pulled a five-dollar bill out of the back pocket of her jeans. She handed it to Xander. "There's a vegan booth toward the end of this row. I bet they have some snacks Esme can eat."

Xander brightened. "Come on," he said to his friends, and the kids took off on their mission.

"That's two romances saved today, yours and Xander's," Gaynell, who'd been watching, said with a grin.

"His could use a little nudge. I'll think on it."

Maggie returned to the booth, and for the next couple of hours business was brisk, some of it stimulated by locals who wanted the latest gossip on "Bomag," the clunky name mash-up for Bo and Maggie's relationship. Maggie politely accepted the good wishes and occasional snarky comment from a single who'd gotten her hopes up when she'd heard Bo was back on the market.

The evening's crowd was the largest yet, which Maggie attributed to the fact that it was the second-to-last night of *Cajun Country Live!*. The mood was festive, with people dancing in the grassy path between the two rows of food booths to a lineup of Cajun, zydeco, and cover bands. Brasstopia, a band comprised of a half-dozen trumpet, trombone, sax, and sousaphone players, marched down the midway playing "When the Saints Go Marchin' In," followed by a second line of fans holding decorated umbrellas and waving handkerchiefs as they sang along.

Meanwhile Maggie, determined to learn more about Toulouse's background, kept an eye out for the young musician. She'd sensed the Cajun performer was emotionally stunted, but his arrest showed he might also be volatile. Any conversation would require a cautious approach. She caught a break when the presence of a TV crew from *Entertainment Now* presaged Tammy's arrival for the evening.

Sure enough, the singing star showed up a few minutes later, entourage in tow, musicians dragging behind. She wore her country duds of jean shorts, tight T-shirt, and high-heeled cowboy boots; Maggie assumed she was saving her blingy new costumes for the sneak-peek pop music set she planned to spring on Jazz Fest.

Gaynell ducked down out of sight. "I'm grateful to Tammy, but I don't want her to see me and drag me onto some TV show."

Tammy autographed a program for a fan as she chatted with the TV show's segment producer. Maggie recognized the autograph seeker as the rude customer who planned on selling her signed mouse pad on the Internet. "There you go, honey," Tammy said to the woman. "I better not see that autograph being auctioned online, ha-ha. Where was I? Pony, right." She put a hand on her heart. When she spoke, her voice quavered with almost theatrical emotion. "I don't want to think about his death; I want to focus on his life. Each time I sing, it's a tribute to him, which is why we added a set tonight, in addition to closing the festival tomorrow. Now, I'd best be getting to the VIP area so I can rest my voice before we go on." Competing for the honor of escorting Tammy to her trailer, Gigi, Narcisse, and Sara ending up tussling with each other as the group walked away from the food booths.

"Coast is clear," Maggie told Gaynell. She then spotted Toulouse buying a pasta dish from a booth across the way. "I'll be right back," she said, and headed straight toward the accordionist.

He waved at her with a plastic fork. "Hey there." He motioned to his bowl. "I'm working my way through all the copycat Crawfish Monica stands," he said, referencing Jazz Fest's most legendary dish. Its ingredients were one of

Louisiana's best-kept secrets and had spawned a raft of imitators trying to come up with their own successful version of the recipe. "So far I been to Crawfish Tomica, Johnica, and Hanukah. That one was a surprise. They said it's kosher, whatever that means. It's not made with real crawfish cuz they can't have shellfish. How can you live in Louisiana and not eat shellfish? I feel sorry for those poor people."

"That's the Metzes' booth, and they're a very nice, very happy family. Toulouse, I wanted to thank you for coming to the courthouse today. Gaynell needs all the support she can get, and getting it from someone in the band, someone who knew Pony, is extra important. It shows you have faith in her."

Toulouse nodded vigorously. "I do. All the faith in the world."

"Bless you." Maggie cringed inwardly at her pious act but continued. "And bless you for changing your life like you did. I'm sorry, I probably shouldn't have brought that up. My grand-mère's the nosy type—*sorry for throwing you under the bus, Gran*—and she's fascinated with y'all, so she looked up the whole band on the computer."

Fortunately, Toulouse was more amused than annoyed by this intrusion. "Grannies and grampies do like looking stuff up on computers, don't they? Must be cuz they don't have much else to do and it beats thinking about their end being so near."

"Yeeessss . . . So she told me about what happened with that girlfriend of yours." Not wanting to put words in Toulouse's mouth, Maggie stopped there.

"You're talking about the arrest," he said. Maggie nodded. The musician finished the last bite of his pasta, then threw away the empty container. "That was rock bottom for me. At least I knew it. The only way out was to quit doing bad stuff. I gave up drinking. I stopped being angry at everyone and everything. I did what they say in AA. I 'let go, let God.' I know Miss Gaynell has a boyfriend. I also know she's a beautiful person with a talent that makes her a threat to performers not as good as her." Toulouse wagged a finger at Maggie. "I see the surprise on your face. Yeah, I'm not as dumb as people think I am."

"I didn't think—"

"You did. It's okay. I'm used to it. But as for Miss Gaynell, I'd never create problems in her relationship. I'm only looking out for her. I'd swear it to you on the Bible, and I'm a guy who takes the Holy Book seriously."

He stared at her with his light-brown eyes, almost daring Maggie to doubt him. "Amen," she said.

His serious demeanor instantly changed to a cheery one. "Amen, sister. Woot woot." He fist-pumped the air with both hands, then ambled away. His departure revealed The Sound leaning against the booth across from Pelican Pralines. "He's a flipping nut job," the keyboardist said. "You know that, don't you?"

Maggie refused to be baited. "I only know he's been incredibly supportive of Gaynell."

"He gets like that. Always trying to save some poor little woman, as if that could make up for assaulting one. A hero complex born from guilt."

"You're making some big assumptions with a lot of confidence."

The Sound ran a hand over his newly shaved head, which was so smooth it reflected light. "When you tour, there's a lot of downtime. Instead of drinking or doing drugs, I read psychology books. Especially about maladaptive personalities. Quite a few on this tour alone." He put a finger to his lips. "But shhh." He removed the finger. "Wouldn't want to alert a murderer we're on to him. Or her." His cell phone buzzed, and he pulled it out of his pocket. "Apologies for ducking out on this interesting conversation, but I need to answer this text. It's about my plan B."

"Your exercise studios?"

"Piloga, yes. That's what separates me from my bandmates. I know what comes after plan A, 'A' being a music career, which could disappear at any time. My future isn't in the hands of some dim diva or aging rock star trying to ignore his creaky old bones when he struts across a stage. As Buddha said, 'No one saves us but ourselves. No one can and no one may. We ourselves must walk the path.'"

With that metaphysical pronouncement, The Sound drifted away. Maggie was put off by his superior attitude, and he replaced Uffen as the musician she most disliked. Yet despite his declaration that the future was his, Maggie picked up a note of bitterness under his boasts, and she wondered if the Piloga-pushing keyboardist might not be as chill as Valeria portrayed him—and he portrayed himself. But The Sound did score points by shaving off his man bun, and she found merit in his evaluation of Toulouse. While the Cajun musician was sweet and sincere, his mission to protect Gaynell smacked of zealotry. Could it have driven him to defend her honor by killing Pony? Was God-fearing Toulouse that "maladaptive"?

Maggie went back to the Crozats' booth. She took her cell phone from her purse and texted Bo a question: WHAT'S THE NAME OF TOULOUSE'S HOMETOWN?

The time had come for a field trip.

Chapter 20

Maggie awoke to rain the next morning. The fact that it was the last day of *Cajun Country Live!* spared her the task of making more pralines. She'd put the Poche siblings in charge of the Crozats' booth and didn't plan on showing up to the festival until early evening or later. This would give her the time she needed before Lia's baby shower to take a deep dive into Toulouse's past.

Not sure what kind of people or atmosphere she'd find in his hometown, Maggie chose her outfit carefully, eschewing her usual jeans and T-shirt for a conservative outfit of beige pencil skirt and cream silk top. Then she grabbed an umbrella and dashed from the cottage to her car. She drove out of the family's graveled parking lot, made a right turn onto the River Road, and crossed over the Mississippi on Veterans Memorial Bridge. Once on the west side of the river, she followed a maze of two-lane roads south to her destination in coastal Cajun Country: the aptly named Petite, Louisiana. Petite was so small that Maggie was in Grand Petite before she realized she'd driven right through its little sister. She pulled a U-turn and backtracked to what was essentially a crossroads at a stop sign.

She parked in front of an old white building with a wide front porch. A painted sign above the front door identified it as the Petite General Grocery. The rain hadn't let up, so Maggie maneuvered her way out of the Falcon while holding an umbrella, then dashed up the grocery store's front steps. She opened the worn screen door and stepped into a time capsule. Wooden shelving stocked with canned goods, some of which looked decades old themselves, lined three of the walls. Refrigerator cases that appeared to date back to the 1950s rested against the fourth wall. The center of the store was taken up with battered shelves featuring everything from cereal to diapers. There was one cash register manned by an African-American woman who could have been anywhere from forty to seventy. Maggie couldn't tell. The woman wore a faded smock and her hair was hidden under a colorful tignon. There were three portraits on the wall behind her: a painting of Jesus on the cross, a faded photo of President John F. Kennedy, and a shiny new photo of Pope Francis.

"Mornin'," the woman said with a wide smile. "You need directions?"

"No."

"You here to shop?" The woman didn't bother to hide her surprise.

"No. Well, of course I'll buy something."

"You don't have to, chère." The woman had a low,

mellifluous voice. There was something innately comforting about her entire presence. "I'm Zenephra."

"Maggie. Maggie Crozat."

"Maggie Crozat," Zenephra repeated. "I heard you and that detective got back together. I'm glad about that."

Maggie's jaw dropped. "How did you hear that here?"

Zenephra chuckled. "Word floats from small town to small town in our part of the world, chère. In the Petites, small and Grand, gossip is less of a grapevine and more of a grape bayou. So how can I help you, Maggie Crozat?"

She gestured to a rickety stool next to her. Maggie carefully took a seat. "I need to ask you about someone named Toulouse Delaroux Caresmeatrand, who grew up here."

A serious expression replaced Zenephra's smile.

"Do you know him?"

"I do." Her tone switched from warm to wary.

"I'm trying to understand him. He appears to be a good person. But he also appears to be troubled in a way I can't figure out. He's . . . devoted to my friend Gaynell, who's been facing some problems."

"Yes, I heard about that."

"Right, the grape bayou. Anyway, he's a passionate defender of her, which is good; she needs all the help she can get. I just worry that he may cross the line to obsession. I wonder if he's—"

"—right in the head."

"Yes," Maggie said, relieved. "Exactly."

Zenephra climbed off her stool and went to one of the

refrigerator cases. She came back with two old-style bottles of Coke. She knocked the caps off on the edge of the register counter and handed one to Maggie. "Poor Toulouse. Sweet, sad Toulouse. If there was ever a child who deserved a break, it was him. He always had a talent for music. Got it from his papa, who died when Toulouse was a baby. Drunk, crashed a car. Yvette, Toulouse's mama, gave the boy a string of stepdads, one worse than t'other. Toulouse took a shovel to the back of the head of one of them when the man started beating on Yvette. Dang near killed him. He spent some time in one of those places where they send troubled kids, but Yvette got him out. Said it was self-defense. He was her protector. She was so proud of him."

"Was?"

"She passed on a few years back. He was just eighteen. That's a tough age. Government says you're an adult, but are you really? Back to his mama—Yvette developed liver cancer. She was a big drinker like his papa. Wouldn't be surprised if Toulouse got some of that fetal inside stuff."

"Fetal alcohol syndrome."

"Right, that. After Yvette passed, Toulouse played with some local bands, bounced around a few houses here. Lived with me for a while; I have an old place out back. He got in trouble with the law again, this time about a girl."

"The arrest for assault."

"The charges were dropped, the way they often are in these cases. After that, he took off for Nashville. I heard he found the Lord." Zenephra took a pull of her Coke. "I don't like when people take refuge behind Him. Too often they're not being honest or true. Still, I always believed Toulouse's heart was in the right place. I wish I could've done more for the boy. But I had my own troubles, don't we all."

Maggie followed Zenephra's gaze to a faded photo of a handsome African-American man hanging above the grocery store's front door. A set of rosary beads was draped over a corner of the photo's frame. "My husband, Jacques. He was in the car with Toulouse's daddy. They were drinking buddies."

"I'm sorry."

Zenephra turned her attention back to Maggie. "They were on their way home from a bordello, which took a little of the pain away. Still, he never got the chance to make things right with me."

Maggie noticed the time on the old wall clock next to Jacques's photo. "I have to go. I'm throwing a baby shower in a couple of hours."

Zenephra's mood instantly lightened. "Well, mercy me, isn't that something. Let me give you a present for the little one–to–be."

"Not one, three. My cousin's expecting triplets."

"Lia Tienne Bruner's babies? My goodness."

Maggie put her hands on her hips and shook her head. "Honestly, Ms. Zenephra, I'm not sure if you're a gossip or a witch."

Zenephra flashed a mischievous smile. "Maybe a little of both." She reached under the counter and took out a small tin. She opened it and showed the contents, a thick white salve, to Maggie. "Calming balm. I make it myself.

All natural. Tell Miss Lia that if the babies fuss, rub a fingerful right here." She pointed to her heart. "They'll settle down in a quick minute."

"Thank you, I know she'll appreciate this." Maggie took the tin. "And I appreciate you being so honest with me about Toulouse."

"When you see him, please tell the boy that Miss Zenephra sends all her love."

"I will."

Maggie left Petite General Grocery and hurried to her car. The rain had lightened to a fading drizzle, so she didn't bother opening her umbrella. She got behind the steering wheel, but before she turned the key in the ignition, she placed the Bluetooth over her left ear and put a call in to Bo. He answered on the first ring. "Hey, how'd it go?"

"Interesting." She filled him in on her conversation with Zenephra. "The Sound said Toulouse has a hero complex. Zenephra called him a protector. Given his background and current instability, he's the perfect candidate for a psychotic break."

"It all makes sense except for—"

Maggie's Bluetooth cut out. She cursed it, then dialed Bo again. "Sorry, having mechanical problems. What were you saying?"

"It all makes sense except for the attack on Bokie."

"True." Maggie pulled out of the parking space and began driving toward Pelican. "Toulouse must've known Bokie had a thing for Valeria. Maybe he thought he was going to assault her. Bokie's loud because of his hearing loss, and he hasn't figured out how to modulate, or doesn't care about it. I think Toulouse is sensitive to violence because of his abusive stepfathers. He could have heard Bokie yell to Valeria and snapped. But on the other hand, I feel like Toulouse is genuinely committed to God and to making up for his past, which would make him fight against any violent instincts he might have."

Bo started laughing.

"What?"

"If we spent as much time planning our wedding as we do talking about murder scenarios, we'd probably be married with a kid on the way by now."

Maggie had to laugh, too. "That is so true. I can promise you this is my last scenario for the next few hours. I have a shower to throw."

*   *   *

Lia and Kyle's living room, formerly the spacious front parlor of the Grove Hall manor house, was festooned with yellow decorations. Crepe paper with cheery ducklings dangling from it crisscrossed the room. The balloon bouquet created by Vanessa took up an entire corner of the room. A disco ball—also Vanessa's idea—hung from the antique carved cypress ceiling medallion, shooting tiny reflective rainbows everywhere. Two large folding tables covered in bright-yellow tablecloths bowed under the weight of beverages and pot luck dishes brought by guests, a feast of gumbos, jambalayas, étouffées, dips, and desserts. The three-tiered cake—one tier for each incoming Baby

Bruner—featured three flavors: vanilla, chocolate, and rum raisin, Ninette's unique creation and usually the first tier to go at any party.

Lia had requested an all-girl shower, bucking the trend of co-ed celebrations. "I just want my tribe," she'd said. And her tribe showed up in full force. Generations of Pelican were represented, from Gran down to Vanessa's baby Charli, who cruised the party in her activity walker. All the action revolved around Lia, positioned in her hospital bed at the forty-five-degree angle approved by her obstetrician, Dr. Fran Vella, who was also at the party.

For the first hour, the thirty or so women played baby shower party games, which was Gran's contribution to the event. First up was her adaptation of the game "Don't Say Baby," where instead of each player surrendering the diaper pin she was wearing on her blouse if she said the word, she had to take a drink. Within fifteen minutes, the women had polished off six bottles of wine. Next, the women took turns trying to guess the baby food inside unlabeled jars. Every time a player guessed wrong, she took a drink.

"I'm sensing a theme to these games," Maggie said to her grandmother.

"I have no idea what you're talking about," Gran replied. "I found them all on the Internet. Then tweaked a few."

After a few more "tweaked" games, the women broke for lunch. Their glasses full and plates piled high, they found places on either the pale-blue brocade couch and love seat or the various antique and rental chairs arranged to form a circle that started and ended with Lia. The self-effacing mom-to-be's café au lait cheeks blushed pink from being the center of attention. "I feel so uncomfortable," she whispered to Maggie after the seventh or eighth "*A votre santé*" toast.

"Don't flatter yourself," Maggie whispered back. "All these toasts are just an excuse to drink more."

Lia stifled a laugh. "Got it." She raised her glass of sparkling water. "I want to propose another toast. To Gaynell. I can't imagine this party without you."

"I can't find the words to say how happy I am to be here." Gaynell, who looked rested and happy for the first time in days, clinked her glass with Lia's.

"To Gaynell!"

The women toasted, drank, and then half the room got up to refill their glasses. They stopped when Vanessa held up her glass. "And to my beloved, Quentin MacIlhoney, whose brilliance makes him the best lawyer around and would've made him the best mayor this town ever saw."

Sandy Sechrest narrowed her eyes at Vanessa, then held up her own glass. "To *my* beloved Rufus Durand, who couldn't be here even if he wanted to because he's busy fighting crime in Pelican with the same passion he would've brought to his role as mayor, which he'd be right now if he'd run."

"With all this toasting, I think I better grab myself a bottle," Gran said, and did so, helping herself to a half-full bottle of champagne.

"Sharesies," Maggie said, holding out her empty glass. Gran filled it.

"Rufus has what Quentin doesn't," Sandy says. "Government experience."

"You say that like it's a good thing."

Van's comeback elicited a few chuckles, but Sandy quickly responded, "It is when the experience is provided by a man who's dedicated his life to public service."

"Oh please, you know Quentin would've made a way better mayor," Vanessa sniped.

"I don't know anything of the kind," Sandy sniped back. "What I do know is that he would've bailed on mayoral duties when the first high-paying criminal asked for representation."

Vanessa gasped. "That is so not true; how dare—"

"Ladies, since I actually *am* the mayor, I'm going to ask that we put aside our differences and all talk of crime," Eula Banks said. "But for anyone who's counting, we're behind three toasts."

"Thanks, I lost track," Dr. Vella said.

The women drank three toasts' worth of beverages, refilled their glasses, and returned to their seats. "It's time to open the gifts," Ione said.

This brought squeals of delight from the women. "Presents, presents, presents," they chanted.

"Dang, I just remembered I left ours in the car," Gaynell said to Maggie. The two women had pooled their resources for Lia's gift, a top-of-the-line stroller designed to hold three infants. Gaynell had offered to pick up the present, wrap it, and bring it to the shower. "Be right back."

Gaynell got up and went out the front door. Vanessa

plopped down in her place next to Maggie. "Move your meat and lose your seat. I got a better view of the presents from here. Hey, when can I tell people we're having a double wedding?"

"Never, because it's not happening," Maggie said. "When it comes to a walk down the aisle, I'm going it alone. Well, except for my mom and dad. But no double wedding."

"Keep thinking on it."

"Vanessa—"

"Oooh, Lia's starting with my gift." Charli had dozed off in her walker, so Vanessa grabbed the edge of it and pulled the baby to her. "If Charli was awake, she'd think all these prezzies were for her, and there would be one ugly scene when she found out they weren't, let me tell you. It's a good thing she passed out."

"I'm surprised she's the only one here who has," Maggie said, glancing around the room at the celebrants, who were in various states of inebriation.

For the next half hour, Lia opened present after present to the oohs and aahs of her guests. Gifts ranged from the practical, like a Diaper Genie, which allowed for easy disposal of dirty diapers, to three sets of hand-knit booties in the Mardi Gras colors of purple, green, and gold. "These are so beautiful I could cry," Lia told Yvonne Rousseau, the elderly resident of Camellia Park Senior Village, whose gnarled hands had somehow created the exquisite items. "Thank you so much."

"Food, booze, and Ninette Crozat's rum raisin cake,"

Yvonne said with a cackle. "I should be thanking *you*." She held up her champagne glass. "Another toast to Lia!"

"To Lia!" the women responded, and then drank.

"There better be some designated drivers in this crowd," Ione muttered to Maggie.

Lia gestured to the piles of wrapping paper and stacks of presents that surrounded her on three sides. "I think that's everything."

"Wait," Maggie said. "You never opened our present. Gaynell went out to get it. Gay?" She looked around the room but didn't see her friend. "She went out to her car a while ago. Has anyone seen her?" The women shook their heads and murmured no. Maggie's heart began to pound, her intuition setting off an alarm bell indicating something was wrong. "I'll look outside. Maybe she got to talking to someone."

Trying to hide her concern, Maggie took a calm walk to the door. Once outside, she ran to Gaynell's car. The trunk of the car was open. Inside lay a large box wrapped in cheery wrapping paper of bears holding balloons.

"Your gift's still in there," said Ione, who'd followed Maggie outside, along with Vanessa, Sandy, Ninette, and Gran.

"I know."

"Where's Gaynell?"

"I don't know."

A wave of anxiety passed through all five women. They called to Gaynell and got no response. "This is bad,"

Vanessa said, wringing her hands. Sandy nodded emphatically, the competition between the two women forgotten.

"I don't like it," Ione said. "I don't like it at all."

"Neither do I." Maggie got a sudden, sick feeling in the pit of her stomach. "I'm calling Pelican PD. I hope I'm wrong, but I have a terrible feeling that Gaynell's been kidnapped."

Chapter 21

Two Pelican PD squad cars showed up at what seemed like warp speed. Per Maggie's request, neither flashed lights or sounded sirens, an attempt to shield pregnant Lia from the drama. Officers Cal and Artie searched the area while Rufus interviewed the women, who shared what little they knew. "Have you talked to Toulouse?" Maggie asked Rufus. Fear made her stutter as she put the question to him.

"Bo's up at Belle Vista looking for him right now."

"Gaynell and I follow each other on the app Locate Me. I checked and it says LOCATION NOT AVAILABLE. That's never happened before."

"Whoever she's with—if she's with someone, and it's sure looking like it—must have turned off her phone." Rufus's two-way radio crackled. Maggie heard Bo's garbled voice. "I need to take this, Maggie."

Rufus stepped away. Maggie took a deep breath and scurried up the front steps into the house, where she was met with a sea of concerned faces and peppered with questions.

"Where's Gaynell? What happened?"

"Is everything all right? Why are the police here?"

"Has she been kidnapped? I heard she's been kidnapped."

"Did they steal your present? I saw it in Gay's trunk; it was a big'un."

Ninette spoke up before Maggie could respond. "Whatever's going on, I'm sure the police are handling it. Rather than worry ourselves and our guest of honor, why don't we focus on cleaning up and getting Lia some rest?"

"Good idea, Mom," Maggie said, giving Ninette a grateful look. She pointed to different women as she assigned tasks, distracting them from Gaynell's mysterious disappearance. "Gin, can you make a list of all the gifts? Eula, how about you put plastic wrap over the leftovers? Ione, why don't you take charge of cleaning up wrapping paper?"

"Happy to," Ione said, grabbing a large black trash bag. "My cousin's girl is expecting, so we can reuse a lot of this."

She and a few friends sorted and bagged bows and wrapping paper while Eula supervised the leftovers. One crew of guests cleaned up the living room; someone else took charge of the kitchen. Maggie presented a calm front that belied her text to Kyle: GET HOME NOW! She'd feel better knowing he was there keeping an eye on his expectant wife.

"Maggie," Lia called to her.

"Hey," Maggie said, forcing a smile. She went to her cousin and took her hand. "What a party, huh?"

"Go." Lia squeezed Maggie's hand. "You can do more out there than here."

"Everything's okay, Lia. Really."

"No. It's not. I appreciate that you're trying to protect me, chère. But what would really give me some peace of mind is knowing you're using whatever it is you've learned about Tammy and her crew to help find Gaynell."

"You sure?"

"*So* sure. Now *go*. I'll tell your mama and grand-mère what all's up."

Maggie gave her cousin a fierce hug, then dashed out of the house to her car. Not trusting her mercurial Bluetooth, she called Bo before starting the engine. "Hey. Are you in a position to tell me what's going on?"

"More than that. We need you. Tammy and Toulouse had a blowout. He accused her of trying to send Gaynell to jail, so she fired him. He took off with one of the band's rental cars. We put out an APB and got a hit on a similar sedan spotted on Larue Road. Artie's running the plates now."

"Larue. Those houses took the worst of the flood last year. Some are still abandoned."

"Exactly. Perfect place to hide out. Wait, what? It's Artie." Maggie heard static on Bo's end; then it stopped. "Plates checked out. It's the rental."

"What can I do?"

"You spoke to that woman in Petite. I'm trained in hostage negotiation, but you have more of a connection to Caresmeatrand's background than any of us. I wouldn't mind having you there in case we need someone who can reach him on a personal level."

"On my way. But send someone to get Miss Zenephra in Petite. She runs the general store."

Maggie stepped on the accelerator, barely heeding stop signs as she raced to Larue Road. She doubted Pelican PD would be worried about speed traps in the midst of a kidnapping. By the time she reached Larue Road ten minutes later, a half-dozen police cars were already lined up outside a decrepit, flood-damaged shack covered with asbestos shingles. One car stood out among the others—a purple rental sedan. Officers, some in SWAT gear, surrounded Bo. He was dressed in his standard investigation attire of jeans, white button-down shirt, and navy sport coat. Maggie guessed this was an intentional choice to disarm Toulouse. She parked and went to Bo.

"He's in there," Bo said. He gestured to Artie Belloise, who held a bullhorn. "We let him know we're here. I've been talking to him. No idea if we're making progress. That Zenephra woman can't get here soon enough."

"Does he have Gaynell?"

Bo nodded.

"I'd like to talk to him."

"Okay. But from a distance." Bo walked over to Artie, took the bullhorn, and brought it back to Maggie. "Press that button to speak."

Maggie did so. "Toulouse? Hey. It's me, Maggie Crozat." Her ears rang from the bullhorn's reverberation.

There was an agonizing moment of silence. Then Toulouse spoke. "Hey, Maggie. I heard you and Bo were back together. That's good news."

Maggie and Bo's eyes widened at this incongruous statement. Artie twirled his fingers around his ears and mouthed the word *cuckoo*.

"Yes, we did get back together, thank you," Maggie said. "I'm worried about Gaynell."

"No need to. She's fine with me. Someone's finally taking care of her."

"That's real kind, Toulouse. But I think it's time the police took over for you."

"No way. They were doing the opposite of caring for her."

"That's on me," Bo called out to the musician. "I was too upset about Maggie breaking my heart to do my job right." Maggie shot him a look, and he whispered to her, "I'm going for sympathy."

Maggie pursed her lips and shook her head, then spoke into the bullhorn. "But that's over now. You can trust Bo. You can trust me. We love Gaynell and would do anything for her."

There was a pause. "I'm sorry," Toulouse said. "I'm just not comfortable with the current situation."

"*You're* not comfortable," Artie muttered.

Maggie closed her eyes and tried to steady her nerves. Bo watched, concerned, but she motioned to him that she was alright. "Toulouse, I'd feel so much better if I could hear from Gaynell. Would that be all right?"

Another pause, then, "Don't see why not."

"Hey, Maggie," came Gaynell's welcome voice.

"Gay," Maggie responded with relief. "Are you okay?"

"Yes." Her friend's voice was calm, but Maggie picked up an undercurrent of fear. "Toulouse is taking real good care of me."

"Way better than the police," Toulouse jumped in. "I

don't care how broke up Bo was about you. Okay, so now you heard Gaynell. We're done."

Bo cursed and reached for the bullhorn. Maggie held on to it. "Wait." She aimed the bullhorn at the shack. "Toulouse, I saw Miss Zenephra today." Maggie had no idea how the disturbed musician would react to this reveal. Her heart pounded.

"Miss Z?" Toulouse's voice wavered.

"Yes. She sends her love."

"She remembers me?"

Bo put a hand on her shoulder. "You've engaged him. Keep going."

Maggie nodded, then spoke through the bullhorn. "She more than remembers you. She cares about you."

"*Care* is a buzzword for him," Bo said under his breath. "Good choice."

"She was almost a mama to me," Toulouse said. "I'd like to see her again sometime."

Maggie's heart beat faster. "And she wants to see you. Very, very much. Matter of fact, she's on her way here."

"She's here," Bo whispered, his tone intense.

Maggie turned and saw Rufus running to them, pulling Zenephra along with him. "I didn't want to turn on my siren and spook him," the police chief said between gasps for breath. "Where we at?"

"Your timing's perfect," Bo said. Then he turned to Zenephra. "Ma'am, he wants to see you. Let's step this out. Maggie, give her the bullhorn. First you'll—"

Zenephra dismissed him with a wave of her hand.

"I don't need no steps or no bullhorn. I've known that child my entire life." She strode across the street. Tension filled the air as the SWAT team took position. Zenephra stepped onto the old home's rickety porch. "Toulouse? You in there?"

"Yeah. Miss Z, that really you?"

"Yes, it is, baby boy. Can I come in? I'd like to have a talk with you."

The front door opened a crack. Zenephra held up her hand to prevent the officers from making a move. Then she disappeared inside the house.

"I sure hope we don't end up with two hostages," Rufus said, his expression grim. He looked around. "What's that thumping sound? Where's it coming from?"

"My heart," Maggie said, embarrassed. "Sorry."

The responders fell silent as they waited for whatever might come next. It was a kind of quiet Maggie had never experienced before—at once taut with anticipation, yet so mute she could hear the rush of I-10 traffic four miles away. The shack's front door opened slightly again. Zenephra's hand appeared, waving a torn white napkin.

"Pull back," Bo ordered, adding to a sharpshooter positioned in a tree, "Not you."

"We're coming out," Zenephra called from inside the shack. "Your friend first, then me and Toulouse."

The door opened wider, and Gaynell took an uneasy step outside. She saw Maggie, Bo, and Rufus, and relaxed. Bo motioned for her to come to them, and she did, slowly at first, then breaking into a run. Maggie opened her arms, and Gaynell fell into them. "Gay, chère," Maggie said, hugging her friend hard. The young woman's baby shower outfit was covered with dust, her hair matted with cobwebs. Tears left rivulets in the streaks of dirt that stained her cheeks.

"I'm okay," Gaynell said. "But man, was it gross in that house." This engendered tension-release giggles from both women.

"It's gonna be us now," Zenephra called, and all attention snapped back to the shack. Zenephra emerged, holding Toulouse by the hand. She held a gun down at her side.

"He looks so broken," Maggie couldn't help murmuring.

Cal and Artie approached Zenephra. Artie held up a pair of handcuffs, and the woman waved the gun at him. "Cuff him and I'll use this thing myself."

"Sorry, ma'am," Cal said. "We have to."

"It's okay, Miss Z," Toulouse said, a quaver in his voice, his tone defeated.

He put his hands behind his back. Artie cuffed Toulouse, then escorted the musician to a police car. Gaynell wept, and Maggie put a reassuring arm around her friend's waist. "I'm not crying for me," Gay said. "I'm crying for him."

* * *

Maggie drove Gaynell to Pelican PD headquarters, where she gave a statement to Bo and Rufus. "I didn't want to press charges," Gaynell told her friend afterward.

"But kidnapping's a felony, so the state has to bring

them," Quentin MacIlhoney, who'd joined them, explained. "The ADA's also going to charge Toulouse in Pickner's murder and the attempt on the drummer's life. The cases are still circumstantial, but much stronger than the one they had against you, Gaynell."

Gaynell released a shaky breath. "I need to get home. I could use a shower and a rest. Maggie, you mind dropping me?"

"Of course not. Let me tell Bo I'm leaving."

She headed down the hallway and found Bo in his office. He looked exhausted but smiled when he saw her. "Hey. Come on in."

Maggie did so, shutting the door behind her.

"You heard about the charges Jerriere's bringing against Toulouse?"

Maggie nodded.

"That'll get Gaynell off the hook."

"Which is good news." Maggie paused. "So why don't I feel relieved? Why do I still feel so . . . unsettled?"

"Because you don't think Toulouse is the killer," Bo said. "And neither do I."

Chapter 22

Maggie dropped into the office chair facing Bo's desk. "I'm so glad I'm not alone on this. But why do we feel this way? Tell me, oh Great Detective."

Bo pushed his own chair back and rested his feet on the desk. "Pony Pickner's murder walked a line between spontaneous and premeditated. By that I mean the urge to kill may have been spontaneous, but the method wasn't. Someone had to know that they needed to remove the safety ground connection. They also had to know when and where to place the water so that Tammy wasn't electrocuted."

"Unless she was the target and they messed up the timing."

Bo lifted a corner of his mouth. "Thank you, devil's advocate. No worries; we haven't ruled that out. Still, no matter who was the target, the killer did some planning. Toulouse is a deeply damaged guy. Frankly, I'm amazed he's held it together this long. There's a lot at war inside of him. His faith versus his anger, his need to be a hero versus his past as an abuser. I think killing Pony would have broken him completely. And my guess is he would have confessed. Instead, he swears on a Bible he didn't kill the guy or attack Bokie, and I believe him." Bo took his feet off the desk and planted them on the floor. "So does Rufus. But that intel doesn't leave this office. We want the murderer to think they're free and clear. We make a lot of collars when over-confidence leads to sloppiness on the part of a killer."

"This is totally inappropriate," Maggie said, "but you are really hot right now."

Bo burst out laughing. "We're gonna have to do something about that once this dang case is closed."

* * *

Maggie drove Gaynell home, then headed to Crozat. As soon as she parked, she saw Tammy stomping toward her in six-inch black patent-leather boots. Narcisse shadowed her as usual. Maggie got out of the Falcon and slammed the heavy car door. Just the sight of the nasty singer annoyed her. She ignored Tammy and trudged toward the shotgun cottage. Tammy didn't take the hint. "So now my accordionist is in jail," she yelled at Maggie's back.

"What do you care? You fired him," Maggie said, continuing to walk.

"Only because every crazy thing that's happened here made him lose his flippin' mind. What is *wrong* with this stupid town? Where am I gonna get a Cajun musician in two hours?"

Maggie, her last nerve worked, stopped and turned

around. "It's Cajun *country*," she yelled back. "They're all over the place."

"You wish. Everyone's booked up for Jazz Fest."

"Yeah," Narcisse said, tossing in his useless two cents.

"You know what, Tammy," Maggie said through gritted teeth, "if you'd been nicer to Gaynell, you would've had the best Cajun musician in the state by your side. Instead, you treated her like something you scrape off your shoe, you bullied her, and made her an outcast with her own band. You deserve every problem you've got."

"Who do you think you are, talking to me that way? Gaynell's the dang reason I got all these problems. I can't believe Toulouse went crazy for her. Probably because he knew he couldn't get to me."

Narcisse puffed out his chest. "You got your security to thank for that."

Maggie's face burned red with anger. "That's it, Tammy, I have *had* it with you." She took a step toward the singer.

"No," Narcisse yelled, jumping in front of Tammy.

"Whoa," the country star cried out. She tried to keep her balance and failed. Tammy tumbled to the ground, taking Narcisse down with her. She screamed as his elbow landed on her hair and pulled out an extension. "Get away from me!" She tried pushing Narcisse away, then grabbed the chunk of hair. "This is American hair, not Pakistani. It's worth a fortune. Ow!"

"Sorry, my watch is caught on your ponytail holder."

"If you ever bully Gaynell again or try and pull some

mean-girl act," Maggie said to the pile of humanity trying to untangle from each other, "or say anything bad about her to Little Earlie or anyone else, I will go public with what a it-rhymes-with-witch you are. I'll back it up with everything I've seen since you've been here, and believe me, I have seen a *lot*."

Maggie stormed off to the manor house front parlor. She poured herself a shot of bourbon and took a sip to calm down. Then she collapsed onto the room's ornately carved settee, pulled out her cell, and called Bo. "You almost had a third attack on your hands. I was seconds away from decking Tammy."

Bo chortled. "Oh, that would've been great. Hey, we've had a development."

Maggie leaned forward. "What?"

"Zenephra's apparently the Toulouse Whisperer. I think she sees herself as a surrogate mother. And thank God for that, because she pulled a crucial piece of information out of him. What triggered the kidnapping was an anonymous note he received threatening Gaynell. *And* he had it in his pocket."

"So you have evidence that could get the charges dropped."

"We may. We sent it to a handwriting expert in Baton Rouge to confirm it's not in Toulouse's handwriting. With his mental state, we can't discount the possibility that he wrote it himself. But my gut tells me he cracked because of the note, not before it."

"I hope you're right." Maggie closed her eyes and rubbed

them. "Today's been such a day, I almost forgot about Valeria's manuscript. Have you found anything interesting in it?"

"To be honest, I've hardly read it. Too busy, plus I'm a slow reader." Bo paused. She heard him drumming his fingers on his office desk. "We're running out of time. I'm sending you the manuscript from a secure account here."

"You don't want one of the other officers to go through it?"

"Between the crimes and the festival, every officer's up to their thinning hairlines in police business. Besides, I don't think a single one of them reads anything except Saints stats. I'm making an executive decision—you read Valeria's book. If you spark to anything, let me know."

Bo ended the call, and Maggie finished her drink. She looked longingly at the bourbon bottle but summoned up the willpower to skip a second shot, instead taking a walk through the house to find her parents. Neither was around, so she texted her mother to see if she needed any help with dinner prep. ALL GOOD, Ninette texted back. DANCERS TOOK THEIR CIGARETTES AND BONY BODIES BACK TO NOLA FOR COSTUME FITTINGS.

Off the B and B clock, Maggie left the manor house for the shotgun cottage. To her relief, Tammy and her sycophant were gone, so she didn't have to worry about another confrontation. She went inside and found Grand-mère sitting on the sofa with yet more boxes around her feet. "No word from Carina," Gran said, "so it's business as usual."

"If you want to call *shugernitzeroggen* that."

"*Döstädning.* You weren't even close. Come. Sit. You look stressed, as the kids say."

"I am," Maggie said. Gran motioned to a spot next to her on the sofa, and she took a seat. "It's been such a rough day that it feels like a week, and it's only three PM."

She told her grandmother about Gaynell's rescue.

"My heavens," Gran said. "A visit to Petite, a baby shower, and a kidnapping, all by midafternoon." She furrowed her brow, a wistful look on her gently lined face. "Sometimes I feel like the world and I have parted ways. Become estranged. There's too much I don't understand anymore about why people do what they do."

"You're not alone, Gran. Lots of people think that, including me." Feeling guilty for upsetting her grandmother, Maggie decided to change the subject. She gestured to the boxes. "What are you going through today?"

"The paraphernalia of yours and your father's child-hoods. I'm only keeping three of his school projects, ones that have meaning for me and I'd like to see live on after Saint Peter has welcomed me through the pearly gates. Stop making that face like you ate a bad crawfish, Magnolia."

"I'll try, but it's hard not to make 'that face' when you talk about the pearly gates." Maggie picked up a construction-paper card that said *Happy Mother's Day* above a rudimentary drawing of a bird. "Aw, this is so cute. How old was Dad when he made it?"

"Fourteen."

"Oh."

"Yes, you did not get your artistic talent from your father, that's for certain." She took the card from Maggie. "Still, these are the items that are particularly hard to death-clean. Every one of them has a memory attached to it." Gran's tablet, resting on the coffee table, pinged an alert, and she picked it up. She read the message, then put a hand on her heart. "It's from her. Carina. She'd love to see me."

"That's . . . wonderful?" Maggie posed this as a question. She wasn't sure if Gran meeting her husband's old flame or even a relative of the woman was a good idea.

"It is," Gran said with confidence. "Like I told you, I have questions I want answered."

"All right then. Find out where she lives. For all we know, it could be a different part of the country—or world. If it is, you can arrange a phone call. If she's local, I'll make sure you meet in person."

"Thank you, chère."

Gran began typing a message to the mysterious Carina, and Maggie retreated to her bedroom. She took her laptop, then sat on her bed resting against its headboard, her feet straight out in front of her. She placed the computer on her lap. Bo's email, with Valeria's file attached to it, was in her inbox. Maggie opened the file and began to skim. The manuscript seemed to revolve around various A- to D-list musicians whose advances Valeria had or hadn't fended off. Maggie raised her eyebrows at a couple of legendary names, wondering how the backup singer planned to skirt the "cease and desist" letters from lawyers that the book was sure to engender. *Wow, have I had a dull life*, she thought after getting caught up in a chapter involving the Greek island of Mykonos, a Dionysian music festival, a few members of the British royal family, and a hookup with rock star royalty.

Focus, Maggie, she scolded herself. She entered the name PONY in the search bar. The word came up thirty-six times. She read each entry, deeply regretting one that involved an impromptu sexcapade at a tech billionaire's Northern California alpaca ranch. *I can't unread that, but at least the alpacas weren't involved.*

By the thirty-fourth PONY, Maggie was fighting to keep her eyes open. Numbers thirty-five and thirty-six repeated the story Valeria had told her about the manager hiring a private investigator to track down old flames. Frustrated, Maggie closed the file and powered down her laptop. She yawned, stretching out on the bed, hands clasped behind her head. Jolie jumped on the bed and burrowed under the covers. Gopher barked his displeasure at Jolie's one-upping him for bed privileges. Maggie bent over the side of the bed and picked him up. "If I ever need back surgery, I know who to blame," she told the basset hound. He ignored her, instead stretching out his full length alongside her as soon as she resumed lying down. Maggie stroked his silky coat, and he muttered an appreciative grunt.

She heard Gran humming in the living room, the hums accompanied by the sound of papers being sorted. Maggie thought of the memories her grandmother was sifting through. Death cleaning was one way of sorting out a person's affairs. She'd read about geriatric physicians who encouraged their patients to have end-of-life discussions with their families, which helped prevent nasty surprises after they passed. *Both are good choices*, Maggie thought. *Still, there's the bigger question . . . do you embrace mortality or run from it?*

Her mind began to wander, and she let it; stream of consciousness often led to revelations. She imagined herself as a mom admiring her child's handiwork from school. Not the extraordinary art young Xander produced, much as she loved everything he created, but the pipe cleaner flower bouquets and handprint Thanksgiving turkeys the average kid brought home, like her father's primitive bird drawing. She recalled a comment East had made when she'd asked if Pony Pickner had children: "None that he knew about." If the music manager had indeed been battling prostate cancer, had he made a choice regarding his mortality?

She finally surrendered to her body's plea for a nap. Her eyelids fluttered shut. A thought occurred to Maggie as she drifted off. *What if Pony wasn't paying a PI to find women he could pay off to avoid harassment accusations? What if he was looking for illegitimate children he sired?*

Then she succumbed to sleep.

Chapter 23

It was twilight when Maggie woke up. The alarm clock by her bed read six thirty PM, which meant she could catch the last few hours of *Cajun Country Live!*. The festival would culminate with Tammy's closing set. The singing star wasn't set to leave for Jazz Fest until the next morning, so Maggie estimated Pelican PD had about twelve hours to pursue her new theory that Pony might have been tracking down offspring instead of dodging sexual harassment lawsuits. She put a call in to Bo and shared it with him.

"Interesting. We'll definitely look into it." He yelled to be heard over the raucous sounds of the festival's final night.

"You sound distracted."

"I am. I'm doing double duty as detective and festival security guard. Using my breaks to work the case from our mobile unit here. Same with Ru. Have I mentioned strong-arming our new mayor into hiring more officers? Hey," he yelled. "Break it up, you two."

"I better let you go."

"Sorry, we got kids from both Pelican and Ville Blanc high school here. Apparently, there's a lot of shade-throwing on account of the upcoming parish baseball playoff. But your idea is solid. Gotta go; I see a coupla kids drinking from brown paper bags, and I'm guessing they're not hiding pop."

Bo signed off. Maggie changed into a clean *Cajun Country Live!* T-shirt. *I'm looking forward to retiring these*, she thought as her chest blasted yet another ad for the festival. She stopped in the kitchen, where she saw a note from Grand-mère, written on her personal stationery in her beautiful Catholic school handwriting. It was propped up against Maggie's to-go coffee cup, which steamed with freshly poured chicory coffee. *No update on Carina*, the note read. *I'm going to the festival with Lee, who wanted to have me carted around on a sedan chair like a pasha. I said no.*

Maggie giggled at the image of Gran gracing festivalgoers with a pageant wave from her sedan chair, then grabbed her car keys and took off for the festival's climax.

* * *

The minute Maggie parked and got out of her car, she sensed the evening had a different energy from past nights. It simmered with tension. The grounds were overcrowded, the green alley between the food booths crammed with cranky, hungry celebrants—"hangry," as the Poche sibs would label them—who traded glares as they bumped up against each other while waiting in long lines. The general mood wasn't helped by humidity topping one hundred percent. In some regions, a temperature drop followed rain. Not in Pelican—at least not on this night. Dry lightning flashed in the distance.

A pickup truck pulled up next to her. Maggie recognized it as belonging to Chret Bertrand, Gaynell's boyfriend. Sure enough, Chret hopped out of the driver's side. "Hey, Maggie."

"Chret, you're back from DC."

"Heard what all was going on with Gay and got here as fast as I could." He opened the truck's passenger door, and Gaynell hopped down from the cab.

"Gay!" Maggie and her friend embraced. "I didn't think you'd make it tonight. I figured you were recuperating."

Gaynell gave her boyfriend a warm smile, which he returned with a shy one. His fair skin turned red. "I felt better the minute Chret showed up," Gaynell said. "She squeezed his hand. "We'll see you later. We're going to the front of the music stage. Who knows, we might even dance tonight."

The couple set off in one direction, Maggie in another. She squeezed through the crowd, navigating knots of festivalgoers. By the time she reached the Crozats' booth, perspiration dripped from her brow and darkened her T-shirt with stains. "Wow, it's brutal tonight," she gasped. She pulled up the edge of her shirt and used it to wipe the sweat off her face. "As soon as you're done selling, you're free to head out."

"Oh, we sold out your stuff a while ago," Clinton said, smiling at a customer as he made change. "Sold out of my sweet potato pralines, too."

"Now we're selling *my* invention." Brianna held up a neatly wrapped praline. "Bacon maple."

She handed one to Maggie, who bit into it. She faked a swoon, then genuflected to the Poches. "I bow to you both. Never tell my mother or anyone from Bon Bon Sweets I said this, but you make the best pralines in town."

"You know it," Clinton said, as he sold six of them to a family.

"We were wondering if you'd pay us to break down the booth tomorrow," Brianna said. "We want to earn money for our new business." She threw her hands in the air in a *ta-da* gesture. "Poch-tastic Pralines."

"I like it," Maggie said. "And not only will I pay you to break down the booth, I'll pay you to pack up whatever artwork I didn't sell. You'd be doing me a big favor." The kids hooted and high-fived each other.

Maggie, who hadn't eaten dinner, slapped a five-dollar bill on the counter, helped herself to a second praline, and went hunting for Rufus. She'd finished both pralines by the time she found him scolding a couple of sullen tween boys. "I'll let you off this time," he said as he confiscated vaping paraphernalia, "but if I catch you Juuling again, you'll be all *Orange Is the New Black*-ing while you pick up roadkill on the side of I-10." The boys skulked off. Rufus took off his police hat and rubbed the top of his head. His sandy hair was so wet with sweat it looked like he'd just gotten out of the shower. "Every time you think kids can't come up with some stupid new thing to do, whaddya know, they do. I'm gonna have to raise my Charli in a tower like that Rapunzel chick."

"Ru, did Bo mention my idea to you?"

"About Pickner hunting down his mystery spawn? Sounds like a road. Artie's in the mobile unit drilling down into the guy's past. He told me to thank you for getting him an inside detail. This weather ain't pleasant for a man of his girth." A large sweat globule dropped from Ru's brow, splattering onto his shirt. "Or mine." He squinted into the distance. Maggie followed his gaze and saw two teen boys exchanging angry words. One wore a green-and-gold jersey in Pelican's team colors, the other Ville Blanc's blue-and-white theme. "Great, that's what this shindig needs," Rufus said. "A good old-fashioned rumble. 'Scuse me."

He tromped off to separate the rivals. Maggie continued toward the VIP trailer by the stage, determined to make use of what little time she had left with Tammy's entourage. She passed Lee and Grand-mère, who were wending their way through the crowds. Lee, although drenched himself, fanned Gran with a leftover I'M A FAN OF RUFUS DURAND swag fan as he walked alongside Pelican's grande dame. "You got yourself a good man," Maggie told her grandmother as they passed.

"I'll keep doing it till my arm gives out," Lee said, rubbing said arm.

"You're welcome to take a break, cher," the octogenarian responded, before stopping to accept a handshake from an appreciative local. "But a quick one."

Maggie kept going toward the VIP trailer. Her mission

was interrupted by Vanessa calling to her from the Fais Dough Dough booth. "Maggie, I got a couple of crawfish pies left. You want one?"

Maggie stopped. Delicious as Clinton's bacon maple pralines were, her stomach was still rumbling. She checked her phone. There was plenty of time before Tammy's last set to satiate her hunger, thus preventing it from being a distraction. She walked over to Van and accepted the offered hand pie. She took a large bite. "Delicious. Your recipe?"

"Sandy's." Vanessa motioned behind her, where, to Maggie's surprise, Sandy sat on a cooler tallying up receipts on a calculator. "We called a truce."

"I made a dozen of them pies as a peace offering," Sandy shared from her perch on the cooler. "We felt bad about getting into it at the baby shower like we did. Gaynell's kidnapping was a wake-up call for both of us. No more silly competition."

"It's all good, except I'm stuck with two hundred of these potholders," Vanessa said glumly. She held up a purple potholder decorated with the slogan MacIlhoney Brings the Heat in bold gold lettering.

Sandy eyed the potholders. "They're pretty. I'll take one. And you know what, since you already had 'em before we declared our truce, why don't you give them out? It'd be a shame if they went to waste."

Van brightened. "Really? You're okay with that?"

"Sure. Go. I'll look after the booth."

Vanessa squealed and hugged Sandy. "You are the *best*.

Back in a jiff." She picked up the box of potholders and darted out from behind the booth into the crowd.

"That was super nice of you, Sandy," Maggie said.

"There's no race, so what does it matter? And honestly, she would've made a much better first lady of Pelican than me. It's not who I am. I don't know why I got so competitive. I think it's because I know Vanessa hurt Ru when she dumped him, so I didn't want her to get a win. But he doesn't care about what happened anymore, so why should I?"

Maggie smiled at the dance instructor. "I think I'm looking at the reason he doesn't care anymore."

Sandy blushed. "That just earned you another crawfish pie."

"Thanks, but I'm okay." It occurred to Maggie that Pony's murderer was probably cooling his or her heels in Tammy's trailer. Butterflies replaced hunger in her stomach. She took a breath to steady her nerves, then left the booth for the trailer.

Tradition Jazz Band, a hometown favorite, had taken the stage. While Maggie waited for the private security guard overseeing the VIP area to vet her by contacting a member of the organizing committee—who happened to be Grand-mère—she listened to Tradition's skilled trumpeter bring the Dixieland favorite "Tailgate Ramble" to life. The guard returned her driver's license and nodded her past the ropes cordoning off the secured section of the festival.

Maggie traipsed through damp grass to the trailer housing Tammy and her collection of musicians and toadies.

She was about to knock on the flimsy trailer door when Valeria emerged. The backup singer wore a tight black tank top, equally tight black jean shorts, and black high-heeled sandals whose ties crossed her calves gladiator-style. Her mass of black hair hung loose, reaching below her shoulder blades. She faced backward into the trailer as she walked down its two steps. "Let me know how Jazz Fest goes," she called to someone inside. "Post lots of pictures." She turned around and saw Maggie. "Oh, hi."

"Hi. I wasn't expecting to see you here."

"I wanted to say goodbye to everyone. When you tour, you develop a bond like nothing else. Hard to fight that." Valeria sounded wistful.

"How's Bokie?"

"Out of the coma but not talking yet. The doctors think he'll be okay eventually, but he's gonna need tons of rehab. His insurance'll cover a big chunk; the rest'll have to come out of pocket. But that won't be a problem, because guess what?" Valeria crossed her arms in front of her chest, a sour look on her face. "I know Bokie's computer password—"

"Let me guess. It's *Valeria*."

The sour look softened. "That man is nothing if not predictable. I was worried about what his copay would be for all the help he's gonna need, so I got into his computer and checked out his online banking. Get this—I saw his direct deposit, and he was making way more than me. The bump was in separate payments from his contract salary. I thought we all were favored nations, but Bokie sure wasn't. Which is good news for him, and I'm glad about that. But still, I am major-league ticked off at that Pony, sneaking someone extra money like that. It's dirty pool."

"Bokie was secretly being paid more than the rest of you?" The revelation sent a jolt through Maggie. Valeria nodded, the sour look returning to her face. "Do you think that's true of any of the other band members? Could one of them be making more than you thought?"

Valeria shook her head. "Pretty much all of them complain all the time about the crappy pay. Wait, no—T.S. didn't. At least not as much."

Maggie's level of excitement surged.

"But that could just be him. He's got that Piloga exercise thing on the side. He probably complained less because he has more money."

"Probably," Maggie said, deflated.

"I gotta get going; I need to pack," Valeria said. "I'm moving to a motel near the hospital until we can fly Bokie back to LA for treatment. It's been nice getting to know you. Thanks for your support with everything. When I sell my book, I'll send you a signed copy."

"I thought you were putting the book on hold."

"On hold don't mean dead, honey." Valeria accompanied this with a Nae Nae dance move, a hand on her hip and another in the air as she rocked her hips. She finished with a finger snap, then strutted off.

Maggie thought about the info bomb Valeria had dropped. Was there a personal connection between Bokie and Pony that motivated the clandestine pay raise? Could the drummer be Pony's son? She closed her eyes and tried to recall Pony's features and then Bokie's, searching for a resemblance between the two. Usually her artist's eye embedded details like that in her brain. But she hadn't spent enough one-on-one time with Bokie to take a mental photograph of his face. She had to acknowledge another possible reason for Bokie's raise: blackmail. Maybe he'd stumbled across some secret Pony paid him to keep.

"Thank you, Pelican, good night!"

Tradition Jazz Band was signing off. Maggie glanced at a dry-erase board listing the evening's order. There was only one more act before Tammy's. She knocked on the trailer door.

"Who is it?" a voice Maggie recognized as Sara's called out.

"Maggie Crozat." There was a pause. Maggie swallowed her pride, then forced herself to add, "I came to apologize to Tammy."

The door flew open, and Sara, holding a phone to her ear, motioned for Maggie to come inside. Maggie did, and was immediately struck by the trailer's slightly cooler but still fetid air. Tammy's musicians were sprawled around in various states of undress. Even The Sound had shed his ubiquitous cotton tunic and gone with a bare chest. "I thought it would be cooler in here."

"Didn't we all," said Gigi, who was on her knees fixing the hem of an intricately beaded seafoam-green gown being modeled by Tammy.

"No sweating on this thing," Tammy said to her cousin. "I won't be able to return it to the designer."

"Don't worry; I'm being careful as can be." Gigi wiped

her brow with her forearm. "I can't wait to move to Los Angeles with ya, cuz. I tell you, I am looking forward to that dry heat."

A look passed between Tammy and Narcisse. Gigi missed it, but Maggie didn't. She forced herself to concentrate on the task at hand: selling a fake apology. "I wanted to stop by and say how sorry I am for blowing up the way I did, Tammy. It's been a stressful week, what with my engagement breaking up and then coming back together. But that's no excuse for my behavior."

"Apology accepted. In fact, let's toast to it. Narcisse, pour me and Maggie here shots of the Macallan. It's a twenty-one-year-old single malt that's heaven in a glass."

Narcisse did as instructed, sneaking a pour for himself as well. While Maggie waited, she glanced around the room, using a bored attitude to mask her goal of scouring each musician for a resemblance to Pony. Narcisse delivered shot glasses to Maggie and Tammy, who raised hers in a toast. "*Laissez les bon temps rouler!*" Maggie seconded this, and the women toasted.

"All right, everyone out, our star has to change," Sara said.

Gigi started for the door, but Tammy pulled her back. "Duh, not *you*, coz; you have to dress me. Everyone else, out, out, *out*."

The musicians roused themselves and shuffled toward the door. "Nice jeans," East said to The Sound. "They new?"

"Uh-huh. From All The Tribe. The only ones that fit me right."

In a flash, a revelation hit Maggie so hard it almost

knocked her off balance. When she'd met Pony, the first thing her artist's eye zeroed in on was his unusual build— short legs and an unusually long torso. *He'd be hard to shop for*, she'd thought. She'd never seen The Sound without his tunic. Now, as he stood in front of her shirtless, it was impossible to ignore the similarity. "You have the same build as Pony," she blurted out. The Sound stared at her. She cursed herself, wishing she could suck the words back in. Instead, she lied. "He complained about that. How it was hard to find pants or anything that fit right." She blathered on. "I can see where that would be a problem. It's hard when you don't have the usual body type. I've got a butt on me. I have trouble buying jeans, too. All The Tribe, huh? I'll have to try them. Do they have a website? Of course they have a website. Everyone does now."

Sara opened the trailer door and began herding everyone out. "Move, people."

"Yeah, why are y'all still here?" Tammy snapped at them. "Get *out*. We go on in, like, ten. Narcisse, make yourself useful."

"What?" Tammy's "security guard" pushed away the second shot of Macallan's he'd helped himself to and waved his arms at the others. "You heard her. Go. Git."

They got. Maggie, at the end of the line, chafed at the slow exit. She was anxious to break away and find Bo to report her discovery about The Sound. They were all finally outside when she suddenly heard an odd rumbling noise.

"What's going on there?" Uffen asked.

"Where?" Maggie strained to see around him.

"There."

Uffen pointed to what looked like a giant ball of humanity. People screamed and tried to get out of the way, but the ball grew as boys and men piled on. "It's a group fight," Maggie said, "and it's heading toward us!"

"Back in the trailer, back in the trailer," Sara yelled to musicians, pulling at them. The others stumbled back inside, but Maggie managed to extricate herself from the group. It was chaos on the field as Pelican and Ville Blanc fans fought each other. Bottles and food flew through the air. Parents grabbed their children and ran. The VIP security guard helplessly pushed back against the warring factions, shouting out "Whoa!" as the melee knocked him down and the VIP ropes with him. Maggie gave up searching for Bo and ran onto the stage to escape harm. From her vantage point, she could see every Pelican police officer on hand trying to break up the brawl. Sirens blared as patrol cars from Ville Blanc raced onto the field, disgorging more officers into the fray.

Maggie heard someone yelling a stream of foul language. Tammy stormed onto the stage, still wearing the green beaded dress she'd had on in the trailer. Gigi skittered behind her, holding up the gown's train. Tammy yanked the stage mic out of its stand. She put two fingers in her mouth, emitting a shrill whistle that prompted deafening feedback. The sound literally brought Maggie to her knees. She covered her ringing ears.

"*Hey*," the country singer yelled into the mic. "Knock it off, all of you." To Maggie's surprise, the crowd, already discombobulated by Tammy's whistle, broke apart. Yelling turned to confused muttering. "I planned my whole dang schedule around closing this dang festival so I could show y'all what it looks like when someone leaves this freaking cow town and gets a life," Tammy yelled at them. "Stop fighting so I can start singing! You hear me? *Now.*"

The combatants staggered to their feet and started to disperse. Maggie could make out Bo and Rufus, their uniforms askew from being caught up in the battle, pulling instigators from the crowd and cuffing them.

"That's better," Tammy said. "Now I'm gonna change, get my band together, and be back in a few. Y'all better behave yourselves till then. Oh, and Pelican PD, don't even think of shutting this shindig down. I came here as a star and I aim to leave as one."

Tammy stomped offstage, Gigi bringing up the rear as always. Maggie saw Bo load a couple of miscreants into the back of a squad car. Rufus was at the wheel. Bo got in on the passenger's side and the car squealed off. She pulled out her cell phone, sat back on her haunches, and called Bo. The call went to voice mail, so she sent him a text: THE SOUND RELATED TO PONY. TRUST ME ON THIS. She thought for a moment, then added, MOVE FAST! Given the circumstances, she knew that was doubtful. Maggie cursed herself for her slip to the keyboardist and vowed to work on her internal editor.

Roadies and technicians appeared on the stage. They fiddled with equipment, setting up for Tammy and her band. Maggie got off the stage and stood to one side. A minute later, East meandered onto it, followed by Uffen, and then Pixie, the Gator Girls' drummer. "Tammy hired me to fill in for that Bokie guy; can you believe the luck?" she called to Maggie as she hurried over to the drum kit.

"Not sure *luck* is the operative word here," Maggie muttered to herself.

A musician Maggie didn't know passed by. The accordion strapped to him marked the man as Toulouse's replacement. Sara, trying not to look frazzled, clambered up the steps. She made a show of checking the speakers. "Are we good to go?"

"Almost," East said, his focus on tuning his guitar. "All we need is a keyboard player."

"I saw him leave the trailer," Sara said. "He's not here?" East shook his head. Sara released a frustrated groan. She spoke into her headset. "Narcisse, find The Sound."

Maggie tried to tamp down a growing sense of foreboding. 'I'll help look for him," she told Sara. She didn't wait for a response. Instead she did a sweep of the VIP area, then searched behind the stage. There was no sign of the keyboardist.

Sara's voice came over the festival's loudspeaker system. "The Sound, please report to the stage. Please report to the stage immediately."

The lack of response confirmed what Maggie suspected.

The Sound was gone.

Chapter 24

"What do you mean, he's gone?"

Tammy's shriek when she found out her keyboard player was missing out-decibeled the sound system's feedback squeals. Maggie wasn't the only person who covered her ears. Tammy had changed into her "country girl" show outfit. Her custom-made high-heeled boots kept sinking into the wet soil, and she fought to keep her balance. "This is like one of those horror movies where people keep disappearing and winding up dead. Only it's *my* people."

She burst into tears backed up by genuine emotion, exposing a vulnerability Maggie had no idea existed. Maggie wanted to race over to Pelican PD and see if they'd tracked down The Sound, but instead she rested a comforting hand on Tammy's shoulder. "The police have been notified. I'm sure he'll be found."

"I really wanted to close the festival," Tammy said, still weeping. "I know I said mean things about the town, but I was angry. It's still my home. A little. Kind of."

"I'll fill in for him." Gaynell stepped through the huddle and stood in front of Tammy.

"You play keyboards too?" Tammy asked. Maggie noted that the singer said this without her usual snarkiness.

"What doesn't she play." Chret appeared behind his girlfriend. He put a protective arm around her waist.

"Here's an idea." This came from Sara. "Tammy, you'll invite the Gator Girls to join you onstage. The rest of you'll whoop and holler." She gestured to the other musicians. "You'll earn back points with the crowd for showcasing local talent, plus we'll fill the empty slots in the band. It's win-win."

"That's a good idea, but do you think they'd do it?" Tammy asked Gaynell. Maggie was surprised by the touch of insecurity in her tone.

Gaynell snorted. "Play with the most famous act outta Pelican? Are you kidding? I'm surprised they didn't hear that idea the way dogs hear a sound we can't, and rush over already."

Sara and Gaynell sprinted to the stage to summon the other Gator Girls. Maggie hastened to her car, positioning her Bluetooth over her ear as she ran. She hopped in and gunned the engine, then drove out of the grassy parking area, clinging to the steering wheel as each grassy bump threatened her control of the car. She finally got out of the lot and onto the side street, which she followed until she made it to the River Road. Her cell rang. She pressed the Bluetooth button to answer the call. "I got your message," Bo said. "I put out an APB about The Sound to everyone, including the state troopers. As soon as I finish processing the numbnuts who started the fight at the festival, I'm on it. Does the guy know you suspect him?"

"Yes," Maggie said, again regretting her slip of the tongue.

Bo sucked in his breath. Then he mustered an even tone and responded, "Drive straight home. Don't stop for a light; just drive. As soon as you get to Crozat, get whatever you need for protection and lock your whole family inside. Don't do anything else until you hear from me. Got that?"

Maggie nodded, then realizing that nerves had made her nod to the air instead of an actual human being, said, "Got it."

"I'll call or text you updates."

The call ended. Maggie gripped the wheel. She stared straight at the road ahead, following Bo's instructions, merely glancing both ways at stop signs and traffic lights before ignoring them. As she drew closer to home, she allowed herself to relax a little. That's when she saw a truck parked on top of the levee—a tricked-out black pickup truck with gold spinners.

Maggie, eager to alert Bo to the sighting, pressed the button on her Bluetooth. No response. "Great, now you choose to die on me?" She pulled it off her ear and threw it on the passenger's side of the bench seat, then pulled off to the side of the road. She texted Bo. A few seconds later, her cell sent an alert that the message hadn't gone through. Certain stretches of the road between cell towers offered spotty service, and Maggie had somehow parked in one of those stretches. She started her engine and pressed the accelerator. The wheels of the Falcon spun, but the car didn't move. She got out to see what was causing the problem and gave another groan when she saw that where she'd parked had been turned into a virtual swamp by the day's earlier rains. Only a tow truck would be able to extricate the old convertible. Maggie tried resending her text and got the same annoying red exclamation mark, plus the words NOT DELIVERED.

Despite the cover of night, Maggie felt exposed. The full moon cast a light on her that she ducked as she crept along the side of the road looking for a cell signal. She heard a car door slam and hid behind bushes. She peeked between branches of dense foliage and saw The Sound had gotten out of the truck. Maggie turned off the ringer on her phone, not wanting to risk a sudden call revealing where she was.

The keyboard player began walking down the river side of the levee toward the batture. The location suddenly looked familiar. On the other side of the levee lay the Harmonie Plantation ruins, the final stop on the "My Memories of Pelican" tour Tammy had forced upon her retinue.

Despite the recent rain, snowfall in the northern reaches of the Mississippi had been light the previous winter, meaning less melt-off flowed into the river. The trip with Tammy had revealed that while part of the batture was underwater, a good chunk of it dodged flooding. *Why is he going there?* Maggie wondered. She recalled the old plantation's disintegrating dock. Could he have arranged to be picked up by boat?

Maggie tapped another text to Bo on her cell, this time with the specifics about Harmonie to help him pinpoint the location. She pocketed the phone, praying there'd be a signal between the road and the ruins, and the message would send. Then she darted across the empty street and climbed up the levee. If The Sound was escaping by boat, at least she'd be able to tell the police which way he'd headed.

At the top of the levee, she hid behind the pickup truck, then peeked around it. There was no sign of the keyboard player. She began the trek down the river side of the levee, moving slowly and carefully, avoiding dead leaves or branches whose crunch might give her away. It grew darker inside the tangle of wild brush, and Maggie longed for the moonlight she'd resented moments earlier. An errant branch caught her hair, yanking her back. She managed to free herself but almost lost her balance. Maggie had serious second thoughts about her plan as she grabbed the branch's tree trunk and righted herself.

For a moment, she debated turning back. Then she heard a splash. Maggie hastened as fast as she could through the plant detritus until she found a viable vantage point. She positioned herself behind a scrubby tree. The view between its branches gave her a clear visual line to the abandoned, rotting dock. But no motorboat sat at its end waiting for The Sound. Instead he was pushing the pirogue, which didn't appear to be in much better shape than the dock, into the water. The musician grabbed a piece of driftwood and jumped into the canoe. He used the driftwood to row, battling against the river's current. Maggie inched closer. The pirogue was taking on water. It was slowly sinking. The Sound was in danger of drowning.

Maggie couldn't watch the man die before her eyes. In the distance was the faint sound of a river patrol boat's siren. She checked her phone. The text had gone through. "The Sound, help's coming," she yelled, remaining behind the tree for security. "Paddle back to shore."

The musician turned at the sound of her voice. "Oh, hey there, Maggie." His tone was bizarrely upbeat. "I guess I shouldn't be surprised you found me. You're a big step above the other yokels around here." He began humming a song. Then he sang a verse: *"When the night comes crashing down, when the darkness is your soul, when there's no one else around, I dream of you to make me whole.* Pretty good, huh? I wrote that."

"I don't know what happened between you and Pony—"

He ignored her. "It's how I felt my whole life. A hole needing to be made whole."

"The Sound, listen to me—"

"You don't have to call me that anymore. Use my real name. Paul. Boring old Paul. You know who else was really named Paul? Pony Pickner."

The police boat siren grew louder, but it was still out of sight. Paul, aka The Sound, stopped rowing. The pirogue continued to sink while being pulled downriver by the Mississippi's current. Maggie hated feeling helpless, but she knew if she waded into the water and tried to pull the boat to safety, Paul would fight her in a battle that could take them both down. Suddenly she saw the police boat round a bend in the river. "Hold on, Paul," she called to him. "Help's almost here."

He cocked his head to one side, an amused look on his face. "You're assuming I want help."

"You don't want the river to take you; it's a terrible way to go," Maggie said. *Please let the police boat get to him, please let it get to him.*

The pirogue picked up speed as it drifted downriver. Maggie noticed the old rope swing suspended from a tree branch by only a few threads. She gave up her hiding place and ran to the tree. "Oh, I see you now," Paul said from his sinking vessel. "Much better."

Maggie yanked on the rope. There was a loud snap and it came down, bringing the branch with it, toppling her to the ground. She clambered to her feet and ran to the shoreline, dragging the branch and rope with her. "You don't want to drown." She was out of breath as she tried to keep pace with the pirogue. She threw the rope into the water, holding tight to the branch at its other end. "Grab the rope. I can help pull you to shore."

Paul ignored her plea and the rope slowly sank, disappearing into the murky water. "You're right," he said. "Drowning would suck. There has to be a different way to end this. Hey, I just came up with a great song title—'It's You or Me.'"

He pulled a semiautomatic pistol out of his back jeans pocket. Maggie dropped to the ground. She didn't see the keyboard player aim the gun at his head.

But she heard him pull the trigger.

Chapter 25

Maggie sat on Crozat's porch swing, still wrapped in the emergency blanket provided by the first responders at the site of Paul's death. She stared into the pitch-black, toward the levee across the River Road from her family's home. The sound of the police boat's siren had faded long ago. It was four in the morning now, but she was too wired from the evening's dramatic events to go to bed. She'd given her statement to a state trooper who'd shown up moments after the keyboard player took his own life. She'd left as soon as she could after that, unnoticed by the law enforcement official's fellow troopers who'd quickly swarmed the scene, along with Bo, Rufus, and other Pelican PD officers.

The air was warm, but with an edge of dampness that added a chill to it. The only sound came from mourning doves nesting in the veranda's rafters. Maggie found their sad coos weirdly comforting. She knew instinctively that Paul, aka The Sound, was Pony's son. She also knew, as a therapist in New York once told her, that feelings weren't facts, although in Pelican intuition was respected enough to be fact-adjacent. What she still couldn't figure out was the circumstances that had driven the musician to murder and attempted murder.

She pulled the blanket tighter and slowly rocked back and forth in the swing, searching for answers. They didn't come. Lulled by the swing's gentle motion and the doves' soft warbling, exhaustion overwhelmed her. The emergency blanket slipped to the ground. She never heard her father, who came out when dawn broke, discovered his sleeping daughter, and covered her with a warm quilt handed down through generations of Crozats.

*　*　*

Sunday morning, Maggie was back on the veranda, rested and rejuvenated, waiting for the friends who would join her for a trip down to the New Orleans Jazz & Heritage Festival. The Gator Girls were performing with Tammy Barker during her set—sans Gaynell. After the brief display of vulnerability during the last night of *Cajun Country Live!*, the singing star had reverted to her old ways. "If we're both onstage, people would get confused," Tammy had told Gaynell. The nonsensical statement was a head-scratcher. Maggie came up with an acidic explanation: "People will get confused because you have more talent than she does, and they'll wonder why she's the headliner." But Gaynell was so relieved to be un-kidnapped and cleared of all criminal charges that she didn't care about Tammy's petty jealousy. Eager to support her bandmates, she was already at Jazz Fest.

Ione pulled up to the front of the manor house in an ancient, battered Honda Civic. She got out and held up the hem of her dashiki-inspired sundress as she climbed Crozat's five front steps. Maggie reached out her arms, and the women hugged. "I haven't seen you since that man shot himself," Ione said.

"It's only been two days. Although it feels much longer."

"Seeing what you saw can do that to a person. Did you ever find out what happened? He's the one who killed the manager, isn't he?"

Bo's SUV turned into the plantation's long, decomposed granite driveway and headed to the manor house, staggering over each bump in the irregular drive like a drunken sailor. "Let's wait until Bo gets here. He knows way more than I do."

Bo parked and hopped out of the truck's cab. He wore his usual jeans, but instead of a button-down shirt and jacket, his torso was clad in a white T-shirt that highlighted a muscular set of abs. He'd picked up a tan while working security at *Cajun Country Live!*. Combined with chiseled features and dark coloring, it enhanced the Native American genes in his bloodline. Maggie was overwhelmed with a sudden desire to grab his hand and yank him into the bushes for a steamy rendezvous. She calmed herself down by imagining a bucket of cold water being dumped on her head.

Bo bounded up the steps and gave Maggie a quick kiss. Then he stepped back and surveyed her with an admiring glance. "You look pretty." Knowing the Jazz Fest fairgrounds could be blistering hot, Maggie had opted for a short, form-fitting romper that offered the added advantage of showcasing her shapely legs. The outfit's olive color brought out the green in her hazel eyes.

Ione mock-fanned herself. "A little hot here. Maybe I should find my own ride to Jazz Fest."

"No worries, we'll control ourselves," Bo said with a grin. "Besides, we're all going with Vanessa and Quentin, who probably wouldn't appreciate us canoodling in his Bentley."

"Although I wouldn't mind throwing our reconciliation in Van's face a bit," added Maggie, who was still smarting from Vanessa's lack of faith in her and Bo's relationship going the distance.

"If you're open to a change of subject, I've got some updates." Bo leaned against one of Crozat's wide pillars. The women both clamored "Yes" and sat opposite him on the B and B's glistening white Adirondack chairs. "Pony's lawyer, Jim Newman, finally finished rehab and got back to me. Since his client is deceased, Newman's allowed to disclose information to me for the purposes of probate."

Ione made a *hurry it along* gesture with her hand. "Okay, disclaimer over, get to the dirt."

"Yes, ma'am. My brilliant and talented fiancée here gets points for her hunch that Pony was looking for offspring, not harassment claims. He did have prostate cancer, which had progressed to stage three by the time it was diagnosed. It was local stage, which means it hadn't spread, so the survival rate is excellent. Still, according to Newman, the scare got Pony thinking about the future and his legacy. His private eye winnowed down the guy's field of conquests over the years and discovered some possible contacts. He posted Pony's DNA to a bunch of genealogy websites, using an alias that disguised the manager's identity. He found four people who might be Pony's birth kids. Two were ruled out. Pony hired the other two, who were musicians, for this tour so he could secretly collect their DNA and confirm the relationships. He'd had affairs with the mothers of the other musicians he hired for the tour, but their families hadn't signed up for any ancestry sites, so he got DNA samples through bottles or cups they drank from and his PI took it from there."

"It makes sense Pony's actual children would be musicians," Maggie said. "According to my online searches, he pretty much slept with either groupies or female artists. There was a good chance any kids he sired would either have music in their genes or gravitate toward the field."

Bo resumed telling the story. "DNA confirmed Pony's paternity in both cases, so he had his PI dig into their backgrounds to vet them. At the end of the tour, Pony planned to reveal to them that he was their father and they'd be the beneficiaries of his estate. But the PI discovered one of the two was engaged in criminal activity. There was evidence this particular offspring—The Sound, aka Paul—was running a thriving opioid ring through his Piloga businesses. There was Downward Dog in the studio and drug sales in the back room. Rather than turn this information over to the police, Pony, being an arrogant control freak, decided to confront his newly discovered son and lay a triple whammy on him: First, he told The Sound he was his birth father. Then he shared what the PI uncovered and said he that the musician was supposed to be in his will but now wouldn't be. And third, he said he'd be reporting The Sound's illegal activities to the authorities. These boneheaded moves set him up to be murdered."

"How do you know all this?" Ione asked.

"Pickner put his plan into a letter he mailed to Newman on the day he died. If it weren't for Newman's rehab stint, we could have ended the whole thing days ago. Instead of a dead keyboard player being fished out of the Mississippi, he'd be in jail facing dealing, money laundering, and murder charges. By the way, LAPD discovered something interesting when they busted the 'Piloga' studio. One of the dealers operating from it was smuggling more than drugs across the border. Want to guess what else?"

Maggie's mind was blank for a minute; then it hit her. "Exotic animals."

Bo nodded. "Snakes, mostly. Venomous ones banned in the U.S. One of the things this guy confessed to when he was scrounging around for a plea deal was selling a Mexican pit viper to The Sound. Pony's offspring was a real sick piece of work."

"One of his offspring," Maggie said. "He had two. The Sound was Cain. So, who's Abel?"

"Valeria Aguilar," Bo said.

Maggie gaped at her fiancé. "Valeria? She's Pony's daughter?" Bo nodded. "I don't know why, but that never occurred to me. I guess because they were so different."

"Valeria was raised by a single mother in Manhattan. The woman was a session singer years ago but got out of the business once her daughter was born and pursued a more stable career as an office manager."

"My money was on Bokie."

"So was Pony's. Literally. That's why he secretly paid Bokie more. According to Newman, he spoke very highly of him and was disappointed the guy wasn't his son. Bokie's mother was one of Pony's flings. But he didn't father her child."

"What a story." Ione made a face and put her hands on her head. "Wait, if Pony thought all these musicians could be his kids—"

"Except for Tammy Barker; she was a legit client. Her tour is what gave him the idea to pull together his potential offspring, some new to him, some musicians he'd actually worked with before."

"But it means he even had a little somethin' somethin' with that boy Toulouse's mama."

"I guess Petite, Louisiana, is as good a place for a fling as any when you're on tour."

"By the way, I gave Miss Zenephra a call yesterday to see how Toulouse is doing," Maggie said. "Quentin got him a plea deal where he'll be sent to a mental health facility rather than do time for Gaynell's kidnapping, since she refused to press charges. When he's ready, Miss Zenephra's s going to bring him home with her. She hopes that eventually he'll start playing with some local bands like he used to. Toulouse is so talented, I think they'll welcome him back."

Bo shifted his weight, then yawned and stretched. His T-shirt rose up, revealing a few inches of a very taut stomach. "Easy, girl," Ione whispered to Maggie, who couldn't help giggling.

"So," he said, oblivious to Maggie's hormonal surge, "the way things shake down, Valeria will inherit Pony's estate. She's putting aside her tell-all for now to focus on helping with Bokie's recovery from the injury he sustained when The Sound conked him on the head at Belle Vista. You were right, Maggie, someone was threatened when they heard Bokie yell to Valeria that he had some good dirt for her book. But it was The Sound, not Toulouse."

"Glad as I am that Valeria will be there for Bokie, it's too bad about her book," Maggie said. "It is one great read."

Ione stood up. Following Bo's lead, she also stretched. "Better get the kinks out now before we stuff ourselves into Quentin's car."

Maggie stared down the end of the driveway. "We're not going in his car."

She pointed to a blinged-out party bus rolling toward them. A speaker on the roof shared Dixieland jazz with the world. White chaser lights surrounded all the windows. Colored lights rimmed the hubcaps. The bus came to a stop and its door sprung open. Quentin, wearing a vest bedecked with musical notes, jumped out, followed by Vanessa, wearing a dress featuring the same pattern. The driver of the bus appeared next. To the surprise of the onlookers, it was Rufus, wearing the same vest as Quentin. Next out was Sandy—wearing the same dress as Vanessa.

"What all's goin' on here?" Bo asked, amused.

Quentin gleefully threw open his arms. "Why wait until Jazz Fest to get this party started?"

"I think Bo means . . ." Maggie gestured back and forth between the couples. "This. Your outfits. It's nice to see détente between y'all, but this is a whole lotta détente."

"We wanted to show the world that we've moved past our petty squabbles," Vanessa said, taking a spin to model her dress. Maggie grew dizzy watching the busy pattern swirl by. "I'm just sorry my dressmaker ran out of fabric before we could make y'all matching outfits."

"Not as sorry as we would've been if she hadn't," Bo muttered to Maggie, who put a hand over her mouth to hide a laugh.

Quentin clapped his hands together. "All righty, my friends, let's get this party on the road. We don't want to miss the Gator Girls' Jazz Fest debut."

"I'd be a lot more excited if Gaynell was debuting with them," Maggie said as they loaded onto the bus.

"We all would, chère." Quentin handed her a frozen daiquiri. "Drown your sorrows in this. And there's more where it came from. *Allons-y*, my friends. *Laissez les bon temps par-tay!*"

Chapter 26

It was one of those days Jazz Fest celebrants pray for—sunny, dry, humidity a mere ninety percent. The fairgrounds were packed with music lovers, many holding gaily decorated umbrellas to shield them from the sun and dance with whenever a second line broke out. The air hummed with a cacophony of sounds—excited conversations, music from the ten stages and tents, cheers for various acts, even band devotees singing along to their favorite group's tunes. A cloud of delicious scents from the food areas hovered over the entire festival, seasoning the air with a mix of Cajun, Creole, Asian, Caribbean, and other foods from cultures all over the world.

"I forgot how much I love Jazz Fest," Maggie said to the others as a security guard led them behind the primary main stage to the area, where acts cooled their heels before their sets. She cast a longing glance at the stand selling the one and only genuine Crawfish Monica. It was eleven fifteen in the morning, and the line already looped around itself. Time wouldn't allow for a wait. She'd have to ask Ninette to make her version of the dish when she got home.

The security guard led the way behind metal barriers and deposited the group in front of trailers that served as both dressing and green rooms for the stage's acts. A few of the Gator Girls lounged at the folding tables and chairs set up in the middle of the area. Pixie waved to them. "If you're looking for Gaynell, she's in that one," the drummer said, pointing to one of the trailers. "She just got back from doing a mascara run for Tammy."

Maggie flushed with anger. "It's not enough for Tammy to dismiss Gaynell? She has to turn her into an errand girl?"

Bo put a hand on her shoulder. "Calm yourself, chère. We're here to support our friends, so leave it be."

Maggie reluctantly held her tongue. Her anger dissipated when she saw Uffen and East emerge from the second trailer on the site. Both men looked exhausted. Uffen didn't even notice the underage teen girls on the other side of the barriers trying to get his attention. "Be right back," she said to Bo. She walked over to the musicians. "I'd ask how you're holding up, but the answer is on your faces."

Uffen responded with a mirthless chuckle. "Finding out that your mother slept with your boss and you might be related to him but you're not, but two of your bandmates *are*, or rather were, and one was also running a lucrative opioid business, but he was about to be busted so he offed himself . . . it can age a fella."

"Uh-huh," East said, nodding vigorously.

"Are you going to continue with Tammy's tour?"

The musicians simultaneously shook their heads. "I'm going home to my girl and our baby-to-be," East said. "I'm gonna be the father I never had. Maybe do some research of my own and find out who he was. My mother either didn't know or didn't want me to know. It's hard growing up with big questions about who you are, where you came from. I don't want that for my kid."

"And I am all about this brave new world of DNA testing," Uffen said. "I'll be crossing the pond to my homeland and acquiring the spittle of my mother and father. Or is he really my father? To be continued. Besides," the guitarist added, this time with a genuine smile, "I can't stand Tammy's new music."

"Dude, it *sucks*," East said. "I'm so glad I'm not alone on that."

Maggie left the two musicians bonding over their mutual hatred of Tammy's new pop sound and returned to the others. The door to Tammy's trailer opened. The singer appeared, carrying a giant travel mug. She was followed down the stairs by Narcisse, Sara, and Gigi. Gaynell was the last one out. Her face lit up when she saw her friends, and she came to them. "Chret's saving us lawn space by the front of the stage," she said.

"You're sure you're okay only watching?" Maggie asked.

"Totally," Gaynell said with an undeniable sincerity. "My turn will come."

"Yes, it will. And you will *own* Jazz Fest."

Maggie said this loudly for Tammy's benefit, but the singer wasn't paying attention. She did a few vocal warm-ups, then took a sip of her beverage. "That's some big container," Rufus said.

"After all that rain up in Pelican, I felt like I might be getting a cold, so Gigi made this brew for me. It better work, because it sure tastes horrible." She waved a hand at Pixie. "Hey, Gator Girls, over here. Not you, Gaynell."

"Why not?" Maggie blurted.

She was instantly the focus of everyone's attention. "It's okay, Maggie," Gaynell said under her breath.

"You know what? It's not." Having opened her mouth, Maggie decided not to shut it. "What exactly is your problem with Gaynell, Tammy?"

"It's not any of your business."

"*Wrong.* It's all of our business. You made it that way by trying to drag our friend down."

The singer's eyes flashed. "Oh, you wanna go there? I'll go there. Miss Gaynell here knows exactly what the problem is."

"Huh?" The expression on Gaynell's face was utter bewilderment.

Tammy snorted. "Oh please, don't pretend you don't know."

"Actually," Gaynell said, "I don't."

"Yes, you do."

"No, I don't, Tammy. Really. I don't."

"She doesn't," Maggie threw in as confirmation. "So tell us, Tammy. What is your big problem with her? Or is it plain old, very ugly, jealousy?"

The others watched transfixed. "If this were a TV show, they'd go to commercial break right now," Rufus said.

"Ain't that right," Quentin agreed.

Tammy's lower lip quivered. She spoke directly to Gaynell. "You broke up me and your brother Arnaud."

"*What?*" Gaynell stared at the singer, dumbfounded. "That's crazy talk. I never did no such thing."

"Yeah, you did. He told me. He said *you* said there could be only one star in the family and it was you, so he had to break up with me." Gaynell opened and closed her mouth, too speechless to form words. But Tammy was on a weepy roll. "I wanted to get married. My whole life would be different. Well, I'd still be one of the biggest stars on the planet, but he'd be by my side cheering me on. Thanks to you, he ain't."

Gaynell found her voice. "Tammy, I never said any of that. I hate to tell you this, but Arnaud made it up as an excuse to break up with you."

Tammy folded her arms in front of her chest and stared down Gaynell. "I don't believe it. You're just saying that cuz you don't want to own what you did."

"I swear on a Bible. It's how he operates. He did the same thing with other girlfriends, only he told different lies."

Tammy uncrossed her arms. "He lied to me to get out of the relationship?"

"'Fraid so. He's always been a big old coward."

The angry expression on the singing star's face faded,

replaced by embarrassment. "I'm sorry, Gaynell. I can't believe Arnaud did that. I have half a mind to call him and tell him off."

"Uh . . ." Gaynell took her phone out of her back pocket. "Maybe you should see what he looks like these days before you make that call." She thumbed through her phone, then held it up to the singer. "Here."

Tammy took the phone and checked out the photo. Embarrassment morphed into an expression of distaste. "Wow. Talk about not aging well." Maggie glanced at the phone and saw a photo of an obese, gap-toothed man in a chef's uniform holding up a thirty-two-ounce beer can as he flashed a victory sign.

"What's he look like? I wanna see."

Pixie and the Gator Girls huddled around Tammy, but the singer quickly handed the phone back to Gaynell. "Best to leave things be."

Sara clapped her hands to get everyone's attention. "Hello, we have a set coming up, anyone remember that? What're we here for? Enough boyfriend drama. Focus, people."

"Right," Tammy said. She took a big swallow of the brew in her travel mug and addressed the Gator Girls. "I just wanna confirm that as soon as I finish 'My Loving Country Heart,' y'all get off the stage and the dancers get on it, so I can show off my new numbers."

"You've told us this a bunch of times, so consider it confirmed." Pixie's tone was bright, but Maggie picked up more than a hint of annoyance.

Tammy took another sip of her drink. "Sara, you got what we need for the quick change into my pop outfit behind the dancers?"

Sara held up a bomber jacket decorated with gangster-style graffiti. "I've got it right here."

"Good, I don't want—I don't want anything—" Tammy's faced turned red. She began gasping for air. She dropped her travel mug and clasped her hands around her throat.

"Oh my God," Sara cried out. "What's happening?"

Tammy's face began to swell up. Rufus and Bo instantly went into law enforcement mode. Rufus called for medical backup while Bo focused on Tammy. "You're having an allergic reaction." Bo reached for her, but she staggered away from him. "Do you have an EpiPen?"

"It's in her purse. I'll get it." Sara ran into the trailer.

"Shellfish," Tammy gasped out. "Poisoned. *You.*"

The singer pointed an accusing finger at Gaynell. Shocked, Gaynell opened her mouth to defend herself. But before she could, Gigi spoke up. "Not her. *Me.*" Tammy's cousin said this with malevolent pride.

Sara flew out of the trailer, almost tumbling down the steps. "It's not there! Her EpiPen's gone."

Gigi hovered over Tammy, who had fallen to her knees. "You think I don't know what's been going on? How you moved in on my husband? How the two of you were planning to move to Los Angeles *without me?*" An ambulance, siren blaring, pulled up next to the holding area. "I know why you stayed at Crozat instead of Belle Vista, why you rented out the whole place. It was easier to cat around with Narcisse. Well, guess what? I loaded that drink of yours with crawfish juice. That's why it tasted so awful. You want your EpiPen? Try and get it."

Gigi pulled the pen out of her pocket and waved it in the air. Bo grabbed the pen from her and stuck it in Tammy's thigh. The singer screamed, and then passed out. But the color began returning to her face and her breathing slowly normalized.

Rufus called NOPD while Bo used his belt to secure Gigi's hands behind her back until law enforcement arrived. The EMTs loaded Tammy onto a gurney. "I'm Tammy's manager; I'll go with her," Sara said. She hopped into the back of the ambulance, which careened off the field.

The others watched, reeling from the whirlwind of events. "Did we get this whole thing wrong?" Maggie asked, trying to make sense of the bizarre new development. "Tammy thought she was the original target." She faced Gigi. "Did you try to kill your cousin and get Pony instead?"

Gigi, who was struggling to break free from Bo's tight grip, gave up the fight. She burst into tears. "No, I swear I didn't," she said between sobs and hiccups. "I only found out about Tammy and Narcisse hooking up when I was making her stupid drink and heard those dumbbell dancers talking about how Narcisse was 'puttin' the body into bodyguard, if you know what I mean. And I knew *exactly* what she meant."

Gigi threw the last comment at her husband with a fury so frightening that the rest of the onlookers took a step back from her. An NOPD patrol car sped up to the scene, and two officers jumped out. They relieved Bo of the attempted murderess and cuffed her. "Thanks, we'll take it from here," the senior officer said.

The officers marched Gigi toward the patrol car. "You might want to go with your wife," Bo said to Narcisse.

"Huh?" Narcisse, who'd stood slack-jawed through the wild turn of events, snapped out of his fog. "Right, yeah, I guess." A smug grin spread across his face. "Never had two chicks fighting over me before."

He loped over to the NOPD patrol car. The officers were about to load Gigi into the back seat when she wriggled away and kicked her leg backward, straight into her husband's groin. He collapsed, moaning in pain. "I'm all yours, fellas," she told the stunned officers, who carefully maneuvered her into the car.

"Pro move," Rufus said.

Bo nodded. "We'll have to watch out for that one in the future."

The patrol car and ambulance left the grounds. For a moment, no one spoke. "So . . ." Pixie said. "Now what?"

"Now," Maggie said, "it's Gaynell's turn."

* * *

Gaynell protested but caved to the entreaties of her own band, backed up by support from East and Uffen, Tammy's two remaining musicians. Adopting the philosophy that it was better to beg forgiveness than ask permission, Maggie hustled everyone onto the stage before the event organizers had a chance to squash her plan. East explained the last-minute change to the audience, whose disappointment changed to enthusiasm as soon as Gaynell and the Gator Girls launched into their impossible-to-resist set. For the final number, Gaynell got to play her song "Forget the Past" as the lovely ballad it had always been meant to be.

"That went pretty well," Rufus commented as Gaynell and the others exited the stage after their third encore.

"And the award for understatement of the year goes to . . ." Maggie motioned to Rufus with both hands.

The group headed to the holding area, where the musicians huddled together congratulating each other. Gaynell extricated herself and approached Maggie. Her blonde curls were matted with perspiration, her T-shirt soaked through. She couldn't have looked happier. Maggie smiled at her friend. "Today was a game-changer for you and the Gator Girls. You know that, right? Everyone's talking about how y'all stepped in and owned the stage."

"I'm just glad it went well," Gaynell, ever modest, said.

Chret came over and handed his girlfriend a towel. Gaynell took it and wiped her face. "We need to celebrate," Chret said. "I'll get some beers."

"Thanks, chère." Gaynell collapsed into a chair, and Maggie sat down next to her. "I don't know how to thank you. For everything."

"Just keep writing and playing music."

Gaynell gave her a half smile. "Yes, ma'am." She blew out a breath. "Phew, what a night. Can you believe Gigi tried to kill her own cousin?"

"Yes, I can, considering the cousin was having an affair with her husband. Nothing like that to unbind the ties that bind." Maggie shaded her eyes with her hand. The sun was beginning to set, casting a glare from the west. "I owe you an apology, Gay. I never should have gotten in Tammy's face like I did. She was right when she said it wasn't any of my business."

"Don't worry about it. At first, I was all *uh-oh*. But then the truth came out and cleared things up."

"Sort of. It didn't stop her from accusing you of doctoring her drink."

"That's true," Gaynell acknowledged.

"I'm still trying to process that photo of your brother. You two don't look anything alike."

Gaynell's half smile turned into a wide grin. "That's because we're not related."

Maggie sat up straight. "Excuse me?"

"I get how Tammy operates now. She wants what she can't have. And I do *not* want that to be my brother Arnaud. Here's what he really looks like."

Gaynell pulled up a photo on her phone and showed Maggie. A drop-dead gorgeous man stared back at her, his blonde hair tousled, a come-hither look in his bright-blue eyes. He was shirtless, clad only in a fireman's rubber pants and suspenders. "Wowee wow wow."

"That's from the Hot Firemen of Shreveport annual calendar. It's a fund raiser. They do really well."

"I bet. But who's the other guy, the one in the photo you showed Tammy?"

Gaynell shrugged. "Got me. I just googled CHUBBY CHEFS."

Maggie's own phone pinged a text, and she checked it. "Bo. It's like he knew I was looking at that picture of your brother."

Gaynell laughed. "Some of the musicians were talking about meeting up at a place on Frenchman Street tonight to jam. Want to come?"

Maggie held up her phone. "Thanks, but I think I'll go for some quality time with my hot policeman." Her cell alerted her to a new text. She read it and squealed. "After we go see Lia and her babies . . . because Kyle just texted me her water broke and they're delivering them right now!"

Gaynell shrieked with glee. The women grabbed each other by the shoulders and jumped up and down. Then Maggie called to the others, "Hey, y'all, fire up the party van. We got some newborns to welcome into the world!"

Epilogue

A week after they debuted, the Bruner triplets—two girls and a boy—left the hospital with their parents. They were welcomed home by godparents Maggie and Bo, along with a freezer full of meals for Mom and Dad provided by the good citizens of Pelican. Kyle and Lia chose to name the infants after her African ancestors. "I found a registry website while I was on bed rest," Lia told her friends. "It goes all the way back to the late eighteenth century and even lists the countries they came from." The baby girls were named Kika and Asha, the baby boy Jabari.

With *Cajun Country Live!* over for the year, Maggie returned to her job as art collection specialist at Doucet Plantation. She also launched a free art class for local children, using the teaching skills she'd developed in her private classes with Xander. The boy joined the group—along with Esme, who, now lovestruck by his talent, made sure her easel was always next to his.

Tammy Barker debuted her new sound at a "listening party" in Los Angeles, and the tabloids gleefully reported that it bombed. She blamed her "inexperienced" manager, Sara Salinas, and fired her. Sara didn't care. She was busy lining up tour dates and a recording deal for Gaynell and the Gator Girls.

Maggie and Bo batted around a few more potential wedding dates, then stopped worrying about it. The drama wrought by Pony Pickner's murder earned them some downtime to simply enjoy each other's company. After a particularly lusty night of enjoyment, Maggie joked that her fiancé could be the cover boy for a "Sexy Cops of Pelican" calendar. When this comment got back to Rufus, the joke became a reality, and a fund-raiser was born—only with Rufus as the cover boy.

And Grand-mère finally got to meet Carina Albieri.

* * *

Carina responded to Gran's messages with an address and a time to meet. GPS led Maggie and Gran to a gaily painted Creole cottage in the Bywater neighborhood of New Orleans. Maggie parked the Falcon on the grassy embankment that ran alongside the street's sidewalk. She helped Grand-mère out of the car's passenger side onto the sidewalk. Gran slammed the heavy car door shut behind her. She smoothed her dark-navy linen slacks and adjusted the bow on her pale-blue silk blouse. She'd dressed in the colors of her sorority, Kappa Kappa Gamma, a choice Maggie knew she made when she needed a boost of confidence. "Are you ready?" she asked.

Gran nodded. They proceeded up the home's front steps

and rang the doorbell. "Coming," a voice called from inside. Seconds later, the door opened and a stunning woman around Ninette's age stood on the threshold. She was taller by a full head than Maggie's petite mother and wore her gray hair in a stylish short cut. She wore khaki slacks and a T-shirt that read LOYOLA NOLA. The woman, who exuded warmth, opted for hugs instead of handshakes. "I'm Carina. Come in, come in."

Maggie and Gran followed Carina into a living room decorated with midcentury furniture that somehow harmonized with the old home's original decorative molding and carved cypress fireplace. Iced tea and a selection of pastries were laid out on a Danish Modern coffee table. Maggie and Gran took seats on the room's sleek, upholstered sofa. Carina settled in a matching chair opposite them. "I'm sorry for my spotty correspondence," she said. "It's the end of the semester and I'm up to my eyeballs in term papers. I'm a classical studies prof at Loyola."

"Please, I'm grateful you responded at all," Gran said. "We've yet to officially introduce ourselves. I'm Charlotte Crozat, and this is my granddaughter, Maggie. Judging by your age, I assume you're Carina's daughter."

Carina shook her head. "Niece. I was named after her."

"Ah. Well, as I mentioned in my messages to you, I found correspondence between Carina and my late husband that indicated he and your aunt had a relationship when they were young." Gran pulled the bundle of letters out of her purse. She'd rewrapped it with the original ribbon. "In all our time together—and we were married over fifty years—Thibault never mentioned your aunt to me. Which makes me quite curious about her."

Carina picked up a framed portrait and handed it to Gran. "Here's a picture."

Gran and Maggie gazed at the image of a young woman with a shy smile and eyes that shone, even in black and white. "She's lovely," Maggie said.

"Wasn't she? That was taken right before she died."

Gran stared at the photo. "Died? She couldn't have been more than twenty in this picture."

"Nineteen. She never saw her twentieth birthday. Leukemia."

Stunned, Maggie and Gran exchanged a glance. "I'm sorry," Gran said. "I had no idea."

"Carina was my dad's little sister by two years."

"By any chance, did your father go to Tulane?" Gran asked.

"Yes."

"I'm guessing he was friends with my husband, and that's how Thibault met Carina. But I never heard my husband mention your father."

"Her death broke everyone's heart. Dad must have sent the letters back to your husband so that my aunt would live in his memories. But I can see why he didn't continue their friendship. They would have had to talk about Carina, and no one could. Not my grandparents, not Dad. No one. It was too painful."

"To lose a loved one like that, at such a young age," Gran murmured. "It must have been unbearable."

Maggie thought of her own mother, who'd battled Hodgkin's lymphoma when she was not much older than Carina. Ninette had survived, married, raised a daughter. Maggie recalled the times her family feared the cancer had reoccurred and they might lose Ninette. Now she was grateful for every moment she spent with her beloved mother. Moments Carina never got to experience with a child of her own.

"You read the letters. Can you tell me anything about her?" the late woman's namesake asked Gran. "I'd love to know what she was like."

"She . . . She was . . ." Gran stopped. She cleared her throat. She looked down at the packet of letters in her lap. Then she handed them to the second Carina Albieri. "These will tell you everything you need to know about your aunt."

The woman hesitated. "Are you sure?"

"Absolutely."

"Thank you so much." Carina took the letters. Her eyes, light like her late aunt's, glistened.

"I can share two things I learned from them." Gran leaned forward. She placed a hand on Carina's knee. "Your aunt was beautiful inside and out. And my husband was very much in love with her."

* * *

Grand-mère placed a large bouquet of flowers in front of the elegant marble tomb located in a far corner of the city's Greenwood Cemetery. She'd insisted on paying her respects, and Maggie was happy to oblige.

An inscription on the tomb read, BUT IT IS FLESH THAT DIES; THE SOUL IS IMMORTAL. Below it, Carina Albieri's dates of birth and death were listed. Gran and Maggie knelt at the foot of the tomb. They said a prayer, crossed themselves, and then stood up.

"It's heartbreaking," Gran said. "The loss."

"I know."

The women were silent, lost in their own thoughts. The only sound came from the rumble and clangs of the Canal Street streetcar line, which passed by the cemetery's entrance. Maggie took her grandmother's hand in hers. "We should go."

"In a minute." Gran ran her hand across the inscription. "Your grand-père and I had a wonderful life together."

"You did. I saw how you looked at each other. The love that was there. It inspired me."

"I never believed this before, but now I know, Magnolia . . . it is possible to have two great loves in your life." She bent down and adjusted the bouquet, releasing the scent of lilies. "Lee proposed to me. I'm going to say yes."

"Oh, Gran," Maggie said, her voice thick with emotion. "That's wonderful."

"I wasn't going to. I thought it would be a betrayal of your grandfather. But I've come to believe he'd understand. And wish the best for me." Gran turned away from the tomb to her granddaughter. "I'm ready."

Maggie offered Gran her arm. "The ground is uneven. I don't want anything to happen to you."

"If it did, we're certainly in a convenient location."

"Gran, you're too much," Maggie said, shaking her head, amused.

They walked toward Maggie's car, down a long row of tombs, each a story to be told of a family's history. "I was wondering . . ." Gran began, and then stopped.

"Yes?" Maggie prompted.

"I don't suppose . . ." There was a rare note of hesitancy in Gran's voice. "I might talk you into a double wedding?"

Maggie got a catch in her throat. She graced her grandmother with a warm, wide smile.

"I can't think of anything that would make me happier."

Recipes

Cauliflower Jambalaya

Ninette likes to play around with this creative take on the traditional Cajun dish. You may want to add more broth or less if you think it needs it or adjust the amount of Cajun spice. I generally opt for less spicy because I like it that way and figure people can add Tabasco to their individual servings. That being said, when I first tasted this, it was pretty spicy. Yet on the second and third servings, it wasn't, so maybe I just hit a hot patch that first time.

Ingredients

2 tablespoons vegetable oil

6 ounces chopped heavy-cut bacon or turkey bacon (about 1 cup)

2 cups finely chopped onions

1 cup finely chopped green bell pepper (generally 1 large pepper)

½ cup finely chopped celery

1 cup Andouille sausage, cut into bite-size Pieces
1 cup chicken broth
1 teaspoon ground thyme
1 teaspoon dried tarragon
2 bay leaves
¼ teaspoon sea salt
1 teaspoon smoked paprika
⅛ teaspoon ground red pepper
¼ teaspoon black pepper
2 cloves minced garlic
1 teaspoon Tony Chachere's Creole seasoning or any
  Cajun seasoning with salt (if there's a lot of pepper in
  your seasoning, you might want to dial back the
  amount)
Dash Tabasco (optional)
Dash Worcestershire Sauce
24 ounces riced cauliflower, cooked (e.g., 2 bags of Trader
  Joe's frozen Riced Cauliflower, defrosted and cooked)
1 pound cooked shrimp
¼ cup finely chopped green onions
¼ cup finely chopped fresh parsley

Instructions

1. Add the oil to a large Dutch oven or cast-iron pot. Then add the bacon and cook until it curls. Add onions, bell pepper, celery, and garlic, and cook until the vegetables are softened, about five minutes. Stir to make sure everything cooks evenly.

2. Add the sausage to the pot and stir to combine with the other ingredients. Then add the chicken broth, thyme, tarragon, bay leaves, sea salt, smoked paprika, red pepper, black pepper, garlic, Tony Chachere's, Tabasco sauce, and Worcestershire sauce and stir together.

3. Reduce heat to simmer and add the cooked cauliflower. Stir and simmer for a few minutes, then add the shrimp. Stir and simmer for 5–10 minutes.

4. Stir in the green onions and parsley and cook for another minute or two. Let sit for five minutes, then serve with sliced French bread. Have a bottle of hot sauce handy for any guest who prefers their jambalaya spicy.

Serves 6–8.

Vegetarian Cauliflower Jambalaya
It's easy to turn this into a vegetarian dish. Skip the shrimp and sausage and substitute meatless bacon for regular bacon. Then just follow the rest of the instructions.

Shrimp Étouffée

Étouffée literally means "smothered" in French. In Cajun cooking, that translates to a delicious dish of shrimp or crawfish smothered in a veggie-laden sauce.

Ninette's version is more Cajun than Creole because she doesn't include tomatoes, a staple of many Creole dishes. Her recipe really lets the flavors of the "Holy Trinity" of Cajun cooking—onions, green pepper, and celery—stand out.

Ingredients

½ pound butter or light butter
1 cup chopped onion
½ cup chopped green bell pepper
¼ cup chopped celery
2 tablespoons minced garlic
2 tablespoons dried parsley flakes
½ teaspoon salt
1 teaspoon Cajun seasoning, such as Tony Chachere's
1 tablespoon flour (or 2 tablespoons if you want to thicken the sauce more)
1 cup either shrimp stock, crawfish stock, chicken stock, or water
1 pound peeled shrimp or peeled crawfish tails
6 cups cooked white rice

Instructions

1. Using medium to high heat, melt the butter in a heavy, large skillet. Add the onion, pepper, celery, garlic, parsley, salt, and Cajun seasoning. Stir well to combine all the ingredients, then reduce the heat a bit and cook until the onion softens.

2. Add the flour, stirring well. As soon as the flour begins to stick to the bottom of the skillet, add the stock slowly until you've added it all to the mixture, stirring well to combine.

3. Simmer the mixture until it bubbles, add the shrimp or crawfish, and stir well. Bring the mixture to a bubble again, then reduce the heat to low. Cover the skillet and simmer the étouffée for ten to fifteen minutes, stirring occasionally.

4. Serve over 1 cup of white rice per serving. Or, if you want to make it low calorie, serve it over riced cauliflower instead of rice.

Serves 6.

Pecan Pralines

Pralines can be deceptively tricky to make. Within one batch, I can wind up with chewy, soft-hard, and crystalized pralines. But you know what? All three consistencies taste delicious. So just have fun with the recipes, and like we told our daughter when she was little, "You get what you get and you don't get upset."

Ingredients

1½ cups white sugar
1½ cups brown sugar
1 cup whole milk
2 tablespoons butter
1 teaspoon vanilla
1 cup pecans
⅛ teaspoon salt

Instructions

1. Cover two cooking trays with tinfoil, spray the foil with cooking spray, and set aside.

2. Mix together the sugars and milk in a sturdy pot such as a Dutch oven, then cook mixture until it's at the firm-ball stage, about 245–250 degrees. Remove and

beat in the butter until it melts, then add the vanilla, salt, and nuts.

3. Drop spoonfuls of the mixture onto the tin-foiled cookie sheets. When the pralines have hardened and cooled— you can place the trays in the freezer to harden them faster—transfer to a container for storage.

Makes around 12–24 pralines, depending on whether you make them small or large.

Variations

For almond pralines, substitute 1 teaspoon almond flavor for the vanilla and a cup of sliced almonds for the pecans.

For coconut pralines, substitute 1 teaspoon coconut flavor for the vanilla and a cup of shredded coconut for the pecans.

For rum pralines, substitute 1 teaspoon of rum for the vanilla, or even two teaspoons.

Note: If you can't get the pralines to harden in some fashion, do what I do—turn the batch into praline topping. I've gifted jars of pralines-turned-topping to friends. Heat up a few tablespoonsful, pour them on ice cream, and you have one delicious dessert.

Maple Bacon Pralines

Ingredients

16 ounces pure-cane confectioner's sugar
1 cup maple syrup
1 cup whipping cream
⅛ teaspoon salt
1 teaspoon vanilla
1 cup bacon bits

Instructions

1. Cover two cooking trays with tinfoil, spray the foil with cooking spray, and set aside.

2. Mix sugar, maple syrup, cream, and salt in a sturdy pot such as a Dutch oven. Cook until the mixture reaches the firm-ball stage, about 245–250 degrees. (Make sure to stir.)

3. Remove the pot from the stove, add vanilla and bacon bits, and beat vigorously for a minute or two.

4. Drop spoonfuls of the mixture onto the tinfoiled cookie sheets. When the pralines have hardened and cooled, transfer to a container for storage.

Makes about two dozen pralines.

R.I.P. Sweet Potato Pralines Recipes

Readers, forgive me. I tried, oh how I tried, but I could not come up with a successful recipe for sweet potato pralines. The inspiration for them came from a delicious patty I sampled at Southern Candymakers, a shop in New Orleans. My fingers were stained orange from a half-dozen attempts at creating my own version of this treat. I finally had to accept that it wasn't going to happen. But I do have a bit of good news. If you come away from this book with a craving for sweet potato pralines, Southern Candymakers can ship them to you. Their website is southerncandymakers.com.

Ninette's Rum Raisin Cake
with Rum Frosting

The Cake

Ingredients

1 cup golden raisins
1 cup rum
1 box white cake mix
¼ cup water
3 egg whites

Instructions

1. Soak golden raisins in rum for thirty minutes to an hour.

2. Preheat oven to 350 degrees.

3. In a mixer on low speed, blend together the cake mix, water, and eggs. Turn off the mixer and add the rum and raisins. Set the mixer to medium and blend all the ingredients for two minutes.

4. Pour the batter into two greased 8-inch cake pans. Bake for 20–30 minutes, making sure to check at 20 minutes because the layers cook faster with liquor substituted for

water as the batter liquid. If you insert a toothpick into the middle, it should come out clean. Do not overbake! The cake will dry out.

5. Let the cake layers cool.

The Frosting

Ingredients

1 cup softened butter
1 teaspoon vanilla
3 tablespoons rum
⅛ teaspoon salt
1–3 tablespoons milk (or use rum, if you like your frosting boozier)
4 cups confectioner's sugar

Instructions

1. Cream the butter with the vanilla, rum, salt, and 1 tablespoon of milk. Slowly add the powdered sugar, blending it well with the other ingredients. If you need to thin the frosting, add another tablespoon or two of milk—or rum!

Assembly

To assemble the cake, slice a thin layer off one of the cake layers so that it will be level on the bottom, then invert the cake layer onto a plate so that the flat side—the bottom—is facing up. (Feel free to eat the thin slice!) Frost this layer.

To add the second layer, invert it onto a plate, then place it on the frosted layer *with the flat side down*. (This is how you get a professional-looking cake—placing flat side to flat side, that is, bottom of the layer to bottom of the layer.) Frost the rest of the cake.

Note: Remember how I recommended turning a failed batch of pralines into a successful batch of praline topping? You can also use this #epicfail as a delicious middle filling in Ninette's rum cake.

Serves 8–16, depending on the size of the slices.

The recipe for Chulanes appears in *Plantation Shudders*.

The recipe for Banana Pancakes with Brown Sugar Butter appears in *Mardi Gras Murder*.

Lagniappe

The batture is the alluvial land that runs between the levees and the Mississippi River. It's comprised of silt deposited by the Mississippi and can play host to a variety of trees, plants, and shrubs. While the Army Corps of Engineers manages the levee between the state's River Road plantations and the Mississippi River, many plantation owners still own and utilize the batture. As the river changed course or flooded during the last two centuries, it often took a plantation with it. That's what happened to the fictional Harmonie Plantation in this book—the Mississippi overwhelmed it and then retreated, leaving behind the ruins of Harmonie.

If you're interested in learning more about the batture, especially around the New Orleans area, I highly recommend *Down on the Batture* by Oliver A. Houck. His wanderings through this almost-otherworldly environment make for some fascinating essays.

* * *

Never been to the New Orleans Jazz & Heritage Festival? Put it on your bucket list. From Thursday through Sunday during the last week of April and the first of May, the Fair

Grounds Race Course in the city's Mid-City neighborhood becomes home to tents and stages featuring music ranging from blues to zydeco to country to pop, and everything in between. The performing artists are as excited to be there as you are. I've seen Paul Simon and David Byrne wandering around the grounds, checking out the amazing array of music, food, and crafts at the festival, all of which celebrate the melting pot of cultures that is the Big Easy. Jazz Fest is where I first met a voodoo priestess who took credit cards, an anomaly that amused me so much it inspired the character of Helene Brevelle in my series. (We've yet to meet Helene because she's on an endless cruise paid for by sorority girls buying her gris-gris bags in the hopes that the bags' mojo will help land them dates for their formals. Yup—I did that in real life!) And there really is a legendary pasta dish sold during Jazz Fest called Crawfish Monica®. Pierre Hilzom created the recipe in 1981 and named it after his wife, Monica. The recipe is a trade secret of their company, Kajun Kettle Foods, Inc., so those of us who love the dish must try to come up with our own take on it or buy the sauce from their company. If you want to learn more about this iconic festival, I highly recommend Kevin McCaffrey's great book *The Incomplete, Year-by-Year, Selectively Quirky, Prime Facts Edition of the History of the New Orleans Jazz & Heritage Festival.*

By the way, the New Orleans Jazz & Heritage Festival may be the best-known music festival in Louisiana, but it's only one of many. Did you know the state has more festivals than days in the year? What a wonderful statistic. I look forward to visiting as many of them as I can someday.

* * *

Since music is such an important aspect of this particular Cajun Country Mystery, I did something I rarely do in my series—I referenced a few real people. Clifton Chenier is a legendary musician considered by many to be the founder of the zydeco genre. His son, C.J. Chenier, has followed in his footsteps with his fantastic group, C.J. Chenier and the Red Hot Louisiana Band. Another legendary performer I'd like to give a shout-out to is the incomparable jazz singer Banu Gibson. I'm going to brag for a minute and share that I've known Banu for years. She was the wife of my beloved late Tulane theater professor, Bruce "Buzz" Podewell. If you've never heard this amazing entertainer perform, check out her itinerary (http://www.banugibson.com/html/bg_homepage.asp) and pencil a gig onto your bucket list. You will thank me for this.

* * *

Carina Albieri's story was inspired by a real-life tragedy. My wonderful hair stylist, Nuria Contreras, had a very talented assistant named Carina. There was something special about her. She was smart, kind, and lovely in a way that seemed to be from another era. Carina had a graciousness about her that would have been rare in anyone but was particularly unusual for a teenager.

During one of our sessions, I noticed Carina was quiet. She seemed pale and tired. Beset with chronic fatigue, she began missing work. Not long after that, she was diagnosed with leukemia.

Carina died a few months later. She had just turned twenty.

Sometimes people come into your life whom you may not know well but who leave a lasting impression. Carina was one of those people. Her heartbreaking, untimely death haunted me. I decided to pay homage to this lovely young woman by letting her inspire a character.

I hope readers are as moved by the fictional Carina as I was by the real girl.

Acknowledgments

A shout-out as always to my indefatigable agent, Doug Grad, and to the extraordinary team at Crooked Lane Books, including Matt Martz, Sarah Poppe, Ashley DiDio, Jenny Chen, and extraordinary cover artist, Stephen Gardner. Mindy Schneider, Kathy McCullough, and Kate Shein—GoWrite rules! As does chicksonthecase.com, and my fab fellow chicks Lisa Q. Mathews, Kellye Garrett, Mariella Krause, Vickie Fee, Cynthia Kuhn, and Leslie Karst. Ladies, I am nothing without your priceless feedback.

Nancy Cole Silverman, our weekly walks have been life-savers. West Donas Walkers Lisa Libatique, Kelly Goode, Kathy Wood, and Nancy McIlvaney, same goes for our power walks! Jan Gilbert and Kevin McCaffrey, I couldn't write this—or any of my books–without your support. Same goes for you, my dear friends Charlotte Allen and Gaynell Bourgeois Moore. A shout-out to the rest of my NOLA krewe as well: Laurie Smith Becker, Shawn Hola-han, and Madelaine Hedgpeth Feldman, plus Debra Jo and Jonathan Burnette. I can't tell you how reassuring it is to know you're all there when I need you.

A special thank-you to my friend Hope Juber and her

brilliant musician husband, Lawrence Juber. Your input helped me paint a realistic picture of concerts, the music industry, and Tammy's band members.

Tammy Barker, thank you for your generosity at the Malice Domestic Convention and hope you enjoy being in print. Your name could not have been more perfect for *Cajun Country Live!*'s diva country star.

I'm blessed to belong to Sisters in Crime and Mystery Writers of America, specifically the chapters SinCLA and SoCalMWA. Without the Guppies, a SinC subgroup, I never would have gotten anywhere in the mystery world. A million fin flaps to all of you! Thanks to all the friends who've supported me throughout this fabulous journey—I'm talking to you, June Stoddard, Denise and Stacy Smithers, Karen Fried, Laurie Graff, Von Rae Wood, and Kim Rose! If I missed anyone, let me know and I'll make it up to you in the next book. And infinite thanks to my mom, my bros, and especially my husband Jerry and daughter Eliza.